Praise for Nico Rosso

"High stakes and sexual tension will keep readers eagerly turning the pages."
—*Publishers Weekly*, starred review, on *Countdown to Zero Hour*

"Rosso's talent for incorporating romance in the midst of a gang war and military mission earns *Countdown to Zero Hour* a spot on every bookshelf. It's an enticing, scorching-hot read!"
—*RT Book Reviews*, Top Pick, 4.5 Stars

"THIS is how romantic suspense should be done!"
—*The Romance Reviews*, Top Pick, on *Countdown to Zero Hour*

"The sexual tension and chemistry are done really well. Highly recommend this one."
—*Smexy Books* on *One Minute to Midnight*

"Mr. Rosso has quickly become one of my must-read authors, and I will recommend his books to anyone who craves INCREDIBLE romantic suspense!"
—*The Romance Reviews*, Top Pick, on *One Minute to Midnight*

**Also Available from Nico Rosso
and Carina Press**

The Last Night

Demon Rock Series

*Heavy Metal Heart
Slam Dance with the Devil
Ménage with the Muse*

And coming soon in the Black Ops: Automatik Series

Seconds to Sunrise

ONE MINUTE TO MIDNIGHT

NICO ROSSO

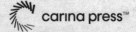

carina press™

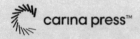

ISBN-13: 978-0-373-00479-9

One Minute to Midnight

Recycling programs
for this product may
not exist in your area.

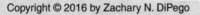

www.CarinaPress.com

Printed in U.S.A.

Dear Reader,

Being a black ops soldier trying to root out gunrunners isn't easy. Just ask former SEAL Ben Jackson and elite sniper "Bolt Action" Mary. But what happens when these teammates find that the flirting of their fake identities starts to feel very real? In my second Black Ops: Automatik book, I wanted to see what it would take for these two seasoned warriors to trust each other with not just their lives, but with their hearts. I hope you enjoy the action and Ben and Mary's journey to discover that there's more to life than just fighting wars.

Best,

Nico

ONE MINUTE
TO MIDNIGHT

ONE

BEN JACKSON KNEW the sign on the side of the highway lied. It read, Welcome to Morris Flats, but they
didn't want him there. Not if the town had any idea
what his mission was. A secret festered behind the
walls of the small burg that had grown up around
agriculture and industry. Automatik had sent him
in to track the rot and strategize how cut it out with
surgical precision.

Ben pulled off the highway and onto the streets.
He had a quarter tank of gas and a full magazine
of 9mm bullets in the pistol strapped to his ankle.
This was the recon stage of the mission, but he
still wanted to be ready for anything. That meant
he needed a gas station, so the SUV was always
topped off in case of a hasty bug out.

The simple homes and single-story businesses
blurred past his windows. Somewhere else in Morris
Flats, another operator was there to pry into the
secrets from a different angle. For the first time
with Automatik, he wasn't backed by his old SEAL
teammate, Harper. Any insertion into possibly hostile territory brought a prickle of nerves. Ben knew
not to ever get too comfortable. The tension between his shoulder blades was heightened by the

unknown variables of working with a new partner. "Bolt Action" Mary, the strike team sniper,
kept herself at a distance. Even when the Automatik operators were sharing a beer after a successful
job, she still seemed like she was a thousand yards
out and viewing it all through her telescopic sight.

Not that he doubted her skills. The woman always came through with precision dialed down to
the millimeter. But what would it be like, just the
two of them trying to gather information in poten-
tially hostile territory? Where would her distance
put their communication? Ben spotted a gas station
and motored that way. He was being selfish. Mary
was attractive, somewhere around his age, fit, and
with dark eyes that had seen the same corners of
the world and the same corners of war fighting as
he had. He'd always tried to shine a light on what
she knew, who she was, but she'd always remained
a shadow operator. Maybe that was why the nerves
prickled. She lit a fuse in him, and he didn't know
where it would lead.

The gas station with a convenience store was the
only pool of light on the block. Ben pulled in and
brought his rental SUV to rest by the pumps. He
got out and stretched in the biting, late fall breeze.
Fourteen hours on the road, just for a cover story.
This job was already more complicated than door
kicking and room clearing, and he hadn't even met
any of the population yet.

First contact came with a shout. Authoritative
voices barked around the far side of the convenience

store. Ben walked to the end of the gas pumps and saw the rear of a police car parked at a sharp angle. The lights were off. He pulled out his phone and faked like he was ambling aimlessly, as if still getting the blood back into his legs after the drive.

As he approached the police car, the scene came into view. Three teenagers, two Latino and one African-American, sat on a curb next to the convenience store. Facing them were two uniformed police officers, white men, thick with hours spent at the gym. They stood with their hands on their hips and loomed. The angriest-looking one, with short black hair, pointed to a pile of broken skateboards. "And don't pretend that you didn't know." The wood had been snapped in half. Not from use, but from someone stomping on them. Everything about the officer was designed to intimidate, all the way down to the polish on his boots.

It wasn't necessary. The kids were terrified. They weren't handcuffed, but they slouched, completely defeated. And if skateboarding was their biggest crime, they'd more than learned their lesson tonight. But the angry cop didn't stop, strutting in front of the teens, his duty belt creaking and his hand close to the gear, including his pistol. Anger choked in Ben's throat. The show of force had gone too far. Was the cop getting his rocks off, or was there a bigger picture? How tight a grip did the police have on this town?

The officers certainly felt like they were the apex predators of the territory. They were so confident, they had both their backs turned to Ben and were unaware as he made it look like he was checking his email while shooting video of them with his phone.

One of the kids caught sight of Ben first and shot him a frightened look. And warning him. Ben's ire flared and his heart broke. How far would this go? The angry officer pulled a can of pepper spray from his belt, though he'd been faced with no opposition. Ben had just shown up in town and needed to maintain his cover through the intelligence gathering, but he couldn't just stand there and do nothing.

"Oh, damn," he exclaimed. "I was looking for the bathroom. Is it over here?" He held his hands up, his phone in one, still recording.

The startled officers turned. Ben suppressed his emotions and concentrated on his battlefield calm. Things could escalate quickly. Either he could diffuse them, or he might have to fight his way out of the town he'd just arrived in. And that would fuck the mission.

The other cop, a blond man, had his hand over his sidearm while assessing Ben. The angry cop seemed paralyzed with rage. He clearly wasn't used to being interrupted or challenged.

The blond cop cocked his head toward the convenience store. "They're inside," he commanded.

"Got it. Thanks." Ben backed up, hands still raised shoulder height. He wanted to be moving toward this fight. Anything to put more distance between these cops and those kids.

He rounded back to the front of the convenience

store, seething. *Be cool*. It would be bad to make enemies on the first night out. He and Mary and Automatik were playing the long game. It had taken at least three years of intelligence operatives tracking illegal guns to bring their focus on Morris Flats. The place was a hub for all kinds of transportation, and the weapons had been hidden parallel to legit shipments across the country. An intercepted crate had linked to one of these aboveboard manifests, which tied to another, and another, until they'd finally zeroed in on this spot on the map. If big-time gunrunning was happening in the area, the cops would know about it. And those two officers certainly behaved like they had a secret to protect.

Ben had to take a long breath to erase the anger in his voice when he spoke to the clerk behind the counter. "Do I need a key for the bathroom?"

"No, sir," the older clerk answered and waved Ben toward the back corner of the room.

Ben locked himself inside and brought up the Automatik communication app on his phone. It tied them all to the shared information on the missions. A big change from the military chain of command he'd left behind. All the doors were open in Automatik. The operators called the shots, and everyone was itching to take down these gunrunners. He explained his brief encounter with the local officers and uploaded the video.

He left the bathroom and bought a candy bar before returning to his SUV. Things seemed quiet on the other side of the store. It would put him too far out on a limb to check, so he pumped gas in his car and tried to keep the frustration from seizing all his muscles.

Then he heard the telltale hiss of pepper spray. The kids yelped and grunted in pain. He halted the urge to rush around the corner. Surprising the cops would only add up to a bullet in Ben's chest. He yanked open the SUV door and leaned across the driver's seat so his shoulder pressed on the horn. The sound blared. He saw the clerk come out of the store behind him. Glancing through the front windshield revealed the blond cop coming around the corner as well, still ready to draw his weapon.

Ben leaned away from the horn and stepped back from the SUV, dragging his coat from the passenger seat. "Sorry, guys." He smiled sheepishly. "Just grabbing my jacket." He pulled it on and turned the collar up.

The clerk watched the cop warily and slipped back into his shop. The blond man approached, cocked for confrontation. At least the sound of the pepper spray had abated.

"You gassing up to get back on the highway?" The cop made the question sound like an order.

"No, sir." Ben kept his hands in plain view, but he was close enough to rush the officer if the man tried to pull his sidearm. "I have some business in town."

The cop looked him up and down. Ben chafed under the scrutiny. He'd done nothing wrong other than interrupting an inappropriate show of force.

He was tempted to list parts of his service record with the SEALs to prove he was a solid citizen. But not the kind of citizen they wanted in town. He was there to seek and destroy the gunrunning business in which this cop was no doubt some kind of player. The cop kept staring. Ben had felt that look before. He was a stranger. A black man. And he wasn't ducking or as quiet as this officer wanted.

"Well, then." The cop smiled without warmth. "Best of luck. Stay out of trouble."

The gas pump clicked off. Ben nodded at the cop and turned to finish fueling his car. Out of the corner of his eye, he saw the cop still staring him down for a moment before moving back to where his partner was with the teens.

Ben was cranked up, ready for action. But he'd have to wait. The fighting would start after he and Mary had found solid evidence and populated the list of major players for the final strike.

The police car backed away from the convenience store and pulled onto the street. The rear seat was empty; the kids hadn't been arrested. But this night was bad enough for them. Ben watched the three boys stagger away, carrying the pieces of their skateboards and rubbing their sleeves across watering eyes.

Ben wrapped up his business at the gas station and drove back into the quiet town. Lies surrounded him. Barely ten minutes into the op, he already felt it balancing on a hair trigger. He wouldn't stay out of trouble, like the cop said. He was there to look for it.

TWO

MARY KURI REACHED past the loaded .38 Special in her purse, found her lip gloss and touched up her color after having left too much of it behind on the rim of a glass of red wine. She preferred to drink whiskey. She also preferred a .40 automatic as a pistol backup. But she was on an operation and had to look more like a real estate developer than a former black ops soldier.

"How's that Pinot?" The other customers' drinks sat dry while the hotel bartender paid her too much attention.

"Nice." It wasn't, but it was the best the Sycamore Inn could offer. "Perfect end to a travel day."

"Where from?" He put his hands on the bar and flexed a little. The guy, in his late twenties, filled out a dress shirt fine. Blond hair, clean features.

"Dallas now, but the boss has me scouting so much, I'm like a vagabond." She sipped the acidic wine and checked the mirror behind the bartender for who might be listening. Two men sat down the bar, paying more attention to the basketball game on the high TV than her. A man and a woman slouched at a table, both looking at their phones and weary from business travel. Slow weeknight at the Sycamore Inn.

The bartender's nametag hung awkwardly from his chest pocket, purporting him to be Will. "You drove up here from Dallas?" He asked it as if recording it to memory and ready to repeat it to the next interested local.

"Anything under ten hours is a dream." Which wasn't part of the act. She'd spent forty-eight hours or more awake during many ops in the Middle East. "I'm just glad to have a little wine and a roof over my head." She glanced about the small bar off the hotel lobby. One security camera looked down from a corner, but it had a blind spot all the way on the opposite side of the room. "The Sycamore Inn is looking mighty fine."

Will topped off her wine with a conspiratorial wink. "The best we got in Morris Flats." A troubling thought brought his brow down. "You're not here to develop another hotel, are you?"

The remote town at the southern tip of Illinois seemed like it could barely support the one four-story hotel.

"Not to worry. We do multi-use spaces. Businesses on the bottom, apartments on the top. That kind of thing." The manufactured shop talk prompted her to fish her phone from her purse and check over the notifications. Her gut tightened as she glanced over Ben's account of the gas station activity. They'd barely started their op, and her new partner had already sparked against the local cops. Not that she blamed him. She blew out a breath and justified her frustration. "Really, Helen?" Her fake boss sending a fake afterhours email. Will started to drift away, but she caught his attention while still looking at her phone. "I just got here, and she's asking about prospects."

"That's the problem with the phone." He patted his back pocket. "They can always get you."

"Well—" she placed her phone facedown on the bar, "—I'm not going to run around an unknown town after dark. You should see the places they send me." She'd been to Iraq, Afghanistan, Chechnya and other locations her service records would deny. "How's Miller Flats? I'll find stuff out here, right?"

Will dialed up the charm with a small smile. Hometown hero. He might get lucky with a guest passing through. "Yeah, you will."

Not with her, though. This intel-gathering trip didn't warrant any extra special investigative techniques. And Will was a lightweight. The kid probably hadn't lived beyond the radius of the local pizza joint delivery. Mary had survived a career in Special Forces and now worked for Automatik. It would take a man with a lot of gravity to move her. Which meant no man these days. Not even a fling with a stranger.

"Looked like a lot of land past the train yard." She took another sip of wine.

Will dismissed the idea with a shake of his head. "Stay away from the east side. There are busted-up warehouses and stuff on the west side, past the high school. That would be good for town."

He'd flinched when he said "east." A small

twitch of the neck and shoulder, as if defending himself against a taller attacker. The bad territory was to the east, and for her job, she always headed toward the bad territory.

"Thanks for the tip." She toasted Will with her wine. "Maybe I can make Helen happy for once." After a meager sip, she resumed reading Ben's account on her phone. From the way he described it, it wasn't just a matter of bored cops and reckless teens. The police were using force to maintain control. The sense of trouble continued to tense her stomach. A town on edge and a brand-new partner.

Will watched her read over her phone for a bit, then finally left to attend to the other patrons at the bar.

Past the bartender and the men talking sports, beyond the door to the bar, a new presence stalked into the lobby. An African-American man. Confident, strong and balanced. Trained for combat.

He was trouble for everyone there except her. Ben Jackson was her Automatik teammate. The former navy SEAL was a solid operator, and she trusted him in a fight.

But maybe he was trouble for her. That easy sway of his shoulders as he removed his coat. Thick muscles in a polo shirt. An even gait and a comfortable smile. And a keen awareness that didn't miss a detail around him. He wheeled his bag into the bar, and an unusual thrill climbed up her spine. She understood him and his past. The way he'd talked to her when the Automatik teammates were hanging out made her think he might understand her history, which had left her exposed and vulnerable. Sensations she wasn't familiar with. But they intrigued her. Like playing with fire, feeling alive at the border of pain.

"Check-in can wait," he said to no one. "I've been on the road too damn long to pass up the bar."

He eased onto one of the stools between her and the men. She'd been polite to him before, but had never revealed more of herself than he needed to know, soldier to soldier. For the first time, she took a long look at him. As if he was a stranger in a bar. Would she have been able to tell he was an elite operator? Fit, yes, and athletic. Sharp eyes. A sexy butt in jeans.

Will came over to him, and Ben held up his fingers, measuring different amounts. "Bourbon. Soda. No ice."

"Got it." The bartender headed off to make the drink.

Ben also used the mirror behind the bar to scope the area. He appeared relaxed, elbows on the bar, but she knew he was as poised as she was. His report of the police encounter had been detailed, yet she'd still felt, and understood, his frustration coming through the curt words. In the bar, he managed to keep the reverberations from the conflict with the cops suppressed without even a line of strain at the corners of his eyes. They'd completed quite a few ops as part of the team, but she was a sniper and he was a close quarters man, so she'd only observed him from a distance.

Will returned with his drink, and Ben opened a tab. The bartender was much less interested in chatting Ben up than he had Mary and moved back to the men at the other end of the bar. Ben sat still for a moment, looking into his drink with an unreadable expression and a new, surprising depth to his quiet.

They'd never been assigned to a recon detail together. The unprecedented arousal spun up through her again. She tried to shock it out of her system with some of the bad wine. Automatik operations weren't the place for liaisons. And Ben wasn't the guy for them. Not if any of the rumors of his exploits were true.

They'd operated on the same team for quite a while, but their current cover stories hadn't met.

He changed that with a crooked smile. "Cheers." He lifted his drink from the bar.

"Cheers." She tipped her glass toward his, and they both drank while watching each other in the mirror.

He had such a casual way of gazing at her. Appreciating but not leering. It could've been disarming, but she never let someone take her weapon away.

"See that?" He set his drink down and scrutinized the basketball game. "Number seventy-three. See that bracelet?"

She, Will and the two men at the bar paid closer attention to the TV.

"Yeah?" Will challenged him.

"It doesn't do anything. It's got the wrong magnets." Ben leaned from his stool and rummaged in an outside pocket on his luggage. "These work." He held up two sporty-looking bracelets made of rubber and fabric cords.

Will came over and took the black one offered to him. The men at the bar waved off Ben's other bracelet, so he held it out to her. And fell into a sales pitch. "Reduces joint pain. Better range of motion. Less fatigue means more focus."

She let him down easy. "No, thanks."

Will already had his on and flexed his arm to test the effects. "Not feeling anything."

"Keep it." Ben curled a strong bicep, showing off his physique and his own bracelet. "You'll thank me in a few days."

"Yeah, I'll let you know." Will kept tensing a fist and shaking his head.

"You in a rec league?" Ben continued the soft pitch to the bartender. For a former SEAL with a quick trigger finger, and he was slick with the line. "I'd love to get more of the regular guys and not super athletes involved to hear what they think."

Will absentmindedly turned the bracelet. "There's a police and firefighter gym." That small flinch returned. Trouble to the east. Trouble with the police. Did Ben see the tell? "Everyone else plays at the park across from the high school."

"Good to know, buddy. Thanks." Ben was able to keep his temper down when talking about the cops. He placed the second bracelet down between him and Mary and returned to his drink. "And don't worry, I won't tell them you sent me." Yes, Ben had picked up on Will's body language. Ben had some chops for espionage work, and that just added to his intrigue.

She skimmed her fingers along the bar and picked up the bracelet. Ben deliberately didn't turn to watch, though she knew he could see from his peripheral vision.

"Does this really work?" She rolled the cord between her fingers. "Really?"

He leaned an elbow on the bar and turned his back on the men and Will. All his attention warmed her like a comforting blanket. "There's one good way to find out." He blinked slow and licked his lips. "Try it."

She put the bracelet back on the bar.

He laughed and nodded. Was it all an act, or was it this easy to sway back and forth in a flirtation?

"Road warrior?" He took the bracelet and pocketed it.

"Does it show?" She checked her phone to give her something to do.

"You're tempered like steel." He didn't sound like he was flirting. "All those miles, they make us hard." He was telling the truth.

"Hard up?" She flashed her own smile.

He laughed louder and toasted her. "Just spinning a little conversation." He took a sip, collected a stripe of condensation from the glass and rubbed it on the back of his neck. His blunt fingers scratched behind his ear and in the tight curls of his hair in a hypnotic little dance. He knew she was watching.

"Sorry." She angled more toward him. "I'm just a little worn-out from the road."

"I hear you." He glanced away from the bar. "I'm going to get a table so I can stretch out and not be bothered by the terrible free throw shooting on the TV. Join me?"

He picked up his drink. She hesitated.

Will came over, warily eyeing Ben. "Everyone good here?" His concern extended to her. Even in a hotel, strangers weren't that welcome. Especially someone as active as Ben. This town didn't trust. They had a secret.

Which was why Automatik had sent her and Ben.

She reassured Will, "It's all good, thanks."

Ben eased away from the bar. She collected her wine, phone and purse and joined him. They took the table farthest from everyone else. The security camera would still see them, but they both knew better than give any visual clues as to who they really were.

The vinyl-covered chair squeaked under Ben as he sat and stretched his legs out under the table. He sighed long and took another drink. She took the seat to his side so she could watch the front door and still see Ben. Her hands rested at the base of her glass.

No one was close enough to hear them and she still kept her voice low as if the flirting continued.

"Is this how you get your bed warmers?" Most of what she'd heard of Ben's reputation with women had come from his SEAL teammate, Harper's, razzing.

"Don't think of them like that." He shook his head. "They're women." He thought for a moment. "We both get got, then we both get gone."

"Romantic." She faked a smile.

"Satisfying," he corrected her. His volume rose, more public. "So I'm going to guess...corporate sales. Big-time stuff. Millions. Billions of dollars."

"Close." She leaned toward his glittering rich brown eyes. "How'd you get that?" He smelled of spiced soap, bourbon and a hint of gasoline. Flammable.

"You've been on the road for hours, dedicated, but not disassembled. Hair's in place. No wrinkles on your blouse." He studied her face. "Lips are perfect."

His attention made her very aware of her mouth. She'd fired thousands of rounds in combat training. Her unit had drilled in anti-interrogation techniques with Korean Special Forces soldiers. She resisted the urge to lick her lips and gave Ben no indication of the rush of excitement the flirting charged through her. But she was impelled to test it. Usually if someone came on this strong, she shut him down. But with Ben there was the foundation of trust. She knew he wouldn't take it too far because they had to stay on task and couldn't let any personal strife affect the mission. It allowed her to tease herself with the very real excitement that came with the fake flirtation.

She kept her hands on the table. His were close. Scarred knuckles. Purposeful fingers.

"We know you're pitching those magic bracelets." If all these lies were true, would she reach out and touch his hand now? "But you didn't say anything about being passed over for a promotion."

He blinked, surprised. "I'm sitting with a damn psychic."

"Your watch." She lifted a finger to point at it. "You bought it in anticipation of the promotion, but instead you're back out on the road."

"Bull's-eye." He shook his head and chuckled. "If I'd gotten that promotion, I could've hired you."

She lifted her glass in a small toast. "You can't afford me."

"Whoever you're working for isn't paying you enough." He toasted her back and they both drank.

A couple of salespeople on the road, in a hotel and no responsibilities until the next day. If she hadn't joined the Army. Or if she'd left after six years and gone into a day job rather than covert special forces. If she was just a woman flirting with a man. How far would the night go?

Ben took another slug of his drink and dropped his voice. "This is a whole hell of a lot better than the detail in the Mexican desert."

"Good bourbon?"

"The bourbon is trash." His gaze took in her face again. "I'm talking about the company."

Was he still flirting with her saleswoman front, or was this warm attention for the combat sniper and undercover operator?

She maintained a cool exterior. "Good to know I'm a step up from a scorpion."

He gave her a slow, deliberate wink. "And more deadly."

"Damn right." She couldn't resist a carnivorous smile. "With me, you don't even feel the sting."

His honest laugh came from deep. The table became more intimate as he slid his hand closer to hers and dropped his voice. "You see my video?"

She shook her head. "I read the report."

His finger drew a spiral on the tabletop. "We're in the right spot."

She nodded. "Something ain't right under the asphalt."

"Locals are hunched under a secret." He glanced at the business travelers at the other table. "Instinct makes the strangers bunker until they can get out."

"East side." Their hands were only inches apart. "Train yard." Hands that had fought to survive across the world. Being this close made her body hum with restraint. Touching him would just be part of the act. Hands like hers, like his, couldn't feel pleasure anymore. Couldn't give pleasure anymore.

"It's a start." He didn't test the distance and leaned away. With a more public voice, he flirted brazenly, "I haven't checked in yet. Otherwise I'd give you my room number."

She took a last pull off her thin wine and smiled

over the rim of the glass. "I'm sure I'll see you at the free breakfast."

He finished his drink and indicated to Will that he wanted another. His gaze moved up and down her as she stood. "I'll save you a bagel."

Was it for the benefit of their covers so the others in the bar could see? Or did she want to feel the heat rise as she put her hands on the arm of his chair and brought her mouth near his ear? "Don't burn it," she whispered.

He licked his lips and turned toward her. Close enough to kiss. The light in his eye promised a lot of pleasure. But it wouldn't be real. She leaned away and left the bar without looking back. The mirror revealed that he watched her with growing intensity. Part of the act again? Will and the other patrons also tracked her departure, but with the more common male gazes that tried to consume her.

She passed through the lobby and waited for the elevator. The brass doors reflected any activity behind her. The space was safe for the moment. This assignment was going to be difficult. She and Ben had to pry at the seams of a very defensive environment in order to trace the gunrunning. That kind of armor was familiar. She used it to survive. Not just her body, but her mind, her soul and her heart. But something in the manufactured flirting with Ben had felt too real. He knew a truth of her few others did. She understood how to protect herself from bullets, but what was she supposed to do when her most hidden self stirred in his warm gaze?

Two TERRIBLE BOURBON and sodas got Ben the name of the high school basketball coach, the times for the hotel shift changes, the closest place to do laundry, a drugstore and the fact that Police Chief Pulaski didn't like people speeding on the frontage road parallel to the east-west train tracks. All he'd given up was too large a tip and more of his cover story.

His first night in town had turned a little better after the confrontation with the police. He sat in his hotel room armchair and used his phone to upload the latest information he'd learned to the Automatik database. The lights in the room were off, and the curtains to the wide window were open. When he'd checked in, he'd asked for the highest room, and they'd given the third floor. The fourth floor was probably completely empty for the off-season. Though in a small town like Morris Flats, he didn't know what would constitute high season.

A crisp fall wind had chased the clouds. Stars glittered, and the few streetlights below mirrored them. Most of the twelve thousand or so residents were asleep. Giant pools of black erased the streets and buildings. His window faced north, toward farmland, swamps and a state park. If only they'd given him a room over the east side. That was the area that had intrigued Mary, and if anyone knew how to scout territory, it was her.

Putting on the little act with her in the bar had been a unique rush into an unknown minefield. They'd never spent any one-on-one time together, and he'd never broken past her poker face.

But to what end tonight, he didn't know. Was it just for the challenge of getting a rise out of the stone-cold supersoldier? She didn't seem too put out by the flirting. They were partners on this mission, so if she'd sent out any indication that he was going too far, he'd shut it down immediately. The mission took precedence. But a little spark in her eyes had revealed an electricity of her own. It wasn't the "Bolt Action" Mary he'd come to know. Then again, he didn't know much about her anyway. Former Army, but that was it. The rumor in Automatik was that she was Delta, but no confirmation. Maybe he should ask. Seemed like if she ever told him the truth, she'd have to kill him.

Ben laughed out loud, put down his phone and picked up the .40 automatic that was resting on the arm of his chair. Good thing he and Mary were on the same team. Otherwise, she'd scare the hell out of him.

He sighted down his pistol to one of the unlit areas in the town below. It was the bad guys of Morris Flats who should be afraid. This place had been hiding for too long. Someone out there turned a profit from death. Ben and Mary were the tip of the knife that would put an end to the gunrunning.

Lives would be saved. For some people, the fight would be over. But not him. He'd be on to the next operation.

He got up and carried his gun and phone to the bed. The king-size expanse was too large for just one person, but an op wasn't the time for hookups.

He slipped the pistol under a pillow. Mary the sales-woman seemed like she'd be fun on all that acreage of crisp white sheets. She was wise. And bit back.

But she wasn't real. The actual Mary was a hunter killer. And it made him feel much safer, just knowing she was out there.

He changed into a tank top and gym shorts, got under the covers and propped himself up on a stack of pillows. Automatik used an app for communicating between team members in close proximity. It didn't rely on phone systems or the internet, so the only thing their phones needed to keep in touch was battery power.

He fired up the app and sent a message to Mary: Do you wear a ghillie suit for pajamas

He'd gone through rudimentary sniper training in the SEALs but had never reached the transcendent level of Mary's craft. He'd seen her checking over her rifle before a strike, and it was like a psychic communication between human and metal.

Her message came back: You must be in your wetsuit and swim fins. Then the words faded away, a failsafe in the app in case someone else got ahold of an Automatik operator's phone.

I can only sleep if *soaked* in seawater and covered in sand, he replied, remembering the hours and hours he and his team had spent drilling in the surf.

Must make you nervous to be landlocked, sailor. She didn't let up. He imagined her voice would be low and smoky in the quiet room.

Must make you nervous not to be on the top floor.

She never did give him her room number. It wouldn't have worked for the early stages of their open flirting, but he needed it for the operation. Before she responded to him, he asked for her room, and she sent the number back quickly.

Second floor. Same side as him, just a few rooms over. Now he could keep watch on her. He replied with his own room location.

Received, was her only response.

Not that he expected her to drift up to his door wearing a flimsy robe over her well-shaped body. But he let the fantasy spin out for a second. White silk to contrast her dusky skin. Her black hair tumbling down to her broad shoulders. The silhouette of her narrow waist. Wicked glitter in her hazel eyes.

But that wasn't "Bolt Action" Mary, so he closed the door on the image of her in the robe and found himself alone in the hotel room again. Whatever she was like when she was intimate was private, between her and whomever she trusted enough to share that self.

For her, he was her teammate. She was his. They had a job in this rotten little town. He sent her another message: This would be a lot easier if we were in the same room

Was she asleep already? No. Her answer appeared on the screen: There's nothing easy about me

He hurried to explain, Talking about mission

specifics. Ease of operations. He wasn't thinking with his crotch when he wished their false identities had been connected. They might be able to cover more ground apart, but coordinating information was a pain his logistics.

Received. Absolutely opaque.

She thought he was a dog. And maybe he was. But not on a mission. And not with her.

See you in the early. He signed off.

Sleep with one eye open. Her message faded out and he shut the app off.

He would, and he knew she would, too. Nothing was safe.

THREE

THE MATTRESS AT the hotel was more comfortable than many of the places she'd stayed around the world, but it didn't make for a better night's sleep. The room had felt just as dangerous as the other bombed-out apartment buildings and mountain shacks, and she'd skimmed along, dreamless, as usual, until a small noise or a change in the air currents brought her fully awake.

The .38 had been close at hand. When she was up for good before the dawn, the firearm was on the floor during her pushups and burpees, then accompanied her into the bathroom for her shower. Toweled off and dressed, she stood at the window and watched the sky brighten.

Sunlight carved the town into relief below her. An east-west wind bent chimney smoke and steam to a hard angle. The breeze would be trouble for any shot over five hundred yards, but she didn't have anything with her that would reach that far out. She hoped her recon assignment wouldn't need that kind of ordnance. Instead, her weapons were a stack of fake business cards, logo pens, stylish but sensible boots and an expensive cardigan she'd bought at an outlet store.

Any business was hours away. She mapped the town from above and overlaid onto it what she'd already learned. Beyond the western border of her view were the high school and old warehouse and factory buildings. To the east, where the low sun seemed to light the earth on fire, was the train yard. The dangerous territory. She knew the gunrunners would kill to defend their business.

She and Ben were just the first wave. Once they found hard evidence and identified the combatants, they'd construct a solid plan and bring in the rest of the strike team to take the bad guys down. Two operators against a town, even as experienced as they were, would make for a bad vacation.

Ben's extracurricular attention still lingered below her skin, in her chest. A warmth, as if from a good dream she couldn't remember. All part of the act, but it still had an effect, making her feel like an operator and a woman. He was damn slick at putting on the moves. If the communication app didn't erase the conversation as it happened, she'd be tempted to look back at last night's exchange to figure out what specifically he'd done to make her keep thinking about the unique intimacy that had resonated since they'd sat down at the bar table.

Was he still sleeping, one floor above her? Not with this much light in the sky. Not with an operation this important. He was right. It would've been easier to coordinate their action if they were staying in the same room. But after the real charge from the fake flirting, she was glad to have her own space.

Once the hour seemed more sensible, she packed her pistol in her purse and headed down to the complimentary breakfast. No sign of Ben. She sat alone at the tall tables in the modest hotel lobby with her toast, yogurt and coffee.

The woman behind the front desk would glance over to Mary every couple of minutes, but it was just good business. Mary knew how to recognize the signs of wary animosity. Narrow eyes, sideways glances. Even outright staring. The hotel worker was merely checking on a customer. Because she didn't know what Mary was really there for. If the truth was revealed, the locals would show their true alignment. Until then, Mary considered them all combatants who weren't to be trusted.

"Don't tell me you took the last peach yogurt." Ben dug through the ice-filled tub of yogurt containers. He wore a coat, simple button-down shirt and stylish jeans. Casual, approachable but with enough style to show he meant business. "Here we go." Victorious, he retrieved one and held it up. "Goddamn mango." He placed it on a table near hers and continued assembling his breakfast.

"You're not going to keep looking?" she asked.

"Too cold." He blew into the side of his fist and rubbed his hands together. "You didn't drink all the coffee, too, did you?" There it was again, that easy thread of communication. No challenge, no commitment. Just a couple of people finding out what worked.

"I'm sure there's mud on the bottom for you."

Actually, the coffee wasn't half bad. The hotel knew what was important to business travelers.

Ben flashed her a knowing smile. "I'm used to it."

She knew what he'd been through. On the last Automatik operation, he'd been stuck in the desert as an information relay. Sun and rain had beaten down on him, and he was still up and running when it came to the final assault. She'd only caught glimpses of his action through her rifle scope, but the man was a crisp practitioner of the art of war.

The lobby was too public to discuss any of that action. In this space, they were still strangers.

He sat with his food and ate eagerly. Between bites, he asked, "Do they give you the good contacts, or do you have to hunt them down?"

She bussed her plates to a bin and turned back to him. "I have to hunt."

He nodded with a sudden gravity in his eyes. "Same."

"Good luck out there." She meant it. Things could turn quickly in this town.

"You, too." He stepped away from his food and extended his hand. "I'm Ben."

She took his hand. "It *is* cold."

"Not always." The smile was an intimate secret. Her breath caught in her throat.

They still held each other.

She found her voice. "Mary."

Was this the first time they'd touched? He'd helped her onto the helicopter during the last op. And after the assault on the house full of domestic terrorists in Michigan, she'd given him a hand up a broken basement stairway. But this moment, skin on skin, sank in. It felt too real. She wasn't susceptible to completely fake flirting. A piece of Ben must not have been lying, and part of her stirred with the attention from a man who might understand her.

She broke the contact and took a step toward the hotel's front doors. "See you around."

He tilted his head back in acknowledgment. "Count on it."

Back to business. Her manufactured persona slid completely into place as she exited the hotel. But beneath it, the connection with Ben lingered. Like a pocketful of bullets that were still warm from his hands. She trusted him with his assignment, even if she didn't trust him while flirting. He wouldn't fuck up the operation. She never did.

An internet search had revealed the one major real estate business in town. She'd memorized the directions across the simple streets and navigated her rental car there. The sky remained bright and clean. Cold. It would get colder. The bottom edges of the buildings were splashed with mud from the summer rains. Once the snow came, all the right angles in the town would be erased by the white drifts.

Morris Flats rolled past her windows, a place in stasis. No new construction. Faded "For Rent" signs in business windows. Cars being eaten from the ground up by the street salt. But occasionally she'd see a brand-new American pickup truck or SUV. Money choked in most areas and flowed strong in others.

Edward Limert's real estate company took up a corner lot. The 1950s building had windows facing both streets of the intersection, as if surveying the territory. Just like she was doing. She pulled up out front. Two of the employees perked up from their desks and tracked her. Other desks remained empty.

She stayed in the cold air as briefly as possible between the car and the offices. Worse weather had battered her skin and dug into her bones, but these people needed to see a real estate developer slightly out of her element, not a sniper who waited three days in a snow bank to fire a single bullet.

The two employees, a man and a woman, were standing by the time she stepped through the door.

The man rushed to speak first, "How can we help you?"

Her business cards were at the ready. "I'm Mary Long, from Strathmore Development." She gave the cards to the man and the woman. "Is Edward Limert available?"

"Yes." A new voice dominated the offices, making the employees wince a little. Edward had been watching from the barely cracked open door of his back office. The blinds to his interior windows were drawn and rattled as he swung his door open and strode out.

The employees sat, faces neutral. This wasn't a genial workplace. These two were putting in their time before escaping. She tried to shoot them a sympathetic look, but they were both pretending to be occupied by their computers.

Edward continued forward, his hand outstretched

like the prow of a ship. He was in his mid-forties, soft and well fed. Expensive slacks and a cheap belt. Wedding ring and a class ring. Sandy-blond hair in a pronounced sweep over his forehead. "What can Eddie do for you?" He flashed a tooth-whitened grin and smelled of this morning's coffee.

She shook his hand. "Mary Long of Strathmore Development. We're looking to enrich select territories around the Midwest, and I'm checking out Morris Flats to see if it's a good candidate." Lying came so easily.

Eddie waved her toward the back. "Well, come into the office and we'll take a look." His hand dipped into his pocket and jingled his keys in a habitual move. The man cried for attention.

He left the blinds closed and shut the door behind her. The office was undisturbed by business. Baseball memorabilia lined a shelf. The wide desk held a quiet computer, a blotter and Eddie's phone. The most valuable asset of the space lined the wall behind the desk.

A map of the town. She immediately located the hotel and where she was. East and West stretched out to the sides, where the houses thinned and larger buildings dominated. Then nothing. Swamps and prairie.

"Please sit." Eddie gestured toward the visitor chair. She complied as he took his own seat. "Now, what kind of developing do you do?"

"Mixed use, mostly. Businesses on the bottom

and residential up top. It really maximizes available lots."

He scanned her face, neck and shoulders as she spoke. Assessing and undressing. Her skin crawled at the thought of him exposing it. His hands remained on the desk, but she could see one twitching a little. He wanted to jingle his keys. "I can imagine something like that here." He turned in his chair to look at the large map. "Construction would make jobs, and the new shops would get people excited."

Railroad tracks cut long scars across the eastern portion of the map. Every direction could be fed from that hub. Perfect for the gunrunners.

"You're talking more like a politician." She smiled at him when his gaze returned to her. "Usually real estate people go for the dollars and cents first."

He twisted his mouth, smug. "Guilty." A glance at the wall directed her toward a photo portrait of him and a woman. "That's the wife talking. Donna's the mayor of Morris Flats."

So this woman would know about the gunrunning. Eddie would as well. They may even be part of it. His monogrammed dress shirt indicated he was the kind of person who'd fight to maintain his power and status. And sell guns to the others around the country with the same agenda.

"So she'll have a good idea of the personality of the town." Though she wanted to put her thumb in the base of his throat until he told her all the details of the gunrunning operation, Mary maintained her businesslike interest. "Is Morris Flats open to new development?"

Eddie tilted his head back and forth in a broad show of considering her question. "Depends on the area and what we're putting in. Some people are pretty well knee-deep in their own concrete, if you know what I mean."

She ignored his obvious metaphor. "Do you have a smaller map of town, like that one?"

He glanced behind him, then sprang into action at his desk. Business must not have been flowing into his office often, considering how many drawers he had to open in his search. Mary sharpened, alert, when a heavy object clad in leather clunked in a drawer. Eddie had a holstered gun in the desk.

Adrenaline flashed through her limbs as he reached in the drawer. She could make it over the desk in a flash and close the drawer on his hand if she had to. But he was too loose, oblivious to what he'd just revealed to her to be an immediate threat. He pulled out a map on standard paper and held it out to her.

She took the map with her left hand, her right ready to reach into her purse for her pistol. "What about the east side?" She pointed at the map and maintained her cool while the muscles in her arms tensed. "The industrial look is very popular right now, and converted old train yard buildings along with new construction could do quite well."

Eddie closed the drawer and leaned closer to her. "East?" He clicked his tongue and scratched at his earlobe. "West is better."

"Too bad." She drew her energy in, sending the message that Eddie was losing a sale.

He shrugged and tried to maintain his smile. "Remember I said some people were damn set in their ways? That's Kit Daily, and the train yard is Kit's business. Family business for a long time, if you know what I mean." Eddie seemed desperate for someone to know what he meant. His wife, the mayor, probably didn't take him too seriously. Mary didn't blame her.

"Well, that's good to know." Mary stood, digging her claws into the name Kit Daily and wanting to tear him open to see what his involvement was. "Let me look around town a bit, see the possibilities while you're thinking about what it is Strathmore Development does." She handed him her card. "We'll meet back up and see what we can do."

He trapped her card against his palm with the fingers of his opposite hand. "Glad to have you looking into Morris Flats." If he knew the real reason she was there, he wouldn't be smiling. He might be reaching for that pistol she'd heard. Even this soft man had hard bullets close at hand. "But leave Kit and his train yard alone. It's not the place for you. The guy's a former Marine, a real hard-ass without a lot of marshmallows in his cocoa, if you know what I mean."

"Sounds like a dead end for me." Kit and his train tracks were exactly where she wanted to be. She itched to pursue the new lead but knew this stage of the mission had to be a careful recon. The people were not to be trusted, and charging into their territory would set off too many alarms.

"Good thinking." Eddie came around his desk and opened the door for her. "Stick with Eddie, I'll show you around." The door closed again after she was midway through the main offices. The lights on the business phones remained unlit. He must be calling his wife on his cell.

Before leaving, Mary got a couple of lunch recommendations from the two employees. She thanked them and stepped back into the cold. At least the weather was honest. Any warmth in Eddie's office was manufactured.

She got into the car and turned the engine on for the heater. The two employees still watched her as she sat in the idling car and texted on her phone. Just as any businessperson would.

But her text to Ben read: I don't trust anyone with money here.

Hell no. His response came quickly, then faded out in the app. Rotten cream at the top.

Hell yeah. She went on to text him the lunch recommendations.

He acknowledged and told her his next destination. Police rec league now. Over and out.

Menace hummed in Morris Flats like the overhead power lines. The more she and Ben searched for answers, the more deadly the current would run. The mayor now knew someone was looking around town. She'd reach out to the police. The same cops

Ben had run against last night. And the same ones he was going to see just then. Everyone had to be counted as the enemy. Ben was her only safety. She was his only backup. And they both had to keep pressing into the danger.

INSTINCT TWISTED A knot in Ben's stomach. This town wasn't right. Mary's text had reinforced what he'd already seen.

He almost wished she was backing him up with her .50 as he walked across the chilly parking lot of the police rec league gym. Right onto the home turf of the officers he'd already tangled with. Every natural urge told him to turn around and find another lead to follow, but if illegal guns were being moved in through town, these cops would know all about it. The building was money. New construction without a single crack in the stucco of the high, imposing walls. The cars outside were just as fresh. None of them were more than two years old, and there wasn't a base model in sight.

The glass doors to the gym were clean. Ben approached them as he did any assault. Where were the blind spots? What was his quickest egress? The door was unlocked and he was grateful for the climate-controlled heat inside. Instead of an assault rifle, he held his soft briefcase full of sport bracelets, business cards and other swag. The mission was recon, not search and destroy. Yet.

A long hallway stretched to both sides of the entryway. Humid air came from the left. Locker rooms, showers, probably a whirlpool and a steam room. He walked to the right. Here the air was scented by the heavy rubber of a weight room. Another glass door revealed the pristine equipment, but no one was lifting at the moment. From the sound of the chirping squeaks down the hall, there was a basketball game in progress.

These doors, the last ones before the fire exit, only had small slits of glass. Glimpses of men, all of them white in shorts and T-shirts, flashed past. One was a decent dribbler. Another, an older guy with reddish hair, couldn't shoot for shit, but set a nice illegal screen. No one called him on it. He must have rank.

Ben took a breath and waited for a missed shot to bounce out of bounds and away from the players. While one of them was chasing it down, Ben opened the doors.

All six men turned and looked at him. The least hostile of them was cautious, curious. But that was the end of the good news. The black-haired angry cop from last night was there, burning Ben with a hard look. His partner, the blond, and two others glanced at their duffels on the side of the gym. Their guns. So they were wary enough to bring the guns in, but not to lock the doors. The cops were feared in this town, and they had little to be afraid of.

The angry cop flexed his arms and broadened his chest. "This is a private gym."

Ben smiled like a salesman. His warrior self

lurked in the shadows. "I'm not looking to join. This is the police rec league, right?"

The blond cop drifted over to his duffel and stood ready next to it.

Angry cop took a step forward and muttered to the senior man, "That's our 10-13."

Ben maintained his smile but felt a jump in his legs, urging him to get the hell out of there. The cop had used the radio code for "civilians present and listening." Last night's activity hadn't been forgotten and had made ripples into the department.

The oldest officer scowled. "You a reporter?"

That would've been the worst cover. An African-American reporter walking into a gym full of cops? Instant trouble. Sporting goods made everything nice and friendly.

"No, sir." Ben took another step onto the floor and watched the cops tense a little more. "I'm Ben Louis from Circulatron Sports Equipment out of New Jersey."

Angry cop and his partner didn't relax. The others did. A little.

The blond officer stared at Ben, skeptical. "That's your business? What does that have to do with us?"

Ben spun. "We're looking for promotional opportunities and sponsorships across the country. Rec leagues, kids, first responders."

The oldest cop smirked but still looked like he wanted to erase Ben from his town.

Ben continued. "I have samples in my bag." He

held it up and pointed at it but knew better than to dive into the interior with a bunch of wary cops around him.

"Let's see." Angry cop used his authority voice and waved Ben forward.

The cops converged around him as he opened the bag of swag. They relaxed further when they saw the contents. The angry cop hissed a laugh.

Ben pulled out one of the bracelets. "Made in the U.S.A. Rare earth magnets tuned in our New Jersey labs to increase circulation, range of motion. Reduce joint fatigue." He'd practiced this all again and again in San Diego with Harper. "Try it." He held it out to the gingery cop, knowing he had seniority. "Don't worry, it's not a bracelet. It's a performance band."

The cop plucked it from his fingers but didn't put it on. Wrinkles spread from the corners of his eyes. But his gaze was still sharp. He was in his mid-fifties, fit. His curly hair had receded a bit.

Ben's sales pitch could go on and on. "Rather than getting high-profile athletes to rep our stuff, we want real people. You see a guy on a court, making millions of dollars, drinking a certain sports drink or wearing a brand of shoes, you know he's getting paid. You don't trust him. But we trust the everyday guy."

He didn't trust any of these men. They peered greedily at the free items while being surrounded by their perfect gym and standing on their perfect hardwood basketball court.

The senior cop put the red bracelet on and waited with his head tilted back, defiant. "Is this a scam?"

Ben chuckled. "Give it a day or two. Seriously, it's science." It was bullshit. Each band contained a magnet on one side and a tiny tracking device on the other. He dug five black bracelets out of his bag and handed them out to the other police officers.

"You understand," the oldest cop said, laying down the law, "that if we wear these we're not endorsing your product and we're not to appear in any of your promotional material."

"Got it." Ben found a business card and held it out to the senior man. "But you might change that tune once you give it a chance and start blowing past these younger guys on the way to the hoop."

The cop took the card, holding it at a distance to read. "Ben Louis."

Ben extended a hand, and the cop shook it.

"Chief Pulaski."

"A pleasure, Chief." Ben nodded to the others. "Fellas."

The cops nodded back, even the blond one. Though the angry one still looked like he was ready to throw down, or at least bench-press a few stacks of plates in the weight room.

Ben edged toward the exit doors. "I'm going to be around town for a few days. You've got my card, so give a call with any questions about the performance band. Or I can stop by the station sometime." Which was very low on his list of fun things to do.

But it might be necessary for recon. "Alright, half-time's over. I'll let you get back to your game."

A couple of the cops waved vaguely. They all put on the bracelets. Chief Pulaski rolled a crackling shoulder. The angry cop flexed his lats and clenched his jaw.

Ben was almost at the door. "Enjoy the increased performance, guys. Though I don't know if it'll do anything for your midrange jumper, Chief."

Small laughs echoed through the gym. Even Pulaski smiled wryly at the dig. But his tolerance was thin, just like the angry cop. Any challenge against their power would have them reaching for their service pistol.

With a wave, Ben exited the court. The rest of the gym remained quiet as he walked up the hall and finally out into the fresh cold air. At least one of the cops must be watching him. Probably the angry one.

Still, he strode to his rental car and climbed in. How far away was Mary? He couldn't linger in the parking lot with his phone. He maintained a calm front and drove off as if it was business as usual, but he wanted to stand on the accelerator until he found her.

They'd both known the town was dangerous when they inserted. Gunrunners made for bloody business. Solo operatives could recon more territory. But Morris Flats was a grenade without a pin. Could they stand and fight if they didn't have each other's backs?

FOUR

THE WAITRESS AT the truck stop diner pursed her smile for almost everyone in the medium-size restaurant. As if she didn't want to laugh, but the customers had broken through her game face and reached her heart of gold. Except Mary. All she got were the businesslike questions of "coffee?" and "what'reyahavin'?"

Alone in the last booth against a wall of windows, Mary was able to survey the restaurant and the parking lot outside. Truckers came and went, mostly eating at the counter opposite the booths. The scene must've played out thousands of times since the place had been built in the postwar boom of the '50s. The country was in the process of being connected by highways, perfect for taking goods coast to coast.

Like illegal guns.

Three of the truckers wore concealed handguns. Barely concealed. They didn't even try to reduce the printing through their down jackets and softshells. Were the firearms for security against someone trying to steal their rig and contents? Or for enforcement and intimidation?

The men were genial enough with the waitress,

and the diner was free from overt menace. Still, the tension of Morris Flats hummed in the walls and tables. Bad business bled just under the surface.

Mary pretended to look over paperwork and sipped iced tea while tracking which truckers went to which rigs. Of the men with handguns, two of the three towed empty flatbeds. They'd either just delivered or were waiting for goods to move. But their stately pace climbing into their rigs or the time they took to smoke their cigarettes told her they weren't on the clock.

The attention of the diner shifted at once to the front door. Ben entered. His easy smile remained in place against the people overtly glaring at the stranger. When he caught her eye, he nodded and his smile warmed. The waitress and the patrons watched as he strode to Mary's booth. A buzz rushed through her blood with his attention, a remnant of the fake flirting from last night. But it had grown stronger.

The locals seemed to sort strangers as a threat or not. No one really bothered with her. Ben, though, wasn't trusted. She could see why. He was potent, very capable. And he didn't shrink or apologize his way into the space. Not that he was a brash bully. He was just being…himself.

"Working lunch, or do you mind company?" He stood a respectful distance at the edge of her booth, his hand on the strap of his soft briefcase.

She took a moment to openly assess him. Her gaze scanned across his broad shoulders, up his neck. He was put together. Adding what she'd seen of his physicality during Automatik strikes made him that much more potent. A sexual charge ran up the backs of her legs. He was a secret that only she knew. Her scan reached his face. He met her look and didn't back down. Did he see that her thoughts had strayed far from the mission? A keen edge of desire seemed to glint in his eyes.

Regaining a semblance of calm, she collected the papers spread across the table. "As long as you're not selling something or trying to buy something from me."

"Truce." He eased into the seat opposite her. "Though I did notice you didn't take the performance band last night."

"I'm juggling enough things and don't need to be beta testing your prototypes." There was enough space between them and the rest of the diner to speak freely, but not as the waitress approached.

"Prototypes?" He did a good job of looking offended. "We're fully ready to field—"

She held up her palm to cut him off. "The amount of miles I put on across the country, I'd have seen them."

"Minutes away from market," he conceded.

The waitress reached them, and Ben scanned the menu quickly and placed his order.

Once the waitress left, Mary asked him, "Are you heavy?"

"I wasn't for the police rec league, but I am now."

He was trained well enough to know not to shift his weight against wherever he wore his pistol. "You?"

"Detective special in my purse." Which was open at her side if she needed quick access.

"Five shots?" He glanced about the diner, then out into the parking lot. "Got a feeling there are more than five bad guys around here."

"Sometimes it only takes one bullet." Though their mission wasn't as clear and simple as a combat op.

He leaned forward. "Said the sniper with one hundred percent accuracy." His voice lowered and slid across the linoleum table. "Where'd you learn how to shoot like that? Delta?"

Ever since she'd been recruited into Automatik after retiring from Special Forces, her teammates had tried to pry out who she'd operated for. Only the top people at Automatik knew. The rest could run out of breath guessing. What would Ben do with the information? He was already closer to knowing her than almost any other man she knew, creating a swirling, frightening thrill that tantalized her.

Instead, she gave up a part of her past few had ever been privileged with. "Balboa13." Maybe his interrogation techniques were so low-key she couldn't have trained for them.

Or maybe he was genuinely interested in learning about her. He didn't laugh. Gravity sank into his gaze as he considered her. "Street gang?"

"Lebanese girls in the San Fernando Valley." She never got caught, though, so there was no record tying her to them.

He leaned his elbows on the table, closer to her. A knowing look in his eyes. "Sounds like trouble." Did just a sliver of her past reveal so much?

"We were." She was hard then and remained hard now.

Ben angled away as their food arrived on heavy plates. But he didn't begin eating once the waitress left. He raised his lemonade glass to Mary in a toast. "Glad you made it out to sit across from me and share a patty melt."

She clinked it with her iced tea. "Almost didn't when the cheap 9mm submachine guns hit the streets."

He drank and got into his food. "Yeah, they're still writing that story."

The blandness of her chicken sandwich felt like an aggressive act from the kitchen, trying to get her out of town. "We're in it."

He chewed and nodded thoughtfully. "My mom would've whupped me if I'd got caught up on the street, but I lost friends in gangs."

All the lies remained. Mary Long. Real Estate. Her reality: Black ops. A pistol in her purse and a map of every exit in a room as soon as she entered it. The cover was intact, so she was able to test her humanity and peel back the armor a bit and share a quiet truth with someone who might understand. With Ben.

"I lost my brother." She'd faced that pain years ago, yet a pang of the agony, confusion and fury still jolted through her heart.

Ben sighed a long breath. He placed a hand on the table and reached it a quarter of the way toward her. "I'm sorry."

The warm comfort that had started by sharing pieces of her past with him rose higher. Up her chest and across her shoulders. As if he were touching her there, releasing the ever-present tension in her muscles. What if she stretched her fingers to him? What would that connection become?

She knocked her knuckles on the tabletop to acknowledge his gesture. "Balboa13 got their revenge. And I joined the Army right out of high school, before the heat came down."

Revealing it was the Army was a clue to her Delta past, but Ben didn't jump on it.

But a little grin did brighten his face. "And you're still bringing the pain."

"To the right people." She glanced about the diner, keeping track of the incoming truckers and outgoing lunch breakers.

His gaze turned out the window and into the parking lot, where a local police car was parking. Two officers, both white men, got out. They both had dark hair and dark sunglasses.

"They the ones from last night?" she asked.

"No." Ben muttered so only she could hear, "Money and attitude. They're protecting and serving whatever's paying for their cars and new gym, and I don't think it's the taxpayers."

The whole infrastructure of the town seemed rotten. "The mayor's got to be in on it." She shared her intel quietly. The cops walked across the parking lot toward the diner doors. "Her husband wasn't scared. He's fed by it. And he has a pistol in his desk. Tried to talk me off a former Marine, Kit Daily, and his train yard."

The smile remained on Ben's face, but his eyes hardened. "Then that's where we've got to go."

The police officers entered the diner and were greeted by the waitress. Ben relaxed his posture further by leaning back in the booth so his legs stretched out beneath the table. His shin slid against hers. She knew the drill and didn't move away. The contact served a tactical purpose. If he flinched with action, she'd feel it and know when to move. Or if she needed to signal what was happening behind him, she could do it with a small press of her legs to his. But she wanted it to be more. A connection. The comfort of one person knowing another. If it wasn't for the potential danger in the diner, this touch could reinforce what they'd shared of their pasts.

To what end? Ben was an expert flirt. Was this just reflex for him?

The lies of the operation and their fake personas had to tighten up with the arrival of the police. But Mary still probed, "Your mom still around?"

A bigger smile lightened him. "Yes, and proud of me and more proud of herself for raising a boy right. Your folks?"

She shook her head. His smile wavered before she explained, "We never had a lot of money for good food or good care. I was…away." In Iraq, protecting a convoy corridor, and couldn't get home while they were both sick.

"Damn…" His leg stayed against her. The rough memory faded faster than usual. She wasn't used to sharing it.

"Old news." She shifted gears quickly as the cops took the booth next to theirs, at Ben's back. "But you're not really interested in a video call, so I can show you how I organize my kitchen cabinets."

"It tells a lot about a person." He pulled out his cell. "Take my phone, call your number with it, then we'll be looped in."

The cops refrained from conversation, obviously listening.

She let some sass whip out. "I'll take your number, and I'll call you if I'm desperate to know what's in your drawers—kitchen drawers."

He laughed and so did the cops. Ben turned as if he just realized they were behind him and nodded at the men. They tipped their heads back at him and pointed to the sport bracelets they wore.

One cop kept chuckling. "Chief stayed late to shoot extra jumpers at the end of the game."

"Did he hit?" Ben split his attention between the cops and taking out his business card and writing a number on the back.

The other cop scoffed. "One out of ten."

Ben clicked his tongue proudly. "Then the sport band's helping." He turned back to her and slid the card across the table. "Personal cell on the back."

The waitress came by and left the check before going to the police officers' table for their order.

Mary collected Ben's card and the check.

He put his hand out to stop her. "Take the card, leave the check. I got this."

She waved him off. "It's expensed. You were a business lunch."

"Bang." He recoiled as if hit. "That hurt."

"You liked it." She collected her bag and stood.

"I did." His gaze slid up her slowly, from her shoes along her legs and chest to her face. She soaked in the attention, allowing it past small gaps in her defenses. Bright awareness danced on her skin. He continued to taste her with his eyes. "You got my number. Use it."

She stared back at him. A new gravity took him. Had she gotten past his defenses as well? "We'll see how cold it gets down here in southern Illinois."

He turned the swagger back on. "I heard it gets *real* cold."

"So do I."

His smile turned wicked and ravenous as she burned him with her ice. God, if this flirtation was real, they'd either run away screaming or tear the sheets off a bed together. She gave him a wink as small solace for the injury, then walked down the row of booths toward the cash register.

As she departed, she heard the cops release a bubble of laughter.

The first one elaborated under his breath, "He puts one up at the buzzer for the win and…brick."

She was too far away to hear the specifics of Ben's defense, but the confident tone of his words was clear. The conversation between him and the police officers continued while she paid the bill. Because of the presence of the cops, the rest of the diner patrons curled more into themselves, just going about business.

The chill air shocked her first breath outside. No heat in the bright sun. But the unusual comfort from the connection with Ben remained. It had started before they'd had to turn up their flirting to keep the cover story going. So what was his angle? Build her trust, get her into bed? But it felt too real, especially when they weren't saying a word.

Footsteps hurried toward her across the parking lot. She'd reached her car and saw in the reflection of the windows that it was Ben striding closer. Her hand eased off the handle of her pistol in her purse.

"I didn't get a chance to thank you for lunch." He was a little louder than he needed to be. They both knew they were being watched. He didn't crowd her space but spoke quieter as he neared. "Or apologize for sounding like a dog. I'm not a dog. I just…" Was this part of the act? He searched for words, staring out at a weedy on-ramp for a four-lane highway. "I'm just figuring out how to talk to you."

She shifted her body from defensive to open and leaned against her car door. "And I'm figuring out if you're worth talking to."

All things their salespeople personas who'd just met would say. Also true for the black ops soldiers who'd run assaults together, drank beers together but had never shared any details from their past like they had in the diner.

"Fair enough." He nodded and took a step closer. She remained where she stood, but wanted to move forward to test how real the connection was.

No one could hear them this far in the parking lot. She maintained her cool smile for appearances and asked, "How did it happen that our covers started flirting so hard?"

He was within a couple of feet of her. Close enough to see the lines in the corners of his eyes as he grinned. Her legs nearly walked her to him on their own. "It happened naturally."

She hadn't cut the flirtation off at the hotel bar. He'd clearly been tuned to her signals. But she'd allowed it. For the sake of the operation? For the sake of the unique charge that shook her when Ben stood this near?

"Did you follow the signs of my attraction?" She ran her fingers through her hair and twisted a thick strand between them. "You did, didn't you?" Her voice raised in pitch and she playfully patted his forearm. "But how could you fall for that?" She licked her lips and kept them parted as she looked him over. He seemed susceptible to the simple symbols of seduction, and a look of desire rose in his eyes. But had she trapped herself? Her own need rose. It felt too good to be regarded that way by a man who knew more than just the soldier in her. She returned her face to neutral. "Just classic fieldwork tricks."

But his heat remained high. "I saw some tricks, but I saw some truth."

"A testament to my skill." He was right, though. And it had been liberating to show a little of herself to someone.

"You might be trained, but I'm experienced." His body remained neutral near her. "Mary Long can tell me to fuck off, and I'll still give one thousand percent of my effort backing up 'Bolt Action' Mary on this op."

She believed he wouldn't let their bizarre flirting get in the way of their safety or the mission. Same went for her.

"I'm afraid Ben Louis is getting to Mary Long." Was she admitting it for her alter ego or herself? It didn't matter what name she operated under, the same heart pounded as she continued this dance with Ben.

"Was it his wit? Or his smile?" He flashed that easy grin and got her blood pumping even faster.

"His honesty."

His face grew serious. "That's hard to come by these days."

Sparks of excitement tingled in her fingers and up her legs. Like doing a HALO jump into foreign territory. She didn't want it to stop. "Mary Long needs a kiss from Ben Louis, to see if he means what he says."

He approached. Her thrill rose higher, into her chest. His hand stroked down her shoulder and arm. She stepped away from the car and closer to him. He wasn't that much taller than her, but broader, and seemed to envelop her and shield her from the world around them. His heated gaze moved over her face, slow and deliberate. No rush toward an end. It was all meant to be savored.

His jacket was thick, but she still felt how solid he was as she moved her hand over his ribs to pull him nearer. He cupped her elbow and the two of them swayed a moment in a dance to find balance. His mouth dipped to hers. She tilted up to meet him.

The kiss surprised. He was confident, but not forceful. Firm lips that communicated there was more potential than just a kiss. Fueling her own needs. Heat spread deep in her belly and between her legs. She pressed harder against him, opening her mouth to him and seeking out her own answers. Was it real? Was it part of their cover? Her tongue darted out, found his and drew him into her mouth.

It felt like the truth. His need and hers. His hand tightening on her elbow. Her wanting to pull him closer to her chest. The heat they shared in the cold parking lot.

It was too real.

She ended the kiss.

Their hands remained on each other. Heat continued to pulse through her. She knew how to fake all the signs of seduction but understood that the desire on Ben's face had to be genuine. And her own rushed breath had been inspired by the kiss.

She glanced over his shoulder at the diner. "We sent a message." But frustration bit into her. The kiss shouldn't be over. There was so much more to discover, now that she felt signs of life beneath her armor.

His focus remained on her. "They'll know Ben Louis is a closer."

She looked up at him. "What's Mary Long?"

He considered for a moment, which was unlike him. Usually the slick answers came quickly. His hand moved from her elbow. "Unafraid to take what she wants."

She slid her hand off his side, and the chill air crept between them. "That explains why she's heading to the train yard when Eddie Limert told her not to."

The cords of his neck tensed with the prospect of danger. "Want backup?"

She shook her head. "Too suspicious. I won't press so hard I can't get out."

"Right." He nodded. "We're here for fact-finding only."

"Until they get too tight." She held up a fist between herself and Ben so only he could see it. "Someone makes a play, they'll regret it."

He bumped her fist with his own. "Be safe."

The small touch bloomed like a grenade between them.

An atmosphere of menace polluted a far corner of the parking lot, where the semis were parked. "You, too," she said.

Three truckers, not the ones she'd marked as carrying handguns, watched her and Ben with more than just passing interest. One of them talked on a cell phone and communicated short sentences to the others. The men hitched their pants up and rolled their shoulders in preparation for a beat down. Ben flicked a look to them then to the police officers in the diner. One of the cops was just hanging up his phone. A serious calm washed over Ben. She recognized it. Battle ready. He knew what was coming.

And he still managed a small wry smile for her. "Time to put on a show."

"Want backup?" She'd seen Ben's capable hand-to-hand work. It shouldn't be too much trouble, three against one. But it didn't feel right leaving a teammate to fight alone.

"Thanks." He gently ran his hand down her arm. "But it's got to look natural."

"You can still punish them." She wished for a little of the action, just so she could control a fragment of the tension building in the town around them.

He brightened with a smile. "You know it."

She got her keys out but hesitated. It still burned her to leave him. A partner. The man she'd just kissed.

He cocked his head toward her car. "I'll be fine." His sly eyes slipped back to the truckers. "The cops are trying to send a message without getting their hands dirty. I'll keep it from impacting our mission."

"I'll circle." She still felt how his lips had slid against hers.

"They'll notice."

Was this how Mary Long and Ben Louis would part?

She brought herself closer to him again and stole

another kiss. Even if she wouldn't be there, she was backing him up. Trusting him to take care of himself. The way he trusted her to operate in her sector.

A kiss between a man and a woman. A kiss between soldiers.

He let out an appreciative growl when they parted. Her frustration wasn't sexual this time as she moved away from him. She burned to stay and help him finish the fight. But he was right. She had to force herself out of the coming conflict. She got into her car and jabbed the key into the ignition. He held the door open for a moment to lean down and give her a wink, then closed it securely.

She turned the engine over, and the radio started blaring pop. She immediately killed the volume as Ben chuckled at the music. But she didn't need to apologize, and his levity was gone in the silence.

The tires rolled slowly out of the parking lot. She had to go. She wanted to stay. Through the rear-view mirror she saw Ben turn from watching her and walk toward his car. There was a bounce in his step, as if he'd just kissed the girl and had no idea the fight was coming. The three truckers detached from their rigs and approached him. She turned a corner and lost sight. Her frustration rose, laced with anger. Was it because of their operation? Or the kiss? She made a silent promise to Ben, one she'd never tell him, that she'd never leave him without backup again.

FIVE

COLD WEATHER ALWAYS made the hard points of a fight ache more. Knuckles and knees and elbows were already raw from the chill. Get them hit, and the pain was like frozen lightning bolts. He blew in his hands and rubbed them together as he approached his car.

Did he still taste her? Was it his imagination that filled his head with the scent of hot roses? The kiss had hit him like one of her sniper rounds. Out of nowhere, and he was on the ground. Flirting was one thing, and the little touches they'd shared had reinforced the act for anyone watching. But there was more to that kiss than their cover. Honest need. And a challenge that he had to be truthful.

He had been. She'd taken his breath away.

He'd wanted another, and he'd gotten it. Totally unexpected. The mysteries of Mary did not end. Pursuing them would take him way out of the safe and distant life he'd been leading, leaving him exposed.

Way more exposed than standing in this half-empty parking lot while three truckers sauntered their thick selves toward him. None of them appeared to be carrying handguns. All three had pock-

etknives clipped to their pockets. He had two knives
on him. If the bullies wanted to get things deadly,
Ben could reach for the compact 9mm strapped
to his ankle, but that escalation would change the
whole profile of the operation. One shot fired, and
he'd have to go completely dark until extraction or
a larger force could arrive to take on a full fight.

"You guys hear I was giving away the performance bands?" He opened his bag. Either the compact flashlight or the collapsible baton inside could
be used to dissuade an attack. "I've got enough for
you. Perfect for your circulation during those long
days in the captain's chair."

They didn't look interested. They just looked
mean. Two were around the same size. Broad shoulders and thick arms. One of them wore a knit cap,
and the other was shaved bald. The third trucker
licked his lips and blinked hard. Whatever he was
cranked on kept him lean. Heavy boots on all three
men.

The big guys made the first wave of the attack
while the tweaker hung back, shifting from side to
side eagerly. The men were brawlers, rushing Ben
with closed fists. Wild fury reddened their eyes. A
primal show of force meant to intimidate the victim
and win the fight before any punches were thrown.

Ben stood his ground, stayed loose and let the
wave of violence crash toward him. The knit cap
trucker led the way. He cocked his fist back for the
first devastating strike. Ben ducked low and kicked

out into the side of the first trucker's knee. Ben's cold shin immediately ached.

The trucker's scowl of rage cracked into a shocked look of pain. He bent awkwardly and listed hard to his left. Bald trucker's attack slowed. He didn't stop to help his friend who fell to the ground; instead his footsteps became lighter as he had to pick his way around the man.

Three openings on the bald trucker would allow Ben to finish the fight: side of the neck, groin, temple. He didn't take any of them. These men, and anyone watching, couldn't know the extent of his skills.

The bald trucker stumbled his way into Ben's guard and grabbed him by the shoulders. Again, he had options. The most flamboyant of which was to completely flip the trucker onto the hard asphalt. But that would reveal martial arts and combat training.

It didn't mean, though, that Ben was willing to lose the fight. He just had to roughen the edges on his usually sweet H2H game. A subtle twist of his torso pulled the bald trucker off balance. He pressed forward awkwardly as Ben maintained his balance and slid backward.

The bald trucker leaned hard on him, open mouth stinking of chewing tobacco. Ben dipped for leverage, balled a fist and drove a hard jab into the man's solar plexus. Bald trucker grunted hard, then ran out of breath. His grip loosened on Ben's shoulders and he fell into his body while convulsing for air. Ben slid sideways out from under the weight of the bald trucker, who went to his hands and knees, wheezing.

From half-standing, the knit cap trucker lunged forward and punched Ben in the stomach. It came from an awkward angle, and the man didn't have his full force behind it, but the blow still stung as Ben tightened his abs and controlled his breath. He'd had worse sparring in the MMA gym where he trained.

The knit cap trucker hobbled onto his one good leg and tried another swing. Ben leaned back from this one and raked a backhand across the man's face. The trucker's head was hard, and pain jabbed into Ben's knuckles. It would take a lot to knock him out. But from the way he blinked, he wasn't quite ready to take another hit just yet.

The tweaker wanted a piece of the action, though. He hissed and rushed Ben.

And all the while, Ben knew the cops sat in the comfort of the diner and watched everything. Wouldn't have taken much for them to saunter out and break up the fight with a casual, "Alright, fellas." But he bet they'd incited the fight in the first place in order to get him out of town. The peace they preserved didn't include Ben.

There were no weapons in the tweaker's hands, so Ben pretended to be overwhelmed by the onslaught and backpedaled. Hard blows rained in from the tweaker, and Ben closed his guard. Quick punches landed on his shoulders and glanced across his forearms. The tweaker jumped from side to side, and Ben caught glimpses of knit cap trucker getting completely to his feet and the bald trucker collecting his breath.

Ben let one of the tweaker's wide punches through his guard. Hard knuckles scraped Ben's jaw. The flash of pain lit his fuse. He wanted to demolish these men. He wanted send this whole town the message that he'd level anyone who came across him.

But he had to do it right. As an operator with Automatik. And Mary's partner in the field. Winning this fight didn't have to look pretty. Total mission success would be the payoff.

Ben slapped another punch from the tweaker away and let his own fist fly into the man's face. The man's teeth rattled and he shuddered, dazed. Ben's adrenaline masked the pain in his fist and he grabbed the tweaker's collar and ran, making him stumble backward. Before the lean trucker collected his footing, Ben slammed him into the man in the knit cap.

The injured knee gave way, and the knit cap trucker fell sideways. Ben pushed the tweaker down with him, and the two men sprawled, tangled, on the asphalt.

Hard metal clicked. Ben angled away from the sound as a new awareness of danger pulsed hot through him. The fight escalated.

The bald trucker rose to his feet. One hand rubbed his chest where Ben had punched him. The other fist held a folding knife with a bright blade.

It could kill. If the trucker knew how to use it. But it seemed like his intent was just to scare the fight out of Ben. The bald man rolled his shoulders and swung the blade out wide in sweeping slashes.

If Ben drew one of his own knives, the fight would be over quickly—with the bald trucker maimed or dead. But that would be the end of Ben's mission. He kept his cool and his balance in the face of the trucker's attempt at primal intimidation.

The resolve on the trucker's scowling face seemed to waver as he came closer and Ben didn't back off. Ben knew it took a lot to stab a man. Not many people were ready for that kind of violent intimacy. But he'd danced that dance and remembered the moves.

The blade arced through the air toward Ben's ribs. He leaped to the side and chopped the edge of his hand down into the trucker's wrist. The grip on the knife held, but the arm jolted away for a moment.

Ben curled two fingers tight and struck them into the bald trucker's exposed throat. Not hard enough to kill. The man sputtered and gasped. Ben grabbed the side of his knife hand and twisted. The trucker's arm bent at an awkward angle and he released the knife. The handle slid into Ben's hand. He let the bald man fall face-first to the asphalt.

The expensive folding knife hummed, like it still wanted to taste blood. He could've used it to end the bald trucker on the ground, or to slash into the other two, who were finally getting to their feet.

Ben took a step back, the knife calm in his hand, even though his pulse was thundering. The knit cap trucker patted his jeans pocket over his own folding knife. The tweaker's hand went to his back pocket.

Ben gave them no sign of surrender. "You ready for that, motherfuckers?"

The muscles in the knit cap trucker's arm shook. He froze with indecision. The tweaker watched Ben's knife, hypnotized.

Ben jabbed with his words. "You ready to bleed?"

The sons of bitches weren't. Roughing someone up in a parking lot was easy until the threat came back at them. Their resolve drained, revealing watery fear in their eyes. But their scowling mouths remained ready to spit venom.

The knit cap trucker barked, "*You're* not ready. You won't be ready when the real pain comes. So get the fuck out of town or be sorry that you stayed."

Ben remained silent. He didn't retreat or lower the weapon. Their move.

The tweaker wiped the blood from the corner of his mouth and checked the streak on the back of his hand. It was enough for him. He helped the coughing bald trucker to his feet and supported the woozy larger man.

The knit cap trucker still seemed to be on the edge of a decision. His hand remained over his knife. But his friends were out of the fight and wouldn't be backing him up.

"I can't help what's going to happen to you." The trucker shook his head, disgusted.

Ben thought about taunting the man back into the fight. Wouldn't have taken much to get his anger back up and have that knife come out. Then Ben could finish things with him, show him how bad an idea it was to fuck with him in the first place. But the op took precedence, so he kept his head, and the knife at his hip.

The knit cap trucker took a step back and winced on his bad knee. The tweaker still bled. The bald man wheezed and held his arm close to his chest. The three of them left with a lot less confidence than they'd attacked Ben with. They walked back toward their trucks, glancing parting shots over their shoulders, as if to tell Ben it wasn't over.

He knew it wasn't. But whatever next escalation the cops had planned wouldn't match the hellfire Ben and Mary and their team would bring down on this place as soon as they identified and mapped the gunrunning operation.

Seeing the knife might've piqued the cops' interest, but they still didn't come out into the parking lot. Maybe once blood had been spilled. Local blood. Ben didn't expect any special treatment.

The heat of the fight diminished, leaving cold aches in his knuckles and on his jaw. He'd made it all look clumsy enough. He was fine with them thinking he was a badass, as long as they didn't identify him as a trained operator.

His former attackers were all the way back at their trucks when he returned to his car. He thought about tossing the knife in a sewer drain along a nearby curb, but knew the cops were watching and would probably arrest him for littering. He folded the knife away and slipped it into his jacket pocket. Now they might arrest him for theft.

But he got into his car and started the engine without incident. The heater took a moment to kick in. He rubbed the ache out of his fingers and knuckles. Pulling his phone to alert Mary about the fight would look too suspicious. Either he'd appear to be snitching or bragging on social media. So he threw the rental into gear and headed out, knowing the truckers and the cops tracked every move.

He'd find another parking lot on the other side of town where he could let Mary know what went down. The crooked police tried to send a message. They got one in return.

Mary was out there alone. The bold, exposed kiss still shocked through him, even after the adrenaline of the throwdown in the parking lot. She'd shaken his understanding of her depths. But it hadn't changed the fact that he'd never known a more squared-away operator than her. Still, bad things happened to good soldiers.

Someone in this town just got closer to pulling the trigger, and he had to let her know.

MARY ARRIVED AT the train yard with the open, optimistic smile of a salesperson. She exited her car and scanned the area, pretending to be excited by the possibilities. Inside, she was furious. Radio silence from Ben. She knew he could take on three local bullies in a street fight. But what if things had escalated? Had the cops come out of the comfort of their diner to get involved? If anyone pulled a gun, the whole complexion of the action would change. Hell, the entire operation in Morris Flats would change.

Her boots crunched on the oily gravel at the edge of the parking area. There was little transition between the city street and the hard industrial environment of the yard. She'd been hoping for an administrative building with clean carpeting and business offices, but only a collection of single-level cinderblock structures with metal doors and metal roofs stood before her.

The cars in the lot were a mix of very expensive and completely rusted out. To track down the gunrunners, she needed to talk to whoever drove the perfectly detailed crew cab pickup truck.

But this was a very private space. None of the building doors had any signs on them, not even a bathroom. Someone either belonged here or they didn't. She definitely didn't and would have to be very careful as she probed into the secrets.

Instead of heading to the first building, she moved around it, farther onto the grimy gravel and closer to where the train tracks cut the earth and the signal towers grew. It all looked like normal business, much of it unchanged for probably a hundred years. Metal clanged and white, black and Latino workers shouted instructions over huge idling engines. On the other side of the iron-and-steel forest were the warehouses.

A direct route wouldn't work. She'd only get thrown out, and they'd be watching for her from then on. She readied herself and strode toward the closest low building.

Her phone buzzed the distinct pattern of the Automatik communication app. She immediately stopped to pull it from her coat pocket. A cold wind knifed over the flats around the train yard, bringing the smell of diesel and wrapping her in worry. Relief and heat rushed through her limbs when she read Ben's message.

They tried. They bled. Be careful out there. Town's all tripwires.

The words faded. The release from her concerns about his immediate safety lifted. He'd made it through the fight. But they were both still in danger.

She wrote back, Glad you're still operational. At the yard. Rendezvous soon

Looking forward to it. Over.

Was he talking strictly about the mission? The kiss that had started for show continued to shake her. Did she want more? Could he give more? Over and out.

Back to her intelligence gathering. Though debriefing Ben later might take on a very non-military bearing.

Beat-up blinds in a window of the closest building shifted. She was already being watched. But they'd only see the real estate developer, a bit out of her element but ready to make deals. She walked along the steel porch in front of the building and opened the front door without knocking.

Stale cigarettes and stale coffee had soaked into the mottled beige carpeting long ago. Three men worked in this long, open space, with more doors along the back wall. One tall and wide man stood. His chair swiveled, revealing where it had scraped bare the wood paneling on the wall.

He squinted, refocusing from his computer screen, and held up a hand as if in warning. They didn't appreciate new business. But he paused before speaking, almost mesmerized. He smelled the air and his hand lowered slightly.

Perfume didn't have to be expensive to be effective. The fresh smell of clean roses transformed the musty offices. The pistol in her purse wasn't her only weapon.

"Hi, I'm Mary Long with Strathmore Development. I was told to talk to Kit Daily out here."

The large man's face fell slightly with disappointment. The other two men sagged in their seats, surrounded by a technological timeline from the '80s to present day. No one had bothered to clean out the fax machines, dot matrix printers and carbon paper as these offices had progressed. Their current computers were top of the line, though, and jarringly sleek among the old tan tube monitors piled on the ground.

"Kit's not here." The standing man's accent had a slight rural twang. He rasped, too, like he yelled a lot. She guessed he wasn't a shouting stock trader by the lines of grease that had worn into his fingers. He was a foreman.

She pulled a card and extended it toward the man. "Any idea where I could find him?"

He took the card, scanned it, squinting harder. "Not right now."

Not in the era of cell phones and instant messages? She let it go, maintaining her genial smile. "Maybe you can help me…" Her voice rose at the end, prompting him.

"Len." This man had no butter for public relations. "And I don't know when Kit's coming back today."

"Let's forget about Kit for a second." Len and the other two men seemed shocked. Evidently, Kit wasn't the kind of man to be forgotten or passed over. "You've got to tell me about these beautiful brick buildings…" She left the offices out the front door, hoping Len would follow.

He did, seeming a bit put out to be on his feet that long and back in the cold. He trailed after her on the steel porch and adjusted his canvas coat, revealing a glimpse of an automatic pistol in a shoulder holster. A jolt of adrenaline sharpened her. She remembered what Ben had said about this town being all tripwires. The cops had already prompted the truckers to make a play for him. What would it take for her to bring out Len's aggressive side? She made sure never to completely turn her back on him.

"These...are these warehouses?" She reached the end of the building, stepped down into the gravel and pointed at the large structures on the other side of the tracks and waiting train cars.

"They are," Len answered grudgingly and ran a hand through his black, greasy hair.

"See, this is the perfect kind of thing for our clients." She continued walking, stepping over tracks and winding around a set of empty cargo cars. "The brick is like an instant yes for them."

"Ma'am, please don't go that way." Len skipped to keep up.

"It's Mary, Len. You've got my card and my number." She ducked under a thick chain meant to separate areas of the yard. "So when you realize what kind of goldmine you guys are sitting on, you'll call me."

"A lot of this is in use." He made it to her side and matched her pace.

"Mixed use," she corrected him. "Businesses on the bottom, loft studio apartments on top."

He made it around her and stood to block her path, about a hundred yards from the warehouses. She suppressed her anger at being corralled. The foreman was clearly annoyed, but did manage to not overtly threaten her. "I can almost guarantee Kit won't be interested in this."

"Industrial chic." She leaned to peer around him at the three-story structures. A few high windows were broken out, but the loading doors below were well maintained, and new lighting had been recently secured to the bricks. She picked up a heavy shard of rusted metal, about the size of a thick marking pen, with threads cut into one end. "You probably have old, unused machinery and equipment lying around here that you could sell for thousands of dollars to the interior designers." She tapped the metal on her palm, reassured by the improvised iron weapon. "A goldmine, I tell you."

Len spread his arms out, a living roadblock. His coat opened to give her a better view of the .40 pistol in a tactical nylon harness. He had two spare mags on the other side of the rig. If trouble came Len's way, he was very ready. She was, too. It would be faster to take his gun than reach for hers, if it came down to it. Len was almost out of patience. "This is a working train yard, ma'am. It's not safe for you out here, and we're not looking to convert anything into trendy loft condominiums." He swung one of his thick arms back toward the parking area. "Now please..." His eyes hardened. A five o'clock shadow framed the serious line of his mouth.

This was his limit. She wanted to test him. Ever since she'd had to leave Ben in the parking lot she'd been itching for payback. But it would have to come down the road, when the strike was planned and ready. Though her fist remained tight around the iron shard.

A chill wind shouldered past the warehouses and brought very specific smells to Mary. She knew Ben would recognize them as well. Gun oil. Packing grease. Military-grade transportation materials. Every airfield and base she'd been on had that smell in at least one building. That was usually where she'd slept, close to the ordnance so she'd be ready. It had been a few years since she'd been so surrounded by it, but it was hard to scrape the thoughts of her different Delta deployments to Iraq and Afghanistan from her mind.

Though she yearned to charge past Len and investigate the warehouses, Mary turned and started walking back with the same pace she'd probed into the yard. "Now, the fact that it's working could actually be a selling point. I wouldn't be surprised if those Chicago hipsters would want to move down here just so they could live next to all this heavy industry."

Len scattered gravel with his large feet as he kept up. "They'd hate it here."

She fished another card from her purse. "They like hating things." The iron shard remained in her other hand. She didn't think she'd let it go until she was completely extricated from Morris Flats.

Of course Len knew which car to herd her toward. A small town kept track of strangers. A small town with a secret would kill those strangers if they found things they weren't supposed to.

She handed him the card. "Now you have two. One for you, one for Kit. I'd love to talk to him when he's available. And you…" Her keys jingled loudly, indicating she wasn't planning on staying too long. "Think about what we talked about. Keep an eye out for any equipment or carts you could liquidate. Good money in that."

He glanced at his custom truck. Len already made good money. "Yeah, I'll think about it." He still stood to block her view of the warehouses. "And we'll call if anything comes up."

"Excellent." She opened the car door and slid in. "Thanks, Len." She tossed her purse and iron fragment on the passenger seat and started the car. Len closed her door and stood by until she put it in gear and drove off.

She'd played it right and should've only left him with a business card in his hand, the annoyance of a city girl talking at him and the fading scent of roses. He wouldn't know about her ability to field strip and reassemble his automatic blindfolded. Or how her readiness alert for the operation ticked up two levels. The guns were there, making her awareness buzz. She and Ben were one step closer. One step into a minefield.

SIX

MONEY FLOWED UPHILL in Morris Flats. After driving around the public park a couple of times to see the mud-tracked baseball diamond and basketball hoops with no nets or chains at all, Ben parked at the high school. While still in his car, he discreetly removed his ankle holster. After squaring it away under the floor mat, he walked onto the campus in search of the gym. He passed cars of various ages. Hand-me-downs and brand-new rides. If the kids of the gunrunners went here, there must not be a private school in town. The cars in the faculty section weren't as nice as many of the student cars.

Like the rest of the town, most of the school buildings seemed to be from the postwar boom. But the tile had cracked, and water stains spread like rusty clouds on the drop ceilings. Slot windows in the classroom doors revealed crowded rooms and the usual assortment of kids of different races being talked at by a teacher. They still used chalkboards—no whiteboards or computer projectors at Lincoln High, home of the Plainsmen.

At least there was a security officer looking after the place. The Latino man in his mid-thirties approached Ben with his thumb hitched in his belt, close to the can of pepper spray. He also wore a collapsible baton, with the end brassed from his palm resting on it, but the holster was tight, so he didn't use it much, if ever.

"Can I help you, sir?" The guard's eyes were wary, hard. He took his job seriously. And he spent time in the weight room, maybe punching on a heavy bag.

"Ben Louis." He handed him a card. "Circulatron Sports Equipment. I'd love a couple of minutes to talk to some of your coaches."

The guard didn't look at the card. His eyes scanned Ben, taking in the scrapes on his knuckles and jaw.

Ben rubbed at the bruise on his face. "Yeah, I didn't order dessert, but a few truckers at the diner brought me a slice anyway."

"Sonny's Diner?" A hint of compassion crept into the guard's voice.

"That's the one."

"Stay away from that place." The guard motioned Ben to follow him. "Go to the Imperial instead."

"I wish you'd told me that an hour and a half ago." Though he'd been able to walk away from the fight, and it helped define which side of the line those town players were on.

The two of them walked to the administration offices, where Ben laid out his pitch about getting quality sports advancements into the hands of real athletes. He'd gone over it so many times it was a struggle not to rush. Especially when a mission clock ticked hard in his head. Mary was at the train yard. He hadn't heard back from her yet. A visitor badge was created by a school administrator, and the guard escorted him back into the main hallway.

Classroom noise created a constant chorus as they walked to the far end of the building.

"I'll hit the Imperial." Ben shifted his phone from his front jeans pocket to the inside of his coat, where he'd definitely feel any notifications. Especially from Mary. "But if I wanted to take a lady out to a nice meal, maybe candles, where's a spot for that?"

The guard didn't hesitate. "El Pantano. In Dansville."

Ben knew the Spanish translation. "The swamp?" He lowered his voice so it didn't echo through the hall. "I already threw down with asshole truckers at a diner. What's going to happen at the swamp?"

An easy chuckle lifted out of the guard. "It's not that bad. It's good. Sit down. With candles."

"I got to trust you on this one, man." Ben put out a fist, and the guard bumped it with his hard knuckles. "Ben."

"Oscar."

They exited the main building, crossed concrete patios with basic tables and benches, and approached the tall, wide gym. Plaster peeled at the corners to reveal the cinderblock structure. The roof sagged in places. A tenth of the money that had been put into the police rec league could bring the exterior of the school gym to top shape.

The interior was just as bad. Oscar held the door open for Ben, then the two of them proceeded onto the water-stained court. Half of the folding bleachers had been pulled out. The old scoreboard still burned with a home loss.

"Romero." Oscar's voice reverberated throughout the gym, all the way to the office doors on the far end. He turned to Ben. "Hopefully he's here. Either this or the math room."

A tall Latino man in his forties exited the offices, a wary look on his face. He walked like an athlete across the floor, a little stiff in one knee and his lower back. But the man Oscar called Romero was still in good shape and had a full head of black hair slicked back.

"What's up, Oscar? Who's this?" Romero still didn't smile.

"No trouble today," Oscar replied.

This town was used to trouble. Ben imagined that if someone was on the outside of the illegal business, they were always on edge.

"Ben Louis." He extended a hand, and Romero shook it.

Oscar angled toward the door but asked Ben, "You good?"

"All good. Thanks for your help."

"You got it." Oscar gave him a small salute before exiting the gym.

Romero's caution remained. "What can I do for you, Mr. Louis?"

"It's more about what I can do for you." Once again, Ben fell into his sales pitch. He produced a bracelet and gave it to Romero, explaining all the benefits. And how coaches and student athletes were really the ones who deserved this kind of leg up. And he kept thinking about Mary. Was she pitching the same BS as him? Or was she taking cover in an alley and picking off bad guys with only five shots in her .38?

"And you're not asking any compensation?" Romero put the bracelet on and stretched his back a little.

"Not at all," Ben reassured.

"And we're not required to be in any ads if we don't want to be?" The coach walked to a worn basketball and dribbled a little as a test. His skills were sharp.

"Only if you get in touch with us." Ben's phone buzzed. He had to slow himself down instead of tearing it from his coat. "I'm sorry, I've been waiting to hear a piece of news from back home and I have to get this." He removed the phone and let out a long breath when he saw the message was from Mary.

In and out of the train yard clean. Warehouses smell like CLP. We have to recon further.

Romero dribbled and shot the ball with good form. It swished through the basket. "Good news?"

"Yeah." CLP was military-grade gun oil. He knew the smell and how it felt on his fingers as he cleaned his weapons. Good news, they had a location. But it didn't make anything easier. He texted back, Received. At high school. Let's go out tonight. Wear black.

It's a date. Her message blinked on, then faded out. If only it was it was goint to be an evening out. Drinks, conversation, exploration. She'd look fine in a little black dress, but he knew her darkest clothes were tactical gear. Business first.

The class bell rang through the school, almost immediately followed by the boisterous chatter of teenagers.

Ben caught the ball as it bounced through the hoop again and passed it back to Romero. "Feels better already, right?"

"Maybe." The man posted up an invisible defender and shot again, making it.

"Sweet." Ben chased the ball down and skipped it over to Romero. "I saw you had a train yard in town. Was thinking about getting some of these on the guys down there."

"I wouldn't." Romero held the ball, face dead serious. "Kit Daily's not interested in new ideas."

"I want to give these to the working men, not the pencil pushers."

"Sean Harris is a good guy at the yard." Romero

watched the doors as the voices grew louder. "Girls' basketball team's training in a minute."

The first person into the gym was an African-American woman around the same age as Romero, but a little shorter than him. Her wary gaze mirrored his as she looked over Ben. "I heard we had a visitor." There was chalk on the sleeves of her blouse. She wore athletic shoes with her jeans.

Romero introduced them. "Sue, this is Mr. Louis." They shook hands. "She's my co-head coach."

Her wedding band was identical to Romero's.

"Call me Ben. Please." He secured his briefcase as the kids started pouring in and spoke in a private voice to Romero and Sue. "Our company deals with other sporting goods entities. I'm going to make a couple of calls and see what we can do about getting new equipment in here. No strings. Seriously." And Romero and Sue would never know that it was really money that Automatik had seized from drug runners and human traffickers that paid for any upgrades Ben could secure for them.

Sue's eyes softened. "Any help is appreciated."

He handed both of them cards. "You'll hear from me. Or be in touch if there's anything I can do for you." He swam upstream through the incoming girls' basketball team, exited the gym and walked back through the outdoor patios.

Groups of kids lingered out there in the growing cold. They chatted with each other or worked over their phones, which ranged from run-of-the-mill to top-of-the-line. The teens with the more expensive phones wore pricey shoes, both the boys and the girls. Blood money kept them in fashion. Some of them would be the next generation of gunrunners, while there was a good chance one or more of their classmates would be the victim of gun violence.

Ben stopped when he recognized a face in the crowd. The black kid he'd seen on the curb at the gas station the night before stood with friends, a solemn expression on his face. His eyes were red, still raw from the pepper spray. The kid caught Ben staring and glared back at him a second before awareness dawned on his face. Ben tipped his head back to ask if the kid was alright. The teen shrugged, nodded. Ben understood there was a lot that wasn't alright. He couldn't fix all of it but he was furious to find and crush the biggest problem that plagued this town. The kid turned back to his friends, and Ben left the patio.

Most of the students were back in rooms by the time the second bell rang. Ben gave Oscar a salute on the way out of the main building and found himself back in the parking lot. Fucking complicated town. A twisted mission. Sitting in a ditch with a finger on his trigger was so much simpler than collecting intel from people who either didn't trust anyone or had a lot to hide.

It had already come to blows. A knife had come out. What was next? Drawn blood? How long until someone started shooting to protect their killing business?

He drove back to the hotel to regroup and rest.

It was going to be a long night. But the complications wouldn't end. Operating with Mary was no problem. He trusted her skills to be top-shelf. But he couldn't quite trust himself with the quiet moments between them. Not after that kiss. Not after it had reached deeper than he'd ever expected and had taken up residence like a truth he wasn't ready to admit.

Two o'clock in the morning. She could finally be herself. Mary drove the last three blocks to the pre-arranged rendezvous point with no headlights. She was dressed all in black and the car was black. She slowed in the black void at the edge of a highway on-ramp. Ben emerged from the shadows and hurried toward the car.

Being active on an op always carried a charge. All her senses had to be sharp and muscles ready. But seeing Ben kitted out in his black fatigues, knit cap and gloves gave her blood an extra kick of speed. He was a good-looking man in jeans and a T-shirt. Dressed as an operator, he was downright sexy.

He swung into the car as she glided past. His door closed. She picked up speed. Light from the town bounced off low clouds in a dim, yellow haze, allowing her to continue navigating without the headlights.

"Company car?" Ben thumped the dash of the American-made sedan with his fist.

"I stole it." The rendezvous had been walking

distance from the hotel, but they'd both taken long routes and zigzagged to cover their tracks.

"I don't know, Ms. Long—" Ben feigned innocence, "—I thought we were just going out for a milkshake. Things are getting a little too wild for me."

"Too late to turn back, Mr. Louis." Those identities had no place in this car, at this hour. "You and me, we're going to get wild down at the train yard."

Ben grunted something carnal. "I do like the sound of that."

She did, too. A quick heat that had no place on the battlefield wrapped around her hips and breasts. The kiss had proven some kind of connection. What would they be like if they took it further?

"But maybe an alternate plan." Ben pulled out his phone and brought up an app. "I got an interesting ping from the bracelet I gave Chief Pulaski." He showed her the screen. A map displayed a fifty-mile radius around them. Several circles dotted the area. Each bracelet Ben had handed out was a tracker, tied to local cell towers, which triangulated their movement. One of the circles moved in an open space to the northeast. Ben shook his head. "What kind of business does a police chief have at this hour in a state park?"

"New plan works for me." She redirected the car in a more northern route. "The warehouse can wait. If the chief is live, we need to be there."

Ben placed the phone on his thigh and moved his awareness out the windows as he spoke from memory. "State park is approximately one thousand square kilometers, forest, rocky canyons, with a highest elevation around three hundred meters."

"We'll get the car close, but not too close. Cover the rest on foot." No time to study a map. They were going in cold.

"NVGs?" Ben patted a pocket on his tactical vest.

"Got 'em." They were both equipped with night vision goggles. "Load out?"

"Have a .40 on my hip, another on my chest and a 9mm on my ankle. Couple of knives and some really good insults I've been saving up." He shifted in his seat to watch a passing car. It paid them no attention. "Don't like traveling this light."

"I feel that." Usually she could only find comfort with a rifle in her arms. "Sidearm, backup and a single-shot, break-barrel pistol chambered for 7.62mm on my back."

"Damn fine." He growled again. "Truth be told, I'd much rather be out late with 'Bolt Action' Mary than Mary Long."

Words. They didn't cost him anything. But did he understand what they meant to her? Did he know how they reached past all the hard years she'd spent fighting and gave her something she'd forgotten? Hope. The flash of pleasure. Enjoyment in the unknown.

"Mary Long *did* make out with you in the parking lot." The streets grew darker farther away from Morris Flats, making her drive more slowly.

"Is that who that was?" Ben wasn't needling her. It seemed he needed to know.

But she didn't have the answer. Doubt eroded her footing, giving way to confusion. The kiss had burned past all the layers. She'd wanted that. To be vulnerable. And now it felt too dangerous. His words had too strong an effect on her. She couldn't afford to get lost in the desire for normal human contact.

"Intersection approaching." She tipped her head toward the front of the car, moving Ben's gaze off her.

He tapped on his phone and pointed. "Veer left. This road skirts the park and should get us to an insertion point near the chief's marker."

"How far to insertion?"

"Forty clicks."

"Just a casual road trip with no headlights on an unknown road." It would be a long night. She conserved what energy she could while maintaining her focus on the road.

"You learn to steal cars in Delta, or was that from Balboa13 as well?" Ben sat back in the seat, his gear creaking. She could see him settling in for the long haul as well.

"Public library."

"Great resource." He whistled low. "That's where I learned how to swim."

"Not the Navy?"

"Already knew how to swim and tie knots from

our local afterschool club. Joined for the travel and the tech."

"But you went elite." It was difficult to concentrate on the road when she wanted to be watching his face for hints at his interior.

"I can get a little…restless." He chuckled. Because of his reputation of jumping from bed to bed? Another reason she couldn't just trust falling into his arms. "And competitive," he continued. A more serious air descended on him. He tugged at the collar of his tactical vest and readjusted his kit.

"Not a lot of African-Americans on the Teams." She couldn't remember meeting another black SEAL.

He smiled, and the atmosphere lightened again. "Someone's got to show those cowboys how it's done."

After a moment he cleared his throat to draw her attention. She saw he had his fist out toward her. She bumped it with hers, and they both returned their attention forward. The landscape grew wilder, and they climbed out of the swampy flats and into low hills.

"Can't even imagine what it was like for a woman in a combat detail." Ben shook his head. "The women sailors I knew had to be extra tough, and they weren't even trigger pullers out with a bunch of dudes."

"I was pulled from supply duty because my complexion fit the current profile for the theater of operations." Having a female operator who could pass as Iraqi or Afghani was a hell of an asset for the Army. "I didn't have much of a choice when I joined up. I had zero choice when they routed me into the shadows."

"You made it out of the shadows."

She laughed with the irony. "Black clothes. Black car. Running dark."

He nodded with understanding. "At least we're calling the shots now."

"And I don't have macho teammates getting butt-hurt when I outshoot them." Not to mention the under-their-breath comments about her breasts getting in the way of her shooting platform, or how they thought she'd go full Rambo and win the war herself during her period. "They mostly shut up after I'd given them cover fire from three quarters of a mile away during a compound search at the edge of Khost."

"We did a little business over there." His voice was flat.

"Probably tracking down the leads we found." The road blackened and took more of her concentration.

"Or cleaning up your mess."

"I'm always clean."

"Yeah," he conceded. "I've seen it." The glow from his phone revealed the calm focus on his face. "Seven more clicks."

She pulled a night vision monocular from a pouch on her vest and held it to her eye. The landscape brightened into shades of grainy green. The road was crisp in the contrast with the trees on each edge, allowing her to pick up her speed.

Ben leaned forward in his seat as his energy charged back up. "No doubt you could outshoot me from range. But door kicking…"

"I've spent plenty of time in the shooting rooms." Practicing and practicing, until drawing her gun and firing into an enemy was purely instinct, without thought. Was she completely thoughtless now, a tactical machine?

"Sounds a lot like Delta training." She heard the smirk in his voice.

"I've heard of Delta. They're real secretive, right?" She tried to keep the sarcasm down, but it leaked out.

"But not as badass as Balboa13."

"Hell no."

Ben handled the piece of history she'd given him with care. She felt less like a machine.

"One click ahead." He tilted his head from side to side, loosening. "For CQC, though, nobody beats me."

"From what I hear, you do a lot of work up close." One side of the road widened to a large turnout edged with tall trees. She drove off the asphalt, over the gravel and into the thick of the forest. They'd be invisible from the highway.

He opened his door, smile flashing in the dim light. "The only complaints come from the bad guys."

A moment later they were both outside the car

and closing the doors as quietly as possible. The forest air was cold and dry. She met Ben in front of the car and they looked over the map on his phone. Her finger traced a route from their location to the pulsing circle that indicated the police chief. Ben nodded his agreement and moved out.

She maintained a close position behind him. They moved by starlight into the thickening forest. Black trees striped against a slate sky. Dry pine needles crackled under their feet. She rested her left hand on Ben's shoulder and followed his path while checking behind them. No signs of activity there.

Even though they hadn't trained together, their movement through the forest remained quiet and fluid. His awareness kept them moving forward. She scanned their perimeter and six o'clock for any threats.

They stopped and lowered themselves into the shelter of the trunk of a large pine and checked over the phone's map. Ben had it dimmed so it barely made more light than the sliver of a moon that slung close to the western horizon. They were still half a kilometer to the target. Anticipation built in her. So far the mission had been a collection of loose ends that needed tying. They had no idea what they'd find in this forest, but hard evidence would allow her to start making a plan of attack.

Ben whispered, "Maybe the chief has a cabin out here for liaisons."

"More like a horseshoe set, the way he's walking

back and forth." The indicator had been moving in a jagged line through a contained area.

"Ain't nothing wrong with late-night country games. Maybe we should just leave him be." Instead, he moved out of his crouch to resume their stalk.

She kept pace with his efficient movement. Careful and calculated. She felt how his muscles propelled him, as if there was no barrier he couldn't get around. He was a real operator. She'd known men like that before. Automatik was populated with them. But she hadn't kissed any of them. And none of them had learned as much of her as Ben had.

Feeling him against her as they progressed through the forest was more than tactical. The mission wasn't jeopardized, but she was certainly aware of how her body soaked in each contact between them. And when they separated for a moment, her nerves yearned for the touch again.

He stopped suddenly, and she pressed close to him. The grip of her holstered pistol knocked against the knife on his belt. With or without their gear, they were both deadly. Together and naked, they could be more than that. She steadied her legs and pushed away the carnal thoughts.

Ben held up a finger and tilted his head. She listened, then caught the faint sound of distant idling engines. He waggled his eyebrows and smiled. They were on target. She leaned against him in the direction of the action. For a moment they pressed together. Like a primer and an explosive.

He moved, and they resumed their trek. But their bodies seemed to remain closer, more coordinated. The sound of the engines grew louder. The forest thinned, and a chill wind chopped in through the trees. She smelled diesel exhaust and tapped Ben on the shoulder. He nodded and motioned the direction he was proceeding.

They broke through the trees and went down to their bellies. A dirt and pine needle carpet brushed away under her hands as she moved forward. Soon she crawled slowly across hard stone with Ben at her side. The wind brought men's voices from nearby. They spoke over the sound of the engines.

She felt her way forward on a rock until there was nothing left to touch. The sounds were coming from below. She and Ben were hidden on the edge of a bluff, fifty feet above a long clearing in the forest below. Semi trucks idled there, and men milled about. A few of the trucks were bare, while most were hitched to trailers or empty flatbeds. The light of the trucks revealed that at least a half dozen men carried assault rifles, most of them military grade.

Ben slowly extended his phone for her to see. They were right on top of the police chief's position. Ben's face remained still and grim. "Target acquired."

SEVEN

BEN HAD LAIN down with a few women in his time. Bar pickups, or friends of friends. The party spots in San Diego he knew were tailor-made for casual hookups. One or two nights. Maybe three, then everyone moved on. Her bed, his bed, it didn't really matter.

But he'd never taken up a tactical position with a woman before. He'd never been this close to Mary during an op. They'd usually been separated by around a thousand meters. Her presence had only been felt through her cool voice over the radio or her hot .50 rounds smashing into the hostile territory around him.

With his shoulder and hip and leg against hers, he felt the unhurried processes of her body as she inhabited the warfighter space. Her steady hands attached a night vision monocular to a telescopic sight and brought it to her eye.

She scowled. "Bad guys."

He stowed his phone and put together his own sighting rig. Despite trying to keep himself from idling too high during the ride in the car, he'd been itching to get out and move. The quiet conversation between him and Mary in the lead-up to the action had put a charge in him. What was the release? They hadn't been driving to her place, wherever that might be, for a glass of wine by the fire and the time and space to find out what the two of them would really be like together. Her strong body fit his during their insertion walk to the rocky over-look. They'd moved perfectly.

He'd barely noticed the cold night. His situational awareness had remained frosty, but heat had pumped through him as he'd felt her hand on his back and leg brushing his. The smallest touch brought back the kiss. Raw and real.

Fifty feet above gunrunners in the middle of the night wasn't the best place for a make-out session. Ben refocused on the op.

Green hues carved out the scene below him as he swept the night vision over the trucks and men. Assault rifles. Holstered pistols. Empty trucks. Steaming cups of coffee and a lot of talk. A group of about ten men huddled together next to one of the flat-beds. The men with the assault rifles maintained perimeter watch.

"There's the chief. Ten-thirty, talking to the group." He heard Mary shift slightly to that view. "Pulaski. Shitty jump shot, but I'm sure he's quick on the trigger when it comes to protecting his interests."

"Two of your BFFs from the diner are there, too." Anger crept into her whisper. "I was hoping you'd put them in the hospital."

"Couldn't sacrifice the mission for a moment of

pleasure." He scanned the area. The knit cap trucker he'd kicked in the knee sat on the step of a semi, his bad leg outstretched. "I mark all three." Another man in the group turned, and Ben recognized his aggressive stance. "And one of the cops from the gas station and rec center. Angry and cocked."

"Second in command?" A hint of anger spiked her words.

"More like muscle. Seems too keyed up for leadership."

"They're going over a plan."

Chief Pulaski held a clipboard and pointed at it, then at different men.

"Routes, distribution, timing." Ben would've loved to get his hands on that clipboard. "A ton of planning to make all this movement not look like an illegal gun convoy."

She huffed out in frustration. "I can't lip-read through the night vision."

The tech helped them see meager details, but the rest was a muddy wash. "So far they're all agreeing with their assignments. All nods, no arguments. The chief doesn't need a second in command."

"But maybe he's not the top dog. We still haven't identified Kit Daily."

"He's probably warm in his bed full of blood money."

Mary's posture tightened slightly as she zeroed in on something. "His foreman isn't. Len's on the perimeter of the group. Tall man at the five o'clock."

Ben identified the figure. The blocky man

watched, shifting from foot to foot and blowing into his hands. "None of the chief's directions go his way."

"The foreman's keeping an eye on his boss's interests."

"Kit Daily needs a talking to."

"Fast." She growled. "Winter is going to completely wipe this area out."

The huddle of men broke up, with Chief Pulaski getting the last word and the guys nodding. The angry cop stayed with his chief as the foreman exchanged a few sentences, then ambled off. The meeting was over and the men returned to their trucks, including Ben's playmates from the parking lot.

"Everything moves before the snow comes in." He stowed his night vision and slid backward from the bluff, away from any possibility of being spotted. Once clear, he pulled out his phone and brought up the messaging app that tied them to the rest of the Automatik team. He murmured as he typed what information they'd learned. "Trains and trucks will be long gone in two weeks. Maximum."

Mary detached herself from the rock and eased back to cover with him. "Maybe we can get hints of a timeline at the train yard." Small clicks indicated she was disassembling her telescopic night vision rig.

More headlights blinked on and glowed in the valley below them. Truck engines revved and moved out.

"And it'll give us an idea of how much merchandise they have to move." He stowed his own gear in preparation for egress. "How big was the warehouse?"

"Two that I could see. Twenty-five thousand square feet each?"

Truck after truck exited the staging area while Ben and Mary lay on the ground and waited for the sounds to disappear. After a few minutes, the forest and hills returned to silence.

His body ached to move. "Now it's cold."

"It's still better than trying to sell mixed-use real estate developments." She pulled herself into a crouch and eased toward the forest. "I don't know what the fuck I'm talking about with this stuff."

He trailed behind her lead position with a hand on her shoulder. "So real estate wasn't your plan B?"

"Prison was my plan B." Her words were as quiet as her footsteps.

He was stunned. "You mentioned Balboa13, but I didn't know what kind of bad news you were into."

"Bad, bad news," she whispered. "I told you we got our revenge for my brother's killing. I was eighteen by then. Prison for sure if I'd been caught."

He stopped in his tracks. Like a weight had been dropped on his shoulders and he couldn't breathe.

She paused and turned back to him. "What is it?"

"You've never had a day off, have you?" No wonder she was so strong, after a lifetime of fighting.

She exhaled a small laugh. "I usually work nights."

The two of them stood and navigated through the trees toward the car.

He didn't know how he could reach through all of her history and offer any solace, so he confessed, "Spent a little time in the brig."

"I thought your mother raised you right."

"She raised me not to take shit from cowboys." He'd had to win each fight and scuffle he'd been in since joining the SEALs in order to prove himself. Any time trial, any race, he'd had to come in first.

"I like her."

"Me, too." His mother's fierce work ethic and support of him had pushed him through to the top. And beyond. Even after retiring from the Navy, he strove to make a difference, which had led him into the secret teams of Automatik.

"What does she think of your parade of women?" Mary didn't turn to look at him and her voice remained flat. Like a razor.

"I don't text her the details." But there'd always been not-so-subtle hints, like when his mother would ask if she should do some extra shopping for his lady friend during the holidays. "My dad would probably want to hear them, though. Shudder."

A forest fog laugh drifted back to him. Trailing behind Mary was like following a spirit. She moved with ease, her body fluid as she snaked around obstacles. A true ghost operator. And a woman revealed in glimpses. He wanted to know her, and that led him into more obscure shadows than the territory around him.

The trees gave way toward the highway. Mary located the car and got in the driver's seat. He took up the passenger position and settled in for the return trip. He brought up his phone's tracking app and showed her the chief's position back toward town. The area should be clear.

She started the engine and moved out. The motor hummed, and the heater fan whirred. Neither he nor Mary spoke. He looked over the map on his phone to track where the trucks would outlet from the state park into the town and surrounding areas. Because there was so much long-range interstate commerce in the area, the web of roads would make hiding the fleet easy. Trains would move out from the area as well, taking the contraband weapons to every corner of the country. The warehouses were the hub. That was where his and Mary's business was.

And there was business between them. Her map wasn't as clear to him. Navigating closer to her surrounded him in the unknown. He didn't even know himself. A stronger trust developed, tied with the personal information passed between them. This connection went beyond functional or tactical. And it made him want to give her more, while she fed him pieces of what made the woman behind the rifle.

They descended from the state park and sped through the planes back toward town. There was no sign of the dispersed trucks. She turned the headlights on.

He sat back in the chair and murmured, "Just a couple of normal people out for a drive."

"Is that what you want?" She glanced at him, then back at the road.

Normal had been drilled out of him years ago. Now he could sleep with his finger on the trigger, half buried in mud. It seemed he seldom woke up and fell asleep on the same continent.

"I want…" He knew the mission specifics and the reason he'd joined Automatik. To make a difference and protect people without the red tape of bad bureaucratic decisions. Other than fieldwork, he hadn't thought about the question. "I want…" The truth was too volatile to hold back. "I want Mary."

"Mary Long?" She scoffed as if he was joking.

"'Bolt Action' Mary," he explained.

Her look of surprise pierced him. Like she was using a knife to pry him open and see if he really meant it. "Damn it," she cursed, eyes growing wider. He saw it, too. A police car parked at an angle on the side of the road.

"Shit." He turned in his seat and saw the police lights turn on and the car pull out after them. "We were riding clean, right?"

"Yeah." Her focus split between the road ahead and the pursuing car in the rearview mirror. "Speed limit, straight line."

"Maybe whoever you stole it from reported it."

The cop car came closer. Ben went into alert, blood pumping and muscles ready to act.

"Not likely." She was still calm as a glacier. "I

requisitioned it from long-term parking at the bus station and there are no busses due until tomorrow morning."

"The cops are shaking down anyone who doesn't belong." They both still wore their black field gear. "And we definitely don't belong."

"There's a backpack in the backseat." She tilted her head in that direction. "Dump the contents, then secure yourself. I'm going to lose them."

The police siren chirped behind them, and their lights loomed. Ben leaned over the backseat and found the small plaid backpack. It rattled when he grabbed it and when he unzipped it, the contents of empty beer cans and energy drink containers spilled out, along with assorted food wrappers.

"Motherfucking teenage joyride." His breath was nearly taken and he looked between the planted evidence and Mary with a flood of respect. He returned to the passenger seat and made sure his seat belt was secure. "You're a genius."

"I'm airtight." She stepped on the accelerator and put more distance between them and the police car.

He gripped the handle above the side window. "Downright scary, that's what you are."

She smiled warmly. "Means a lot coming from an operator like you."

The police car charged harder after them, siren screaming full strength. If those sons of bitches could disappear, then he and Mary could finish the conversation he'd leaped into.

"Pull to the right," the megaphone on the cop car blared. "Pull to the right. Now!"

He gritted his teeth, hating being a passenger. "Test their authority a little bit and they get pissed."

"They're white-knuckling it." She shifted, readying herself. "We're boogying."

She pulled hard to the left and swerved into the opposite lane. The police car took a moment to react. Ben could've leaned out the window with his pistol and taken out the tires and cooling system. But shots fired at a cop would light the area up like dropping a nuke.

When the cop car got back behind them, Mary stood harder on the accelerator and swerved back into the correct lane. The police started to come alongside them. Mary toyed with them, pulling ahead a bit and drawing them into a faster chase.

"They're squawking for backup." Ben didn't recognize either cop from the rec center. The passenger looked like he was howling into his radio. The tint on the stolen car's windows kept Ben's and Mary's identity hidden.

She shrugged coolly. "There won't be time."

Ben knew that tone of voice from their other field ops. It was right before she pulled the trigger. He braced himself.

She tapped on the brakes and let the police car speed mostly past them. When the cops' back fender lined up with Mary and Ben's front bumper, she tugged the wheel in their direction. Ben slammed against the inside of the door as the impact shook the car. Metal crunched, and tires screeched. She gave the car more gas and turned farther into the rear side of the cops. Their back end wobbled off track, and their car was quickly sliding sideways along the highway in front of them.

Mary and Ben ducked so they couldn't be seen through the front windshield. Driving blind, she sped faster until they impacted the cops again. Her head pressed into his shoulder. There wasn't a trace of panic in her body. After the impacts, they were traveling about forty miles an hour. If they had to, they could deploy from the doors and maybe not get too hurt as they rolled along the asphalt.

But she maintained her tactic. Their car ground into the cops', then broke free. As soon as they sped unhindered on the highway, Mary and Ben both popped up to assess. He turned and saw the cop car spinning into a steep shoulder on the side of the road. Neither of the men should be injured, but the car was out of commission in the ditch. Its headlights streaked up into the dust cloud the car had twisted out of the dirt.

Mary didn't let up. She sped along the highway and to the edge of town. The car thundered over train tracks and bounced along rutted alleys. She flicked the headlights off and wove through backstreets, moving farther from the highway.

Red and blue police lights strobed against the buildings closer to the center of town. Ben watched three cars blast along the empty roads. One car stayed on the highway toward the immobilized officers. The other cars split at the edge of the highway. One searched one side of town, the other came toward their area.

But he and Mary were already gone.

The black car slipped ghostlike through the fringe of Morris Flats. Mary slowed further when they reached the north-south four-lane highway.

"Here's where we bail." She undid her seat belt and drove with one hand on the door handle. "Make it look like friends picked them up and busted out of town."

Ben readied himself. "I like partying with you."

She drove them toward a weedy crescent in the hollow of an on-ramp. They both opened their doors and dove out while the car was still rolling. Ben was already up to speed, running, when he hit the pavement. Mary tracked right with him. Neither looked back as the car churned through dirt and crunched into the thick greenery.

A full-out sprint narrowed the field of action. If problems came on, they came on fast, so Ben downshifted into a jog. The quiet of the early hours and the shadows next to the highway enveloped him and Mary. As they ran, they knocked off any remaining dirt or pine needles from their stalk in the state park.

To an enemy, she'd be terrifying. Her expressionless face showed no effort from the run. All her gear remained completely silent, not a single tap from any of the straps on her rig. As a teammate, he couldn't ask for anything more. But he had. He still didn't know the consequence of exposing the truth to her. And himself.

Police cars continued to zip through town, in all the wrong places. Ben spoke under his breath, "By the time they find the car, we'll be the ghosts of fuck-you past."

She cracked a small smile. "Then we'll be coming back to haunt them."

They made it past the rendezvous point where Mary had picked Ben up earlier in the morning. Two blocks later, they approached the hotel. They circled around the lit parking lot and found a path of shadows to the backside of the building. A service ladder led to a second-story patio, but a locked metal plate blocked the rungs. Ben straddled the ladder and shimmied up, holding only the sides.

He half expected Mary to be waiting for him on the patio, as if she'd just slithered up the wall. But he saw her using the same technique on the ladder behind him. Usually her movements were so contained, but now he got to see her body stretching out and revealing lean strength. His own limbs ached to match hers, find the push and pull between them.

But not on the run.

They still weren't secured for the night and continued into the hotel. A locked service door at the side of the patio blocked them. Ben took a knee and pulled out a set of lock picks. Mary hovered close, watching their backs.

She barely whispered, "SEALs teach lock picking?"

"I can be subtle." The lock conceded to him, and he opened the door for her.

She slipped in. He scanned behind them one last time before joining her and closing the door as quietly as possible. They'd made it to the hotel clean. Now they just had to get to their rooms.

The metal service stairs threatened to clang like church bells, waking the whole hotel. Ben and Mary's pace slowed. They stopped at the first landing and untucked their pants cuffs from their boots. At the second landing, they pulled off their tactical vests. She undid her black field shirt, revealing a vivid blue silk top.

He marveled at her transformation. Something so soft beneath such a deadly exterior. Anything he wanted to say about how amazing she looked—warrior and woman—was lost in his suddenly dry throat. She wrapped her vest in the black shirt, making the whole thing look like she was carrying a coat. Under his tactical clothes was a simple maroon polo. He bundled his rig the same way she did and they stood at the door to the floor.

She cracked it open and peered out. After her nod, they exited the service stairs and proceeded into the long, door-lined corridor. Her posture immediately changed. She strode with a wider swing in her hips and shoulders. He walked more casually at her side and draped his hand on her waist.

Recon of the hotel had already revealed no cameras on the floors, but there could be no loose ends. The service door had let them out near the elevator, which dinged as they started to pass it on the way to Mary's room. She immediately punched the up button and slinked on the wall. He leaned next to her, bringing their faces close together.

She spoke playfully as the elevator doors opened. "Whatever you've got to show me in your room had better be good." Her ability to turn her game on and off so quickly threw him off balance. It took a moment to get his head in the op and not just think about what he and Mary might get to doing when alone.

A uniformed hotel security officer he hadn't seen before stepped out of the elevator.

Ben ignored him and murmured to her, "Baby, it's better than good." He placed his hands on her hips and drew her close. His body immediately responded with a rush faster than the car chase. She swiveled under his grip. He bit back a growl as his cock thickened.

The two of them turned like tango dancers into the elevator. The guard watched them a moment, shaking his head at the display of awkward seduction, then continued down the hallway.

The doors closed, Mary pushed the button for his floor, then pulled away to burn him with a look. "Baby?"

He tried to calm the building need in him and winked at her, slow and sleazy. "Beans knows how to treat a lady."

She remained unmoved. "Nickname from the Teams?"

The doors opened, and the two of them ambled toward his room.

"My mom," he explained, putting his hand back on her hip. When they were apart, it was too far. When he touched her, it wasn't close enough. "Listened to this old song, 'Beans and Cornbread,' and I'd dance along."

"You must've been a cute kid." Was the warmth in her voice part of the act? God, he wanted it to be. It reached right into him as if she could see everything he was describing and asked more.

"This was in high school."

Her laugh was surprised and genuine. "Seriously?"

"Nah, baby, I was five." He slipped his key card in and out of the lock, and the two of them tumbled into his room.

As soon as he closed and locked the door, she put her wrapped-up gear down and sorted through her pockets. They were operators again, and he was rocked by her distance. Her movements were all business, but her voice was light. "You keep calling me 'baby' and I'm gonna put a hurt on you."

He ditched his vest on the bed and checked under the mattress and frame. Then he felt the HVAC vent covers for any scratched paint or replaced screws. "Maybe that's what I go for."

She attached a small antenna device to her phone and brought up an app. The display showed several scans, from Wi-Fi to radio bugs. All came up clean.

They both finally let out a long breath. He took his phone to the window and peeked through the slit between the closed curtains. Police lights flashed in several areas, searching. It looked like they still hadn't found the stolen car. The tracker on his phone indicated Chief Pulaski was beyond the edge of town.

Ben held up his phone for Mary to see. "The chief is out where you grounded his officers."

"We kicked the hive. They'll buzz hard for a while." She switched apps on her phone. "The mock real estate website took hits from a Daily Engine Yard server this afternoon. Kit Daily's looking in."

"We can't make too many waves. They're gearing up and on the trigger." He stepped away from the window and into the shadows of the room. "Who knew this hotel even had security?"

Dim yellow light from the town below edged in around the curtains.

"It's not to keep the guests safe." She was only a silhouette against the light walls. "Everything's built to protect their business." When she turned, her silk top gleamed like a night sea.

Quiet thickened around them. Tonight's mission was over. A success, with good intelligence gathered while evading detection. He was out of the field and still his heart pounded. His muscles urged him to move. Not because there was danger, but because Mary was so close. The lingering question that loomed between them had nothing to do with the operation.

He remained still. They were alone. They were relatively safe. They had connected and could again. The kiss. The truths. He'd revealed what he'd discovered. He wanted her but couldn't press. She'd disappear into smoke if she was cornered.

She didn't move. Only a few feet separated them. The bed was close. He'd known what to say with other women. He could be playful or seductive. Or a meaningful look, and the woman would understand his intent and let him know hers. He was lost with Mary. His truest words had been blunt. Could she see his face now? See how he needed to follow the connection they'd started?

"I'm a sniper," she explained with the shade of emotion shaking her voice. The light caught her eyes and revealed a deeper shimmer than he'd ever seen. "I prefer a long-distance relationship."

He wanted to reach out to her. For himself, and to let her know that she wasn't alone. But maybe they were. A thick pain stabbed through his chest. Maybe they'd seen too much and had done too much to find their humanity again.

"You know where to find me." And he was still trying to find himself.

"I do." Her voice was barely louder than the rustle of her clothes as she turned away. She collected her gear and headed toward the door. He followed, and she paused. "I can handle myself."

"I know it. I've seen it." He maintained a distance but didn't back away. "Ben Louis wouldn't just leave you to walk down there alone. And neither would I."

She nodded and opened the door. Hall light revealed her neutral face, unreadable. The two of them took their time getting to the elevator and leaned against opposite walls once inside. A thousand yards apart. She was dressed casually except for the combat boots, and her gear was hidden in the roll. But she was still alert and deadly.

They exited the elevator and walked down her hall, neither touching the other. The pretense of the cover wasn't shattered. It was early in the morning; they were tired and could be completely spent. She unlocked her door and scanned the interior of her room quickly while he checked up and down the hall. They were safe.

"Thanks," she whispered.

"Anything for an extra minute." He smiled. She returned it cautiously.

The night was over. She receded into her room. He waited until he heard all the locks click before walking back up the hall to the elevator. The mission charged forward. Tonight's op had allowed him to flex his muscles. More action was coming. He couldn't wait and could've scaled the exterior of the hotel just to burn off the energy that still crackled through him. But it wasn't the operation that tore the balance out from under him and pitched him into the unknown of want and need. The mystery of Mary—what he was with her and to her—remained unanswered.

EIGHT

THE FREE HOTEL breakfast had no flavor for Mary. She ate to fuel her day. The burned coffee was the first thing to register on her palette and make her realize she was already halfway through her meal. She was alone in a corner of the hotel lobby. Ben had messaged earlier in the morning to let her know he was out in the field. The mission continued.

Last night hadn't needed to end. Ben had been close enough to touch in his room and it had taken all her effort to maintain her distance. Their contact throughout the operation had sparked her imagination. They'd already revealed so much with the kiss in the parking lot. Sharing themselves in the quiet of the car had brought more of her need to the surface. When he'd told her, flat out, that he wanted her, she'd been flooded with a rush of desire and fear. What would it be like to give herself so completely?

She'd found that the distraction of escape and evasion from the cops hadn't taken away the excitement of being that close to Ben. So much potential. Where would she go if she had more from him like that kiss? The bed had been right next to them. He was ready. She could see it in the rise and fall of his chest. And that desire had charged through her as well. She didn't doubt his honesty but also knew his reputation. Would he still be there after they'd detonated all the explosives that had been building up?

She finished the last of her food and pushed the tray away.

It had seemed like protection to leave last night, but how could being safe tear her apart like this?

Sleep had come and gone, then she'd woken to a message from Automatik. They'd tracked Kit Daily's service with the Marines. Most of the men from his unit had retired, except for a major serving as senior staff at the Blount Island support base in Florida. They handled logistics for deploying troops and equipment. The perfect spot for someone to skim weapons for a profit. While other Automatik assets were working that angle, she and Ben needed to maintain their penetration of Morris Flats.

This morning, the operation came to her before she had to seek it out. Eddie Limert entered the lobby with a woman around his age. She wore a crisp pantsuit, sensible heels and a necklace that matched her earrings. Salon-blond hair and bright blue eyes. This must be the mayor. She waved at the woman behind the hotel counter like she was connecting with the working class while on the campaign trail. Mary almost expected an enthusiastic thumbs-up from the mayor.

Instead she just got an outstretched hand as the woman and Eddie approached. "Mayor Donna Limert, but you can call me Donna."

Mary stood and shook her hand. "Mary Long.

It's been a pleasure discovering your town for the last couple of days."

"Eddie explained what you're looking into, and I'm very intrigued." Donna cupped Mary's elbow in her manicured fingers and turned her toward the front door. "I happen to have a free morning, and there are a couple of areas you're going to want to see firsthand."

The positive energy flowing from the mayor was not to be questioned. She called the shots, and it looked like the woman would maintain that same glossy smile if she was pouring you tea or dousing your living room with gasoline.

"Trust me," Eddie interjected, "you'll fall in love with these possibilities."

"Sounds too good to pass up." Mary gently removed herself from the mayor's grip so she could collect her purse. "We'll caravan."

"Don't worry about it." Eddie already had his keys out. "I'll drive."

Before Mary could accept or refuse, Donna redirected. "Now, when you say mixed use—" she started walking mid-sentence as a way to force Mary to follow, "—do you mean to bring in new businesses, or relocate the locals?"

The three of them made their way across the lobby.

"Both," Mary answered. "It's always good to get established businesses into new facilities for the familiarity of the residents. The last thing we want to do is edge anyone out."

"Good." Donna pointed at the opening automatic doors, as if they were following her direction. "You'll see that we're very committed to local business. Very few chains in Morris Flats."

Meaning less scrutiny from the outside and the ability of the power structure to control the population.

The cold, windy day swirled over the parking lot. Mary zipped her coat higher, smiling sheepishly at her intolerance of the weather. Donna and Eddie smiled knowingly. But they knew nothing of what Mary really was and who they were letting into their excessively large SUV. One non-standard feature in the vehicle was the police radio slung under the center of the dash. It was switched off for now, but it revealed how quickly information could move through Morris Flats. The two of them seemed too chipper to have been up all night with the police activity, but Mary was sure they'd been briefed that morning.

Once they were all inside, Mary made a show of shivering in the backseat. "Younger buyers are very interested in one-of-a-kind goods and services, so you'll have a great selling point down here."

Eddie drove. West, as Mary expected. Away from the train yard. Ben should be there by now, on the front line, while she was moving farther from it and him. And if anything happened in this car, or wherever they were taking her, his support would take a while to reach her.

"Lincoln High." Eddie didn't linger as he drove

past the old buildings that needed new paint and windows.

Mary added limply, "Good central location." She wanted to ask what the graduation rate was but knew Donna would've already boasted if it had been good.

Donna sang, "People love to be close to schools."

"Infrastructure is a huge selling point." Mary watched the homes blur past. Nothing older than the fifties. Working class, most with fenced yards. Maintained with pride. As they moved closer to the west edge of town, the houses slumped with neglect. Weedy lots stretched out and blended with the plains. Old industrial buildings sat, forgotten in the muddy fields.

Perfect place to end a life.

Neither Donna nor Eddie had any flinch about them that indicated death was close. Their hands and eyes were too soft for professional killers. If the hit was on, they'd be tight, even if they weren't the ones pulling the trigger.

"Plenty of parking," Mary mused. Her .38 remained close in her purse.

Donna tapped her fingernail on the window glass. "Development could mean state bond money for improved roads, too."

Bullshit small talk. Donna and Eddie didn't want any state attention on their town. They didn't want any new money or residents. They wanted her as far from the train yard as possible while she was in Morris Flats, then they wanted her long gone so they didn't have to return her phone calls or emails.

She smiled and nodded while her insides ground together. Time wasted. Ben was across town in Kit Daily's territory. Anything could happen as they tore at the sutures that held this town's festering secrets tight. She needed to be there. For the mission. For Ben.

MARY WAS RIGHT—the train yard reeked of military gun oil. To anyone who hadn't been in the service, it would've blended in with the diesel fuel and axle grease, but Ben knew it well. He nearly rubbed his fingers together while remembering the slick of it. Would that have given him away? Maybe. The gesture was the kind of detail he'd notice.

And after last night's police action, everyone would be on alert. He remained edgy. Too much time had passed since contact with Mary. It wasn't outside the operational bounds, but it would've made him breathe a little easier if he knew her position and could relate his current action.

He approached the train yard administrative buildings as a salesman full of optimism. Bounding up the stairs, he reached the metal patio when a large, rectangular man stepped out of a door to confront him. Ben recognized the shape of the foreman from last night's grainy view. Now he had the details, from the man's shoulder holster under his coat to the tired eyes that were clearly not interested in buying what Ben was selling.

"You're going to have to call first to make an appointment." The foreman hadn't shaved and looked to be propped up on several cups of coffee.

"My business isn't that serious." He pushed up his coat sleeve to reveal his bracelet. "We make these performance bands and thought your hard workers might benefit from them."

The foreman shook his head. "We're too busy down here." The clanging of bells and heavy equipment proved his point. Men's voices shouted from the tracks on the other side of the admin buildings.

"Fair enough." Ben relaxed his pitch and saw the relief on the foreman's face. "I can come back around the lunch hour. When's that?"

The lines drew out again down the corners of the foreman's face. "Depends on the shift." His patience was being strained. He looked like he wanted to take a threatening step toward Ben, but only teetered at the edge of it. The door he came out of cracked, and he glanced back at it before hitting Ben with a stern, "I really don't think this is the place for you."

The door opened wider. If a shooter was coming, Ben could keep the foreman between him and the trouble end of a gun. He had his compact auto on his ankle. Or he could take the foreman's piece before his clumsy hands could pull it.

"Now, he's just trying to do his job." A barrel of a man in his fifties stepped out of the door. Blue jeans and a wool blazer. A .45 1911 rested in a tooled leather holster on his hip. Clean cowboy boots. He smiled like he didn't mean it, spreading a white mustache across his broad face. He still had the old-school jarhead haircut. This had to be Kit Daily.

Chief Pulaski walked out behind him onto the metal porch. "Careful, Kit, this kid's a baller." Exhaustion rimmed his eyes red but he still managed a look of disdain for Ben.

"Good to see you, Chief." Ben played it like he didn't see it and skirted around the foreman and shook Pulaski's hand. The policeman still wore the bracelet. "Starting to feel the benefits?"

Pulaski rolled his wrist and it cracked loudly. "Been a little busy to notice." Chasing ghosts. It would've been great to gloat, but there was more important business.

Ben extended his hand to Kit Daily. "Ben Louis."

Daily shook it like he was indulging a precocious toddler. "Kit Daily. You've come down to my train yard for a reason?"

The pitch glided off Ben's tongue once again. The foreman left midway through, going back in the door he'd come out. Pulaski yawned broadly and hooked his hands on his duty belt.

Ben wrapped it up with, "We'd love to give the bands to the men in your yard. Those are the kinds of guys who deserve them."

Daily snorted. "If it makes them work harder."

Ben bristled at the man's contempt for his employees and countered, "It might make the work easier."

Daily didn't like being talked back to. The challenge was met with eyes as hard as bullets. "Then I can give them more work."

Neither backed down right away. Pulaski glanced from one to the other, shocked that Ben would stand up to Daily. There was an excited, expectant look in the policeman's eye when he stared at the boss of the town, waiting to see what he was going to do.

"Go on." The pompous Daily dismissed Ben with a wave toward the entrance to the yard. "You won't do any harm."

Kit Daily was dead wrong. Ben and Mary were there to do a lot of harm to him.

"Thanks much." Ben started in that direction, then paused. "Would you like one for yourself?"

Daily snorted again. "I don't think so."

Ben kept it genial. "Once you see the chief's brand new jumper, you might change your mind." He didn't wait for a response and moved along the porch to the entrance. As he turned toward the yard, he saw Daily and Pulaski still watching him and talking under their breaths. Would the cops send another round of truckers after him, or would the next try be more overt?

Only a few steps past the admin building put Ben into the hard world of heavy industry. Black gravel, steel train tracks and iron machinery. Smoke spewed from exhaust pipes, and train cars locked together with clanging metal. Everything there seemed like it could easily crush flesh and bone to dust.

The men had to be extra hard. Kit Daily could

swagger with his throwback pistol on his hip and immaculate boots, but he didn't work the yard. The men Ben approached wore grease and diesel dust on their heavy canvas clothes. Blacks, whites and Hispanics all eyed him warily.

Mary had already probed this area, dressed for civilian business, no less. The woman could walk through a tiger cage wearing a flank steak suit and still come out on top. How far afield was she now? If she was in trouble, he'd hear the explosions. Then the whole town would go up.

"You guys have a second?" Ben approached nine workers and once they'd locked down what they were doing and came over to him, laid out the same old pitch. He made sure to extend his appreciation for the labor these guys sweat out. As he handed out several bracelets, he ventured, "Coach down at the high school spoke highly of Sean Harris. He got some game?"

"A little." An African-American man a bit younger than Ben stepped forward. His tight beard was broken by a short scar along his jaw.

Ben gave him a green bracelet. "Maybe you can go down to the police rec league and show them how it's done."

Sean scoffed, along with the other guys. "We're all better off if they think they're the ones with the skills."

Ben glanced over his shoulder; no sign of Daily and Pulaski in the yard. "Yeah, seems like this place is on lockdown."

"Except for the truckers." Sean smiled wryly. News had traveled.

Ben shrugged. "I've got game."

"That's the word." The other men in the group stared at Ben along with Sean, waiting for the story.

"They came on strong, talking shit." Ben shifted to his right and put up his guard loosely to show the moves. "Got one in the side of the knee. Went at it with the second one for a bit. The third guy was a fucked-up tweaker, so he got wild and I had to put him on the ground."

Sean wasn't satisfied. "I heard they pulled a knife on you."

"I'm from Chicago," was answer enough.

"But you can't stop a bullet." Sean also kept an eye on the admin buildings. "I'd get your business done quick and get out of town."

"Kit Daily shoot off that antique .45 of his a lot?" The cowboy would probably look like those old Department of Defense training films from the 1950s.

"Back behind the warehouses." Sean swung his hand in that direction. "Him and his buddies shoot off all kinds of things."

"That doesn't sound safe." What better way to intimidate people than the sound of gunfire?

"This isn't a safe place," Sean warned while revealing his own burden.

A new presence behind Ben shifted the men's attention. A boss would've had them dispersing to resume their work. Instead they puffed up and flexed, rugged and manly. Ben turned. Mary stood on the

path to the yard between the administrative buildings. A spike of worry was removed from the side
of his neck and he sighed a little relief at seeing her.

"Is she the one?" Sean's question struck Ben with
more impact than was intended. "Is she the one
you were with before those truckers jumped you?"

Ben nodded as a slow grin spread. "It was worth
it." And he'd endure a hell of a lot more for her.

She stalled on the path, looking up to the porch
of one of the buildings and talking to someone hidden there. Her black hair was pulled back into a ponytail, highlighting the piercing awareness of her
dark eyes. A heavy coat hid the curves of her ribs
and hips, but her tight jeans revealed strong thighs.
High boots covered her calves in shining black
leather. Ben couldn't hold back a grunt of appreciation while the memories of her moving against
him through the forest rolled a wave of heat up his
back, around his chest and down to his groin.

Other sounds of approval came from the men
around him.

Sean muttered, "Nice."

"Right?" Ben agreed.

"She looks put together, man. Good luck." With a
nod, Sean turned back to his work. The others took
another eyeful of Mary, then tore themselves away.
No one said anything crass or made any gestures
toward her. If they had, Ben wouldn't have been
quiet. Metal rang against metal like an industrial
church behind Ben as he approached her.

She remained in the midst of a conversation. He

stepped up the path and saw Daily and Pulaski on the porch looking down to her.

"Yeah, I got your card from Len." Daily hooked his thumbs on each side of his large belt buckle. "And he explained your whole angle, but as much as I'd love doing business with you…" He showed teeth with a leering smile. "I don't think my train yard fits what you're looking for."

Daily spotted Ben and called louder to him with a skeptical laugh. "Any takers?"

Ben stopped near Mary. "A few. You've got a good crew out there."

Daily waggled a finger and instructed, "But I can't tell them that. It'll go to their heads."

How long did Ben have to play nice? He struggled to maintain a neutral face and not scowl at the smug son of a bitch standing three feet above him.

Mary jumped in. "I'm glad I had a chance to meet you, Chief Pulaski. I was curious about crime rates in Morris Flats."

Pulaski stepped forward, but not as far as Daily, who gave no ground. "Nothing out of the ordinary. Nothing to scare off investors."

"A little excitement last night," Daily reminded Pulaski with a hint of disappointment.

The chief waved it off. "Just some kids out for a joy ride."

Ben couldn't hold back. "I heard the sirens."

Daily smiled knowingly and shared a glance with Pulaski. "Now what were you doing up at that hour?"

Both men shifted sticky looks between Ben and Mary. The hotel guard must've reported back. The town had eyes. None of them could be trusted.

Ben kept his voice flat. "I never sleep well when I'm not in my own bed."

Kit Daily barked a laugh. Pulaski's mouth turned down in an almost outright expression of disgust. Mary acted shy and shot Ben a quick accusatory look before taking out her phone and pretending to deal with pressing business.

Daily took too long examining Mary's body, top to bottom and back. Ben seethed and almost stepped between them before Daily asked, "Were you in the service, Miss Long?"

Where was this going? Their cover had been seamless. And Automatik operated in such shady territory that even retired military men with good contacts couldn't shine a light on them. Were they exposed? Pulaski wasn't twitching to reach for his gun. Yet.

"No." She cocked her head. "Why do you ask?"

"Your physique." He awarded himself another opportunity to take her in. "Thought you might've gone through basic."

"I was an athlete in college. Swimmer."

Daily sucked his teeth. "That's it. The shoulders." But his gaze was on her legs.

Pulaski added, "We know Ben was an athlete."

"Yeah." Ben deliberately slung his bag higher on his shoulder to show he was moving out. If he stayed around Daily and Pulaski any longer, he'd jeopardize the mission by teaching them a lesson in mindfulness. With his fists. "I was on the darts team."

No laughs from either man.

Daily didn't even address him as he walked toward the parking lot. "I've got your card, Miss Long. But don't count on a call."

She answered with continued politeness. "I appreciate any consideration."

Ben was still in earshot for the dismissal from Daily. "Now, we've got business to attend to. Have a safe trip out of Morris Flats."

Everyone wanted them gone.

He walked slowly to his rental SUV.

Mary's quick steps caught up to him. "Hey there." A flirty twinkle glimmered in her eyes. "Didn't expect to see you down here. Are you looking to poach my real estate deal?"

"You don't have to worry about that, Miss Long." He aped Daily's drawl on her name. "I'm not cut out to run down contracts and handshakes with those guys."

"I don't blame you." Her sharp edge revealed itself for a split second as she glanced at the admin building. Both men were back inside.

Ben opened the rear hatch to the SUV and placed his bag inside. Mary stood at his hip, her thigh on his. It was for show. They were being watched. He still savored the heat.

"I got a recommendation on a good place for dinner." He kept his hand on the top of the open trunk lid so his arm blocked the admin building's view of them.

"Isn't that what got you beat up last time?"

"*They* got beat up." He flexed his chest and biceps. "And this restaurant is in the next town and comes from a reputable source."

"After last night…" She inspected the building and the police car parked out front. "We need to let them relax a little."

"Too tight for the warehouse," he murmured in agreement, bringing his face closer to hers. Her scent of roses surrounded him and transported him to a much cleaner and safer place.

"Tomorrow night." Her husky voice turned the roses to black velvet. She looked up at him. Lips parted. "Didn't look like they were ready to move the goods before then. We'll crack them open."

"And tonight." He leaned down to kiss her. She didn't move away. It was light, quick. The connection he'd discovered from the last kiss was there, waiting just below the surface. "I'll pick you up at seven."

Hunger for more bore through him.

NINE

She waited in plain view in front of the hotel and tried not to look uncomfortable. It was much easier to operate with an extra twenty pounds of gear strapped to her chest and back. Instead she wore her coat over a glowing champagne cardigan and a simple black top. The sun had set. She should be in the shadows.

At least she had her .38 in her purse and a slim automatic knife tucked into her boot.

A few business travelers hurried through the cold into or out of the hotel. They shared polite smiles with Mary. Nothing out of the ordinary. Except that she hadn't been on a date in years.

Headlights swung through the parking lot, and Ben arrived in front of her in his SUV. Who was he picking up? Mary Long? Her cover blurred when she was with him. Their second kiss at the train yard had been so comfortable and familiar. And it had jolted her senses into overdrive. She'd felt the beginning of his stubble rasp on her face. Her speeding pulse had pushed awareness into her breasts and between her legs.

Seeing his smiling eyes through the open passenger window, that same awareness spread in lush

waves across her body. She lit up under his attention. No one had looked at her with that kind of real
appreciation. No one knew her better than him. And
now she ached to learn more of Ben. She'd been
scared back from the connection and retreated, but
that had only left her feeling hollow.

"Ready?" He reached for the inside passenger
door latch.

She hadn't moved.

The door swung open, and she stepped into the
SUV. The clean, warm scent of his soap surrounded
her. He wore a dark button-down shirt under his
coat and nice jeans. Ben held his hand out. She
stared at the simple gesture for a moment, then
placed her hand in his. Any chill from outside was
chased by the touch. He kissed her knuckles, something no one had ever done. A flush spread across
her chest and up her neck.

"Thanks for coming out." He returned himself
to the driving position. She secured herself in the
passenger seat. They moved out, closed up in the
car and private.

"Thanks for getting me out." The mark of his lips
on her hand remained hot. "Ben Louis has moves."

"Tonight, Ben Louis is in his room alone watching sports and working on his fantasy team." He
took his eyes from the road to glance her way with
a small, personal smile.

Traces of fear rose. It was a real date, without
cover stories. Could she be herself as well? "Mary

Long has home renovation shows on while she does her Kegel exercises."

Ben laughed with a pronounced shiver. "Tight."

He steered them west, heading out of town. A few cars collected around restaurants, bars and taverns, but the neighborhoods were quiet. When they'd been driving out to their recon in the state park, each had been locked and loaded. Tonight Ben sat back and drove with one hand.

His attention was split between the road and her. "So when was the last time you were picked up by a car that wasn't moving?"

"If you really knew how to treat a girl right—" she turned her mouth with disappointment, "—you'd have dusted me off with a Pave Low."

He let out a whistle. "Those pilots are crazy."

"They get us in and out."

"Pitch black, hundred miles an hour and ten feet over the ground."

She remembered the rush, speeding into the inky void, knowing her skills would get her through. But there wasn't anything she could train for that could prepare her for the unknown she headed toward tonight with Ben.

"Where are we going?" The question seemed too vast. She clarified, "For dinner."

"Dansville. Under fifty clicks away. I hear the place even has candles."

"Fancy." For the first time in a very long time, she was self-conscious about being underdressed.

"If you can shoot an eraser off a pencil from half a mile away, you get fancy."

Her mind spun off into setting up for a shot like that. "I'll need a spotter."

A serious edge crept into his voice. "You've got one."

She wanted to fall into that kind of sure confidence but couldn't match him yet and still felt like she was stumbling awkwardly on what should be normal human interaction. "What's the name of this place?"

He hesitated. "El Pantano."

"You're taking me to The Swamp?" She was suddenly way overdressed. "I should've brought a bigger gun."

He put up a hand to slow her down. "I have it on good authority from Oscar, the high school security guard, that this is a nice place we're going to."

"Sounds like a setup."

"Those are all in Morris Flats." He hooked a thumb behind them. "Won't take much to get Kit and Pulaski and his men to draw."

"They'll get their chance." The best Automatik operations didn't spend a single bullet. But none of the bad guys here were going to roll over without a fight. "They'll get hammered down."

Ben put out his fist, and she bumped it.

They sped into the fringe of town, where the old agribusiness buildings loomed like crippled giants on the planes. She recounted to Ben her field trip with Donna and Eddie Limert, where they tried to distract her away from anything near the train yard.

"But you came back anyway." Fewer streetlights meant she couldn't read his face in the glow of the dashboard.

"I don't think we should operate alone anymore." Now she was the one being opaque. To Ben and herself. While it sounded like tactical planning, she was testing how it felt to extend herself and let him know her needs.

"Agreed." His eyes remained on the road ahead of them.

The two-lane highway appeared to stretch all the way to the sharp horizon. Night surrounded them, pierced by stars and distant yellow lights in the planes.

"Delta." A long breath moved through her and released a weight she hadn't known was there.

He didn't look at her with surprise or victory. Ben didn't grin with success where everyone else had failed. His eyes reflected a new depth she couldn't see the bottom of. He took his own breath. "You're fucking amazing. You're fucking fearless."

She couldn't look at herself that way. "They chose me."

"For telling me," he clarified. "They didn't make you anything you weren't already."

That truth sank in. "The good and the bad."

He shrugged it off. "We've all got it."

"Some of us have more bad." The storm of violence in her youth had turned to a steady rain she'd been living under for a long time.

"Whatever we've done—" the energy in his voice started to lift her up, "—it's nowhere near as bad as Kit Daily and Chief Pulaski. The mayor." His jaw set. "Making money, making people die."

His fist tightened on the steering wheel. Her own hand was clenched. They both wanted mission success.

Ben didn't let them sink into the dire thoughts. "We're in the game for the right reasons. That's why we're with Automatik. Special Forces done right. We're not just taking orders, but making them, too."

The process of discharging from the Army after years in the field had left her hollow. Automatik had changed that. If people were hurting, she'd be there. "Putting pressure on the bleeding."

He reached out and glanced his knuckles on her thigh. "Healing our own."

She nodded and tapped the side of her fist on his shoulder. Small contact rang with significance. She wasn't alone.

"How'd they find you?" He brightened. "You were sitting in a twig shack on the side of a mountain in Nepal with birds on your shoulders, and Loftis or Gold showed up to get you back into the fight."

She chuckled and sat back, stretching her legs with the thought of that kind of solitude. "You find me a twig shack, and I'll meditate the hell out of it."

"I'll build you one." It sounded like more of a

promise than a joke. But he couldn't be serious, could he? Not when she'd never allowed herself to plan past the current op.

"I got into Automatik a few weeks before I was out of Delta." Three years ago. "I thought my C.O. was angling me toward a contractor gig, and I was ready to say no. But then he laid it out, and it sounded a hell of a lot better than bodyguarding dignitaries or riding around in an armored SUV with a hit squad."

"You get to ride in an SUV with me." His eyes smiled.

It didn't take much for his warm presence to wrap around her like silk. "And they found you working as a bouncer in a strip club, living in an apartment with no kitchen, but two king-sized beds."

"Hey." Was he actually angry? "I had a kitchen."

"Nothing in the fridge but a bottle of mustard and a bottle of vodka."

"Vodka? I'm not fancy." He sat up, sharpening his attention as they approached the edge of the next town. "Me and my man, Harper, had retired from the Teams and I was back in San Diego, consulting for a security firm and prepping some brothers of color in the Navy who wanted to be SEALs. Gold showed up when we were at a sports bar and lured us into the shadows."

"And now you get to ride in an SUV with me."

"Best decision I ever made." His honesty carried farther into her than any slick line. More of her armor fell away and her skin woke up. Her sweater was sleek on her arms, and she wanted to contrast that with Ben's calloused hands. Then to feel those hands tugging her shirt up and searching up her back and over her chest.

She shook herself back to earth. Ben glanced a question at her.

"Hungry," she explained. "You?"

"Hell yeah." His voice was low, and scratched in the way she wanted his touch to. .

Dansville transformed from a constellation of streetlights in the distance to an old-fashioned agricultural town filled with small homes and low, brick businesses. Morris Flats thrived on the commerce of the train tracks and the highway. The bright future of the '50s. Dansville had been around a lot longer than that and huddled close against the elements as the buildings weathered the years.

Stoplights slowed traffic. The highway became Main Street. Market, a couple of taverns and a hardware store. Worn lettering painted on the sides of buildings marked the evolution of the businesses. Many hadn't changed.

"El Pantano." Ben pointed up and to the left. A lighted sign spelled out the name over an orange door flanked by warmly lit windows.

"Looks good so far." She saw several occupied tables as they passed.

"It's either this or the Iron Plow." The run-down tavern with half-lit neon beer signs lurked at the end of the block. Ben hung a U-turn and parked close to

El Pantano. He was out of the SUV quickly, standing at her door once she'd opened it and extending a hand for her.

She didn't move. "I'm not fragile."

He kept his hand out. "I handle all my explosives with care."

"You're a smooth motherfucker." She placed her hand in his. He curled his fingers around her. Maybe she did need help getting out of the car. Her balance suddenly shifted. The touch rushed her blood. She collected herself and stepped down, holding him as strongly as he held her.

He closed the door; their hands remained together. They walked to the restaurant against a cold wind cutting across the plains and through town with the scent of mineral-rich soil. Cantina music strummed them into the warm room that glowed with bright colors and low, golden light.

She marveled, "There are candles."

Ben held up two fingers to the hostess as she approached. They exchanged the requisite pleasantries and were led to a relatively secluded, thick pine table against a wall and next to a large wooden hutch filled with hand-painted pottery. Their momentum stalled awkwardly when it was time to sit. Each of them angled toward the seat facing the front door. Ben backed off and took the opposite position. They both hung their coats on the backs of the chairs and sat.

Once the hostess was gone, he spoke over his open menu. "I'll cover the kitchen."

She had a good view of the front door and windows. "Carrying?"

"Ankle," he answered casually. "You?"

"Purse."

Each of them looked over the menu as the light conversation continued. He asked, "For knife work, you stick or slash?"

"Slash." The food smelled amazing as it traveled from the kitchen to the other tables. All the plates were vibrantly colored, like the large abstract paintings on the walls. Everything in the place seemed handmade, giving the sense of being a guest in a long-standing family home. "Picked up some Indonesian techniques, some Filipino."

"Fancy." He drew the word out with a high-toned accent.

"Like dancing." The footwork had been easy to pick up during training.

"You dance?" He folded his menu and gazed across the table at her. The candle burnished an outline around the strong features of his jaw and mouth. Another kiss was necessary. But to feel that mouth on her neck, her breast, seemed impossible. And that was why she had to have it.

"I do." In her condo, alone, while she had music on cooking or when she needed to stretch out after hand loading rifle rounds. "With a knife in my hand."

"We can tango." Smoky seduction rasped his voice and caressed over her skin and into her. She wasn't thinking about knife fights. The awareness in her breasts and up the insides of her thighs came from the image of her dancing with Ben. Naked. Muscle balancing muscle. Each strong enough to move the other.

The waitress came over before Mary overheated and they placed their order. No booze for either. Even out of the immediate danger of Morris Flats, they had to remain sharp.

Ben looked the place over once the waitress had departed. "This is nice. Next time I'm at the high school, I'll thank Oscar."

"The school looked pretty beat-up." Anything shining and new in that town belonged to the gun-runners.

"Like a limb without blood."

Their mood lifted with the arrival of chips and salsa and their drinks. Two lemonades in thick glasses for the ghost operators.

Ben held his up. "To candlelight."

"And the shadows who surround it." She clinked him and drank.

Two men came into the restaurant but were greeted as regulars and didn't resonate as an immediate threat.

Ben ate chips and salsa with appreciative sounds. "We've got to get back to Hayley and Art's place. She can cook."

More than the quality of the food, which was excellent, Mary had been touched by Hayley remembering the kind of cuisine she'd requested. She hadn't eaten like that since being at home with her family. "Hayley's tough. She can do anything."

"Surviving a week in that house full of mob goons, then getting out alive while the bullets were flying?" He shook his head with respect. "Badass."

"Badass enough for Art." She'd seen the profound connection between them during the after-hours dinner Hayley had put together at their restaurant. Not a minute went by that they weren't in contact.

"If a surly bastard like that can find something good in the world, then there's hope for the rest of us hunter killers."

She ate the chips and salsa and didn't respond. She didn't hope. She trained, stalked and acted. But she wanted to feel now. The rush of breath. The possibility of two bodies together. The connection with Ben grew stronger, lit by the way the candle shined off his deep brown eyes and the way he navigated the layers of her life. Where would it go? She hadn't trained for anything like this. Could she dive into the unknown if victory wasn't guaranteed?

And there was her problem. Words like "victory" had no place in matters of the heart.

"Is that what you're looking for when you're finding a hookup at a club?" She studied his face. "Something good in the world?"

He started a smile, almost responded quickly, then quieted. A glib line would've come easily. She saw that he searched for a truth. "I'm…" He looked at his hands on the table. "I'm looking to not fight. I've been fighting for a while now. This is a good one I'm in now." He brought his gaze to her. "But I can't be in combat all the time."

That same pressure had wrapped around her for years. On base, she never knew when she'd be deployed. In the field, death could come from any angle, any time. She'd lived in a constant state of readiness. With Automatik, the pace had let up and the open and direct communication kept her up to the minute, but the danger on an op hadn't changed.

When she was a soldier, she'd avoided any emotional ties to the men. A few had tried for her as a trophy; others might've been genuine. It didn't matter. She had to focus on her job to stay alive. In the civilian world, no one had been able to unwind the tense coils that dug through her. No one had understood her.

Ben understood her.

Slowly, she skimmed her hand across the table until it rested next to his. "How do we not fight?"

"We let go." His thumb moved against the side of her hand and stopped there. "And we hold on."

She slipped her hand over his and curled her fingers around him. He made a fist that wove their fingers together. Heat spread from her joints as tension released through her body. As if he were touching all those spots, easing his strength along the knots of her muscles and loosening them. Allowing herself to take a long breath was more freedom than she'd ever felt.

Her eyes opened and she realized she'd closed them. Ben gazed at her with a heat of his own.

And a secret smile, just curling on the ends of his mouth. He licked his lips. She tightened her grip on his hand. Their first kiss had opened so many possibilities. They echoed back harder through her now. In a hot stripe down between her breasts that took her breath.

She drew him toward her and they stood to lean over the table. His mouth took hers in an honest kiss, revealing he had her same needs. Both of them kept their eyes open and aware of their surroundings.

They parted and sat again, hands still wound together.

She held his gaze. "Handle with care."

"Nitroglycerine," he vowed. Their food arrived, and they parted hands. But Ben kept his look on her and continued after the waitress had left. "Sexy, tough, ass-kicking, bangin' body nitroglycerine."

She laughed, yet each word caressed up and down her spine. She had to grind her hips in the chair. His smile disappeared into a heated look as he watched her.

The plates of food cooled until she and Ben tore their attention away from each other and turned to dinner. She was vaguely aware of good steak and beans and rice. When Ben stretched his leg out to touch hers, she nearly swept the heavy table out of the way so she could push him against the wall and slam her body into his.

"Enjoying your meal?" His voice was so steady.

Cold disappointment splashed through her chest.

Here she was, ready to tear his clothes off in the middle of a restaurant, and he was as calm as a helicopter pilot.

He must've noticed the shift in her mood because he leaned forward with concern on his face. "You good?"

"I'm fine." She collected herself and allowed gravity to take her back to earth. "I'm just eating dinner."

He studied her. "We weren't *just* eating dinner."

She could've slammed on the brakes. Contained the emotions and the carnal thoughts, locked them away and focused only on the mission. She risked herself. "Then how can you be so cold-blooded?"

His brow lifted, showing the light in his eyes. "I'm making conversation. Getting by." He moved closer, containing his words for only her over the table. "But Mary, I'm dying a death over here. I don't need a fucking dinner. A table and chairs. A restaurant. You and I can survive anywhere." His breath quickened and the cords of his neck flexed. Her own pulse raced again. "I want you everywhere."

She was too contained. In public. In her clothes. Within herself. "I... I need that. I need..." Had she ever admitted this? "You."

But they were still in the restaurant, though wicked intent glimmered in Ben's look. "You've got me. Right here." He growled, "Wherever you need me."

She suppressed a moan. It was hard enough to

free her emotions and erotic desires. But in an unsecured space? Part of her wanted to shut Ben down. The dizzy rush, though, charged through her, and each spot he mentioned blazed with the possibility.

He continued, voice dropping to a carnal secret across the table. "And with my hands around your waist, I'm going to kiss down your chest. Your breasts." He swallowed and showed his teeth in a sensual smile. "My mouth around your nipple, I'm going to bite, just enough so you dig your nails into my shoulders."

Her nipples tightened. Wet heat gathered in her pussy. She cleared her throat to keep from growling like an animal. She waved at the waitress and motioned for the check.

Thankfully, it arrived quickly. If not, she may have thrown a wad of cash on the table as she dragged Ben out, stripping their clothes off as they went.

Ben put his hand on the bill and slid it toward him before she could get to it. "My turn. You paid at the diner." He counted cash out.

"But you paid in the parking lot." She remembered how hard it had been to drive away.

He breathed a small laugh. "Hopefully this is an easier exit." With the bill squared away, he poised to stand and waited for her.

She rose; he joined her. They put on their coats, gave a wave to the waitress and exchanged the warm restaurant for the cold street. His heat remained close to her, though his hip fit comfortably against hers. He wrapped an arm around her waist as they moved toward the car.

"I didn't want to leave you there," she confessed. "In the diner parking lot. I should've been there to finish them with you."

He shrugged it off. "It was part of the mission parameters. We both knew I could handle them. What are a couple of scrapes if it gets us the big target at the end?"

She stopped their progress and faced him. "I didn't like it."

His swagger receded as still emotion and appreciation rose in his face. "Thanks."

His hand tightened on her hip. She drew into him and slid her hand across his chest under his jacket. He rumbled beneath her touch and his broad muscles tightened. She and Ben came together in a soft kiss. An exchange of quiet trust. Once they balanced together, the intensity grew. She opened her mouth, flicked her tongue against his. He dove into her. She wanted to swallow him completely. To fill the hollow, hot and needy ache that spread through her.

She snuck her fingers in between the buttons of his shirt to find his skin. He reached into her coat. Cold fingers swept under the hem of her shirt and soon warmed on the naked skin of her hip. She leaned harder and rubbed her tight nipples against him. And when their hips pressed together, she felt the rigid length of his cock in his jeans. She was wet and needed to wrap herself around him.

"Car," she whispered when they separated to take a breath.

They walked without completely disentangling themselves. His hand skimmed her hip. She hooked her fingers in his back pocket. They had to separate at the SUV, but it was quick, and they were soon sitting in the closed car, kissing again.

He stroked her cheek, held the side of her neck. She brushed her fingers down the front of his throat. Her body had endured the rigors of fighting wars and hadn't been broken, but she discovered new strength. Lost sensations were found. Pleasure in a light touch. The hint of things to come. The needy ache that pressed her closer to Ben. He responded with his own craving.

She had to find what they were together. "Get us somewhere private."

TEN

EACH INCH CLOSER to Morris Flats brought the danger, the chill of unspoken threats and the intense focus of the mission. Mary's body pulsed with need as she rode next to Ben, but as the tension increased, her joints and muscles lost the fleeting pleasure and took on the steel she needed to survive as an operator.

Ben drove with both fists on the steering wheel. Tight, like he was feeling the same increase in pressure she was. They both knew how to soldier. But she was lost trying to figure out how to hold on to the safety that had allowed them to flirt and kiss and bring themselves to the edge of passion. Was the night over?

He let go of the steering wheel with one hand and rested it on her thigh. She pressed into his touch and couldn't get enough. The connection remained alive. Her ache hadn't been satisfied. She put her hand on top of his and the skin burned with delicious fire.

He seduced her with a murmur. "It's dark out here."

They'd left the lights of Dansville behind and were surrounded by miles of inky farm fields.

She scratched along the back of his hand and heard his breath hitch. She whispered to lead him toward her. "Dark enough for ghosts like us."

With a flick, he turned off the headlights. Her eyes adjusted quickly and divided the view into the slate planes of the highway, the fields and the starry sky. They were alone on the road. The farmhouses were set far back and wouldn't be able to see them in the black SUV.

Ben slowed. The silhouette of a large tree stretched against the sky. The car rumbled over the dirt of the highway shoulder and pulled to the far side of the tree, completely hidden from the highway. He shut down the engine and they both sat, silent and still, to assess the environment. It was always the first thing she did when inserting into hostile territory. Open the senses and wait. Become part of the shadows while detecting anything out of the ordinary.

Wind hummed a chorus through the bare tree branches. The stars glittered, and a tremble ran through Mary. She savored the excitement. Nothing had felt this new for a very long time.

Ben turned toward her, gently ran his fingers through her hair. The rough pads scratched deliciously against her scalp. She tilted to rub her head against him.

"You deserve a five-star hotel." He caressed with his voice, too. "King-sized bed with crisp sheets. Bathtub for two."

"We're not going to find that out here." Feeling his words like a blush on her skin was one thing. She needed something more real to match the pulsing awareness over her skin. She reached out and unbuttoned the top button of his shirt and tipped her head toward the backseat.

He swung out of the driver's side door. She crawled between the seats and was at the next row by the time he opened the back door and met her there. A brief blast of cold air chased him in, but it quickly dissipated when she brought herself close to Ben again. The smell of his refined soap was surrounded by the aromas of soft earth and dry leaves. He was at once sophisticated and primal.

She traced her finger along his lips and memorized the firm lines. What she'd been watching was now real. What she'd been wanting was within reach. She held him by the back of the neck and pulled him into a kiss. It didn't matter that they were in a rented SUV on the side of the road. Need and pleasure and exploration took over. She'd made her need known, and he didn't hold back. His kiss grew more intense as he swept his tongue along hers. He tugged her coat off, and she did his. The night took the details away, so she had to learn them by touch. The breadth of his shoulders. The strength of his neck and how it rose into his defined jaw. She undid more of his buttons and smoothed her hands along his chest to remove his shirt. Hot skin slid beneath her palms. His muscles bunched firm, then stretched as he helped her take off the clothing. Her nipples tightened, wanting to be pressed against his chest. Heat flashed up her legs and centered in her pussy. There was enough light to see the hints of his wicked smile.

His fingers plucked at the buttons of her cardigan. He slipped the thin fabric off her and ran his rough palms down her arms, the way she'd imagined. She sighed with the simple touch. He was careful and deliberate and explored more of her shoulders and arms and back, making her skin feel bright in the dark. She allowed herself to be moved by him, and the tremble of freedom returned.

"Cold?" he asked with concern.

"Not if you're close."

He wrapped himself around her. She twined her arms behind his neck and kissed his cheek and along the edge of his ear. The spice of his soap mixed with the salt on his skin. She learned more, like the way his jaw muscles flexed when she kissed over them. He moved them so he was sitting on the bench seat and she straddled him.

His hand ran up the back of her head and through her hair, bringing tingling awareness. She tilted back into his touch, and his mouth found the side of her neck in a series of kisses that stole her breath. She ground her hips against his and felt how wet her pussy was. Sparks rained up from where they met. His erect cock rubbed against her sex through the layers of their clothes. He growled and gripped her firm around the waist, holding the two of them tighter together.

Oh, God, could she come like this? She felt like she was already on the edge. His hands moving up her ribs, under her shirt, almost brought the climax on. But she was a chaos of sensations, trying to take it all in, and couldn't focus on the one way to that pleasure. He continued higher until one palm stroked over her bra. Her nipple pressed forward. He dipped his fingers over the top of her bra to skim over the areola and tease next to the hardened point.

She tried to whisper how good he felt touching her but only managed broken syllables through rushed breath. Her cheek rubbed against his stubble; the simplest sensation became exquisite.

He slid his hands behind her back and unclasped her bra. Her shirt and bra were quickly swept over her head. The naked flesh of her chest pressed against his. She moaned. He murmured words of heat onto her throat.

Then his lips found the top of her chest. She gripped his shoulders to ground herself as his kisses moved down over her breasts. His tongue flicked against her nipple. She gasped. Her sounds were animal when his teeth bit into the tip. She dug her nails into his shoulders and urged him closer. With his teeth still gently holding her sensitive point, he surrounded her nipple with his mouth. She shook with pleasure and rode her hips harder into him.

His broad hands splayed across her back. She was surrounded and safe to pursue all her needs. She ran her fingers along the muscles of his neck and over his tight hair. He licked across her nipple, sending a jolt of electric need straight down between her legs.

"You're a very dangerous man." She tilted his head up so she could kiss him.

"And still you scare the hell out of me." There was truth in his voice, along with a sexual smoke.

She swung off his lap and sat next to him. The tip of her finger traced a line down his chest. His abs tightened under her touch. Yes, she could move him, too, and that fueled her pleasure. He surged up when her hand slid over his belt and to his erection in his jeans. She ached to know all his flesh. Along her body. Inside her.

"Your belt." She whispered her commands. "Your jeans."

"And my gun and my knife." He kicked off his shoes and undid his jeans. A pistol in a nylon holster released from his ankle. She heard him stow a folding knife on the floorboard.

She ventured over his hips, his boxer briefs and down his strong thighs. He moaned and searched her as well, with warm hands over her breasts and ribs and waist.

She found his cock again, and his movement slowed. His length pressed through the fabric of the boxer briefs. She teased at the waistband, then dove past it to take him in her hand. He was firm and hot and so potent. Having his raw sexuality in her grip brought out her own. Leaving her armor behind was deliciously scary.

He quickly shucked his underwear and was now completely naked. Exposed to her. She kissed his mouth and stroked up and down his cock. He thrust with her. She opened her mouth wider to take his tongue in. Her pace on his cock sped. Her body swiveled, longing to feel all of him. He growled into her.

The sound turned to frustration as he felt along her jeans-covered legs. "Get naked with me."

She released her hold on him to pull the knife from her boot. He helped her tug off the shoes, then undid the button and zipper of her jeans. She braced her feet and tilted up so he could drag the denim and her panties away. His hands instantly returned to her legs, exploring the length, tracing the curves and rasping pleasure along her skin.

"Deadly," he murmured.

His movements slowed as his hands reached higher up her thighs. The shiver returned. She'd never been this nude with someone. Unclothed, yes, but not this open. She sat back and spread her legs.

He moved close and wrapped an arm around her to bring her into his chest. He kissed her temple. She turned her head so their mouths could meet. The connection strengthened with each touch. Each move into the unknown. They trusted.

His fingers skimmed up the inside of her thigh. She writhed. The sensation was so real it nearly blinded her nerves. Her vision went completely white when his finger drew up along her cleft.

"Oh, God, yeah," he whispered reverently.

He slicked back and forth in an easy, long line. She rocked with him in an attempt to push the pace. But he maintained the steady stroke. She discovered why when she breathed into the pleasure and allowed it to soak through her skin and nerves to places she hadn't yet felt. His body remained next to her, solid, as she writhed. Her nails scratched along his arm and over his chest. She searched lower until she found his cock.

His length felt even firmer, more ready for her. She gasped when his finger dipped into her. She wrapped her hand around him. Her back arched further, legs spread wider. She ached, craving complete release. The brief tease of his finger had centered her attention at her pussy. With him in her hand, she could imagine what he would be inside her. What she would be wrapped around him. Completely connected and real.

He thrust in her grip at the same time he slid two fingers over her opening and up to her clit. Bright heat spread out from that point, shaking her limbs. She and Ben moved with each other, hands on each other, mouths meeting and parting. But still the climax couldn't rise through the chaos of sensations.

"You good?" He must've picked up on her disarray and slowed the pace.

"Yeah," she reassured him. "I'm just... It's just..." The answer wasn't exactly clear to her, but the trust she had with Ben allowed her to admit quietly, "It's been a while."

His arm around her shoulders supported her. "I got you."

She released her hold of his cock and rested her hand on his leg. "I'm finding my way."

He shook his head. "We'll find it together. Alright?"

She'd thought she'd known all about Ben and his quick-strike tactic with women, but he'd been straight with her every step of the way. If he'd been lying or playing her to get them to the side of this highway in the middle of nowhere, she would've known.

"Alright," she answered, and tingled with a scary flutter of trust.

He pulled his arm out from behind her. His shadowy presence slid in front of her, eyes glittering in the shadows. "I'm going to taste you—" he spoke slowly, each word a seduction, "—and you're going to tell me what feels good, so I can give you what you need."

She leaned forward and found him for a kiss. He held her trust with care. She rubbed her cheek against his and whispered in his ear, "Taste me."

He moved down her body like a thundercloud, full of electric power and silent strength. She quivered, anticipation growing with each kiss he placed on her chest, then belly. He took her hips in his hands and slid her forward on the seat to perch her at the edge. Hot breath rolled across her open thighs. He crouched in the foot well, and his broad shoulders widened her legs farther.

She'd never been this exposed for a man. She'd never allowed someone this close. But Ben shared her experience in the world, in the wars. He'd revealed his truths and had accepted her, even wanted more of her as she'd peeled back her armor. Still, she shivered.

His mouth on her inner thigh slammed her attention back to her body and the waves of electricity he invoked with each touch. He kissed her thigh again, higher. And higher toward her sex. She'd shatter when he finally reached her wetness.

He paused. She was ready to break. His tongue licked, warm and firm, up her pussy. She moaned, her voice tight around them in the contained car. He drew closer and dragged the flat of his tongue over her clit. Her legs locked around him as she held on to the delicious shock of pleasure.

Ben wrapped his hands around her waist and pulled her tighter to him. She let herself be moved. It felt like the two of them were spinning through the darkness together. The pace accelerated with Ben licking up and back, again and again.

He probed his tongue into her opening, and all the chaos collected to a single bright point. Her breath raced faster and she dug her heels into his sides.

"Right there," she gasped.

"This?" He slipped his tongue up her pussy and flicked against her clit. She jolted with the quick wash of sparkling pleasure. "Or this?" He dove back inside her with his firm heat.

She couldn't answer. She could only run her hand over his hair and hold his head harder to her sex. He alternated between thrusting into her and sweeping up through her lips and around her bud. Her encouraging words rasped in hurried fragments. The climax sped close and wound tight, charged by Ben's mouth and tongue on her pussy.

His relentless pace continued. She gulped one last breath and shattered. The orgasm spread through her hot and fast. Ben didn't let up. He kept licking into her, driving the pleasure higher and higher until she thought she couldn't take it. But she did. She relished pushing herself that far and feeling the lost corners of herself brighten, alive.

The climax crested, and she let out a long moan. Ben slowed until he held her clit in his mouth in a long kiss. Warm, wet and dark. Her hurried pulse throbbed, and her limbs felt limp. But not calm. She stroked his shoulders, encouraging him back up to her.

Her personal storm cloud rose back up. She wrapped her arms around him. He enveloped her. The two of them remained still as her heart continued to thunder. More potential resonated in their bodies. Her awakened desires hadn't been satisfied.

She kissed his mouth. Tasting her sex on him flared her desire, unashamed. "Don't stop."

"I won't ever stop until you tell me to." His voice was as shadowed as the surrounding night. Her heart opened to take in the promise. But how real was it? Right then, she wanted it all to be true.

Swiveling her hips signaled her need. He responded by separating their bodies and leaning between the front seats to search through his jacket. It was taking too long.

She tugged at his hip. "You got it?"

"I got it." But he continued his hunt.

"I have some in my purse."

"I got it…somewhere." The crinkle of the wrapper marked his success. He returned to the back and sat next to her. "Why don't you put it on?"

She extended her hand, and he placed the condom in her palm. She unwrapped it and turned to him. He didn't move. She took her time exploring his chest and stomach until her fingers found his erect cock. He rumbled. Using both hands, she slowly unrolled the condom down his length. She imagined him sliding into her bit by bit. Her need roared louder.

Once he was sheathed, Ben took her by the waist and guided her so she straddled him, kneeling on the seat. She arched her back and aligned the tip of his cock with her opening. Supporting herself on his shoulders, she lowered down until he just entered her. She hovered there. He remained still for her. It had been at least a year since any fling, and her body had to adjust. Ben was patient and held her while she balanced. She sank onto him. Pleasure replaced any pinch of discomfort. Her wetness slicked him, easing his cock further. They both breathed out together when she took him completely inside.

She ground and stirred warm, thick waves of sensation up through her. He rocked with her. One hand moved from her waist to her breast. He rolled her nipple between his fingers. She tilted her head back to savor the tight rush.

Their pace increased. She ground down, and he thrust up, plunging him even deeper. Her sex accommodated him, filling her. His firm length contrasted perfectly against her softest, most sensitive skin. The SUV swayed, but the night beyond the windows was unmoved. The inside of the car filled with the sound of their moans. They moved faster and faster. The edges of the orgasm collected around her again.

"Yeah, Mary." Her name in his mouth was as erotic as all their flesh and sweat. "Come." He held his thumb against her clit so she could spark against it while she rode him.

Her pleasure shined much brighter than she'd expected. The climax was close. Her arms ached from holding herself on Ben and her legs shook. "I'm coming." The release started infinitely far away, then quickly swept into her. She gasped, "I need you to come, too."

The connection had to be complete.

"Mary…" Ben's muscles bunched and lengthened as he thrust harder into her.

Her climax rocketed higher through her, fueled by his increased intensity. She clutched to his chest, and he wrapped his arms around her. They were locked together, each taking and giving. Pleasure spun her head. She bit into his collarbone. He buried himself, then came. Her own orgasm glowed hotter with his. He continued to slide in and out while his cock pulsed and his arms held her so tight.

Chest to chest, their hearts pounded together. They exhaled and caught their breath. She rested her head on his shoulder while he stroked through her hair. The air cooled on her sweat, but everywhere she contacted Ben remained hot.

They couldn't stay nude and alone like this forever. Miles to the west, their mission waited. She eased off him and they disentangled themselves.

He shucked the condom and got dressed. She pulled all her clothes on, the fabric too cool on her skin.

He secured his pistol to his ankle and sat back. Neither of them moved.

She asked, lightly, "What do you want to do for dinner?"

His smoky laugh reminded her of the taste of his mouth. "I already ate." He rubbed at his shoulder. "So did you."

"You inspired me." She brushed her knuckles along the outside of his thigh.

He caught her hand in his. "I'd love to go on inspiring you." He lifted her hand to his mouth and kissed the top. "You could eat me alive."

She understood the melancholy note in his voice. They had to go. Without having to speak or agree, they climbed back into the front seats and put their coats on. Ben started the engine and pulled the car back onto the highway. After a mile, he turned the headlights on. They were back in the world.

And driving toward Morris Flats.

The languid heat in her limbs cooled as she sharpened herself. She could see it in Ben as well. He sat straighter, eyes alert and scanning the black fields and distant lights. Was it possible to explore their passion and return to the mission? Or did the operation take precedence and the connection with Ben would have to be severed before it had been completely discovered? And after the business in Morris Flats had been wrapped up, would that be too late to find again what they'd ventured into to-night?

He stole glances at her, passion remaining in his eyes. "Thanks for coming to dinner with me."

"I'm glad I did." Living in the moment had been a rare freedom. Plans and tactics and strategies returned with the approach of Morris Flats. "But we need to be extra frosty back in the mix."

He nodded, face stoic. "Mission ready. One hundred percent."

"I don't want…" This territory was unknown. She didn't know how to pick her steps. "I don't want to be frosty…" Fear choked her. She felt so vulnerable without her armor. But she couldn't let it stop her from telling him, "…with you."

A glimmer in his eyes cracked his mask. "You're a gift… I'm not sure I deserve." The serious soldier returned quickly. "And I understand. We have an op. Success is critical. We'll stay on target."

"Affirmative." She understood why Ben would fly from woman to woman. No attachments to complicate the transition from bed to battlefield. But could she just turn off the attraction to him? Her body still hummed from their sex. She knew she'd crave more when the night was quiet again. Him just sitting there drew her attention like a magnet.

"Tomorrow night." He was all business. "They should be relaxed by then, and we can recon the warehouse."

Mission planning eased the churning questions

of their personal future. "Too bad we couldn't get a bracelet on Kit Daily."

"Yeah." He stretched his neck, tilting his head from side to side, as if they were heading to the op right then. "We go in dark and slow. Their patrols can't be that tight from what we've seen."

"Egress out the back of the hotel." She imagined the map of the town and the best routes through it. "Rendezvous at the abandoned gas station. We can get to the train yard on foot from there. Just follow the tracks."

"Damn." He clicked his tongue.

"What is it?" The plan had sounded good so far.

"I was hoping a little shop talk might distract me, but you are one sexy operator."

Was the sudden heat across her chest and face a girlish blush? She could tease, too. "Only for you, sailor. For the rest, I'm a nightmare."

He curled his lip in a sneer. "The ones who live."

"Stay on my good side."

"That's where you want me."

Maybe this was their balance. They didn't have to be all operator or all lover. Could she be both?

With the mood lighter in the car, they drove in silence to Morris Flats. The town was asleep, and they wound through the residential streets, past the businesses, then to the hotel. They walked in the front doors together. The bartender didn't even look up from watching the TV in the corner. He was alone in the bar. They passed the desk clerk, who gave a polite nod, and continued to the elevators.

They both got off on her floor, but their steps became less certain as they progressed down the hall. She stopped at the snack machine alcove.

"I'm…still hungry."

"Yeah." He fished bills out of his wallet. "I wasn't paying much attention to dinner."

She selected trail mix, and he got chocolate-covered raisins. They bought drinks, too, and carried it all to her door. He remained with her but didn't loom over her or push her.

It took only the slightest pause while she held her key card for him to nod and take a half step back. They were back in the operation. She wouldn't sleep much, but she needed rest. And time to sort what had happened. Who she was and who Ben was.

He let his hand hang gently against hers. "Come running with me in the morning?"

"I'm in."

His head tilted and he leaned forward. A kiss would shatter any calm she'd found. They'd be in her bed in an instant. The two of them fit together too well. None of the questions would be answered. She tipped her chin down and felt a pang in her chest as she shut off something she wanted so deeply.

He nodded again and stepped away. "Have a good night, Mary."

"Good night, Ben." She watched him walk halfway down the hall before moving into her room. She left all the lights out and listened to the silence.

ELEVEN

IT WAS A bad morning. It had been a strange night. But the evening had been incredible. Ben had barely slept, though he'd collected enough rest to be ready for the day. His bed had never felt so empty. Every time he'd shifted, the exposed sheets had sliced cold into him. Mary had been one floor beneath him. Like he could see her heat signature through the walls. Close, but not close enough to feel.

Their time in the car had burned her onto him. Completely wrapped around each other, breathing each other. Being apart after that was a new wound. A hollow ache he'd never known. He'd paced through his hotel room, hoping to clear his mind. The late-night hot shower hadn't done much to calm his thoughts either. More than the memory of her body kept returning to him. Loops of their conversations echoed. They'd knotted their connection tighter. It seemed like there was nothing he could say that she didn't understand. And then she'd probe him for deeper meanings he hadn't found yet.

With his body rested and mind still turning, he'd risen early in the morning. The operation took over. He'd checked the tracking app on his phone. Pulaski was at home. But so were all the rail yard workers

Ben had given bracelets to. They should've been on the clock by now.

The sun fought its way into a steel-gray sky, and Ben dressed for his run. He went downstairs and hadn't knocked on Mary's door when she opened it, looking as if she'd had twelve hours of sleep after a spa day.

His voice was still morning rough. "You've got to teach me some of those Delta spy tricks."

She smirked. "Maybe I was just born with it."

He breathed in her rosy perfume as she bounded past him and shut the door. But he couldn't follow her. He stood rooted and watched her jog up the hallway in her tight leggings and slim-fitting, long-sleeved hoodie. Now his body was really awake. Blood stirred in his legs and crotch.

She made it a few rooms down, then turned and hit him with a nasty look. Like she could take him apart if she wanted. He wanted her to.

"Move it, sailor." Her growl immediately tugged him forward.

He reached her and they walked shoulder to shoulder toward the elevator. The hollow ache from the night before cut through him. She was close. He needed to be closer, but didn't know how to bridge the gap.

Their job in Morris Flats, though, wasn't compromised. "Local rail workers are all still home," he informed her.

Her brow lowered in thought. "Their day should be started."

"That's what I was thinking." They had to wait longer than usual for the elevator. "Maybe we take a jog by the yard."

"We can recon tonight's route." The elevator arrived, and they stepped inside. Awkward silence tightened now that their immediate business had been taken care of. She ventured, "Sleep?"

"More like a twelve-round title fight with my pillow." Her hair was pulled back in a ponytail, allowing him to see the strong lines of her cheekbones and the sharp eyes under her dark eyebrows. "How'd you do?"

"I've had worse. On a rooftop in Odessa." She shrugged it off. "In the freezing rain."

"Luxurious." A black ops soldier had to be something other than human. He'd been there. He hated to think of her being that uncomfortable. But she was human, just like him. She hadn't passed the night after their time together with completely cold blood.

But could he tell her about how he'd been wanting her in his bed? Next to him, her head on his shoulder, his fingers through her hair. Would that push her away? She operated on her terms.

All he could do was tell her and not expect anything in return. "I missed you."

Her eyes shined with emotion. She hesitated before speaking. "It was…lonely."

The elevator doors opened, and they were thrown back into the world, back into the operation. Three men in their thirties waited to get on. They all looked weary from traveling, mouths thin lines. But their eyes were alert, and strong hands held heavy duffel bags. Ben and Mary exited the elevator, and the men paid more attention to her than him.

They were trouble.

He and Mary walked through the lobby, where three more men just like the others in heavy coats and flannel shirts waited at the front desk. Two duffel bags and a suitcase. They smelled of protein powder and gunpowder. The hotel security guard who'd seen Ben and Mary in the hall the other night leaned on the front desk and chatted familiarly with one of the men.

Ben and Mary got out of the hotel and immediately started jogging. Cold air tightened his lungs, and it took a minute for his legs to loosen.

A block away from the parking lot, she muttered, "Hitters."

"Not their first time in town." His awareness bristled. Morris Flats was turning into a hot zone. "Security for the shipments?"

"I'd bet." Her gaze didn't rest as she scanned over the buildings and intersections. "Nine o'clock."

He looked down the left side of an intersection and saw a police car parked sideways across a street a block away. The roof lights rolled, and one of the cops was placing traffic cones in a line as a barrier to the street.

Ben extrapolated, "They're locking down their routes." He and Mary skirted the edge of town, near the train tracks, and saw another police-enforced road closure.

"Pretty fucking bold." She was barely winded from the run. "Right through the middle of everything."

"Escalation to deadline." New security forces, road closures, the meeting in the state park. The gunrunners would move soon.

A police car eased up a street parallel to theirs. It tracked with them for a moment, and Ben could see the cops staring. One of them was the angry officer from the rec center. He waved forward, and the driver accelerated.

More train tracks collected near the two he and Mary had been following. They approached the yard. The parking lot should've been empty without workers. But there were plenty of cars in the spaces.

"Too many out-of-state plates." He couldn't see any of the workers at this far end of the yard.

Mary's eyes narrowed on the cars. "Florida, Mass, Texas." Anger chopped into her words. "I'm seeing out-of-date military base permits."

"Mercs." The population of Morris Flats was transforming from civilians to some kind of private army.

Mary slowed her pace and muttered, "The brass is here."

Kit Daily and the mayor and her husband all stood at the edge of the parking lot. Their cold breath swirled with the steam rising from their paper cups of coffee. The Limerts hunched like conspirators and flinched when they caught sight of Ben and Mary approaching. Daily only smirked smugly and hooked his thumb in his wide belt.

After a second, the mayor mustered her usual vote-getting smile. "Of all the places to jog. You know we have a nice greenbelt on the other side of town?"

Ben had seen the muddy tract punctuated by high power lines. "This is only the first leg." He and Mary stopped and stretched. Past Daily, the rail yard was in full swing. Men used forklifts to move pallets of crates from a freight car into a warehouse.

Mary shook hands with the three locals. "Yeah, we'll see how far Mr. Louis is willing to chase me this morning."

Daily leered at her calves. "I reckon he'll never stop running."

She ignored him and directed a question to the mayor. "Is there a problem in town? We saw police cars blocking roads."

Donna Limert rolled her eyes at the nuisance. "Road maintenance. Nothing to worry about."

Her husband chimed in, "Yeah, nothing that'll drive down property prices."

Ben chuckled. "I thought they were setting up for a parade."

Mary was a pro and knew when to cut out so they didn't look too suspicious. She bounced on the balls of her feet, ready to run again. "Come on, let's see if you can chase me all the way to Chicago."

"My old home turf?" He readied himself to resume the job. "You won't escape me there."

Daily looked Ben over. "You're a Chicago boy?"

Ben rolled his shoulders and tried not to tense at being called a boy. "It's my city." And if Daily showed himself there, he wouldn't last a second in an alley with no witnesses.

The boss of the train yard still looked down his nose at Ben. "Go Cubbies."

It felt good to laugh outright in Daily's face. "Sox."

Mary waved at the group and took off running. Ben followed without looking back, and they were quickly around a corner and out of sight from the rail yard.

She glared at him when he caught up to her. "You want to blow it?"

"I'm not really trying to sell bracelets." Their pace picked up. "And I don't need him as a friend." He wanted to run back to Daily, take the pistol from his belt and smash it into the side of his head. "I'm on target and won't fail the op. But that doesn't mean I have to let myself get buried by that fucker."

She eased up, and he wanted to keep charging ahead. Her sincere voice brought him back to her. "You're right. I'm sorry."

"It's not you." Had he snapped too hard at her?

"I know." She slowed to a walk. He stayed with her. "And I'm still sorry."

He stopped walking, the rage still bubbled up through him. "Sons of bitches like Kit Daily smile, throwing guns in the streets and counting their money. We've both seen what that does."

She nodded. "I want him, too." Her jaw set. "I want to stick my knife in so deep it cuts his roots and there's none of them left." She patted Ben's chest. The small touch shocked him with her comfort. "That's how we do it. With Automatik. With the plan."

He took her hand in his. "All the way to the bone." Her sleeves covered her knuckles, so he pushed the cuff back and kissed the top of her hand. Not something he'd ever done with a teammate or operator before, but it felt right. A promise, not just to get the job done, but to not let her down at any cost.

Her hard eyes softened and she took a long breath. "All the way."

They resumed their run, seeing more police cars and roads blocked with cones or city sawhorses. Their route took them across the north-south highway and into the more residential neighborhoods. The greenbelt wasn't green. Neither was the park across from the high school. Teachers and administrators were just starting to arrive in the parking lot and chatting as they walked into the main buildings. Ben angled the run toward there when he saw Romero and his wife, Sue, getting out of their car.

He waved and got a questioning squint back from Romero. But as they approached, the man seemed to recognize Ben and smiled politely. Sue extended a "good morning" and Ben introduced Mary to the couple.

Sue's eyebrows raised when she heard what kind of real estate Mary was involved in. "Sounds like an uphill battle in Morris Flats."

Romero nodded and scratched at his freshly shaved chin. "I'll bet there are other towns that would be open to it."

"But not with the highway access," Mary corrected. "It makes this town perfect for development." And for gunrunners.

"Well, the best of luck to you." Sue sounded sincere.

Before parting, Ben asked, "What's with the streets being blocked off? We going to get trapped by construction?"

Frustration flared in Romero. "That's just… truckers getting the right of way. Doesn't matter who else they inconvenience."

"How long?" Ben tried to map the town and the newly protected routes. "I mean, what if I need to get out of town or something?"

Romero glared out toward the east side. "Usually under a week. Three days?"

The timeframe sped up. Ben knew Mary would be feeling it as well but was experienced enough to know not to share a glance with her. He shook Romero's hand. "Thanks. Glad we ran into you."

They said their goodbyes and parted. The teachers walked into their school as Ben and Mary jogged back toward the center of town. Private security forces. Street closures. Activity at the rail yard.

He watched her processing his same thoughts. "They're gearing up," she said, flat.

"I'll let Automatik know." As soon as he had a second alone with his phone. "They're the trigger."

"Security is tightening. They'll have to leak in slowly."

Hopefully the strike team could assemble in time to stop the guns from leaving this hub. "Until then, it's us."

Her face was calm. She was a warfighter. "We're the hammer."

MARY HAD DROPPED into deadly territory from airplanes, helicopters and trucks. She'd hiked over a mountain range with her Delta team and inserted invisibly into hostile land. But she'd never watched a town transform into a combat zone around her. The tension she already felt being in the field dialed up. Every rooftop, every passing car was scrutinized. Her legs couldn't rest, ready to run. And her hand was never far from her pistol.

After her jog with Ben, she'd gone through the motions of scouting more of the town from her rented car. She'd eaten lunch alone, then returned to the hotel, where she now sat in the bar, paperwork spread out across the small table and her phone at the ready. A regular woman, working on her regular job.

But in fact, she was positioned to track the traffic in the lobby and front desk. The private security forces she and Ben had seen earlier came and went. Their pace had been measured and calm. They weren't on the job yet. And they didn't perceive any threats around them. She could tell from their slow reactions to the front doors opening that their radar wasn't tuned for trouble in town.

Two other men had arrived while she'd been observing the lobby. They were like the others. In their thirties, strong, athletic and kitted with heavy luggage. The count was up to at least eight. And that didn't include the armed men from the state park meeting or the newcomers at the rail yard. Former military. Probably networked to Daily through his old contacts with the Marines. The corruption rotted deep and the betrayal fueled her anger. No, she wasn't a Marine, but had known plenty of good men and women, Art Diaz the latest, and hated that the military was being used this way.

"You sure I can't mix you a cocktail to take the edge off all that work?" Will the bartender held up a shaker hopefully.

"The way I've been burning the candle—" she shook her head and looked up from her files, "—it would put me right to sleep. And the boss might call any minute."

He put the shaker down and busied his hands rearranging little cups of garnishes. "As soon as you clock out, let me know."

It was just the two of them in the bar. She had a feeling that would change when the evening descended. The security men clearly knew each other and were familiar with the hotel. They'd take over.

From the size and weight of their luggage, she assumed they carried pistols and submachine guns. Small arms for intimidation but not real fighting. If they'd fired any shots protecting the cargo over the years, there would've been news and it wouldn't have taken Automatik so long to track the center point for the gunrunning operation.

By now, Ben had informed the rest of her team about the escalation. He'd gone about his own business during the day and was now perched at one of the tall tables at the back of the lobby where the breakfast was served. Another working stiff who didn't arouse suspicion.

She couldn't see him but trusted his presence. He had her back, just as she had his. Teammates. And something else. She couldn't name it, but she couldn't ignore it.

"Is your job going to keep you in Morris Flats long?" Will ran out of things to organize.

"A few days, I think." She shuffled papers. "It depends on how things pan out."

A silent alert appeared on her phone. She opened Ben's message: Hitter in the gray coat currently armed. 9mm on right hip.

She glanced into the lobby and saw the man leaning on the front desk, talking to the girl behind it while she politely smiled and went about her tasks.

Will came out from behind the bar and sat on one of the stools with a groan as he stretched his back. "Days get long out here without much to do. Sure you can't bounce early?"

"Not unless I want to find another job." She texted Ben back: Identified.

"Too bad. This place kind of sucks." He stared out of the bar and through the front doors of the hotel. "And this is a shitty season."

A hint of pain in his eyes. Just like that little flinch when she'd mentioned the rail yard on her first day. Kit Daily and his operation had crushed this town.

"You making your own escape plan?" She put down her work and focused on Will.

For a second he looked like a high school senior posing for his portrait and having no idea what was coming next, then he rallied and gathered more swagger about him. "It's all in motion. A few more paychecks, and I'm up to Chicago. There's always work for a bartender. And I can cook a little."

"A friend of mine owns a restaurant in California. Tough business." Being in Hayley's kitchen when it was in full dinner mode was like trying to dance between helicopter rotor blades. "But she's a tough chick." An understatement, considering the story Art told about Hayley going toe-to-toe with a Russian mob goon, armed only with a cooking spoon. And she showed her grit fighting not just for herself, but to protect what she had with Art.

Will kept gazing out of the hotel. "Just a few more paychecks."

That dream might stay alive if he kept his head

down and let Daily and the others roll over him. Just like the rest of town. She saw it in the teachers Ben had introduced her to. No ability to fight back. The crime was too entrenched. And when Mary and Ben and their team shined a light on it, aimed their weapons at it, the gunrunners were going to fight hard to keep their bloody dollars. Morris Flats could crash quickly into a battle zone. Civilians would be in the crossfire and her blood ran cold thinking of any of them being hurt.

Will got off his stool and walked back behind the bar with more purpose. "I'm out of here soon. And you should be out of here sooner." It was the most serious she'd ever seen the bartender. He seemed to age ten years with just the somber look in his eyes.

She shrugged and fanned her hands over her paperwork. "I can't." She had to stop Daily and the Limerts and Pulaski. She had to stay for the fight, shoulder to shoulder with Ben.

TWELVE

DEAD OF NIGHT, she came alive. It was after 3:00 a.m. when she opened her hotel room door and crept into the hallway. Like before, she kept her tactical gear bundled so it looked like she was carrying her coat, but no one was out to observe her silently move to the service stairs and descend.

She reached the cold, abandoned terrace, pulled on her vest and secured the buckles along the front. Every strap was squared away and silent. Any piece of metal—from her knife to her pistols—had been muted to the point that it would reflect no light and give away her position. She climbed down to street level and started the route to the rail yard.

The private security forces who'd arrived at the hotel wouldn't be patrolling tonight. As she'd suspected, they'd taken the bar over around five and closed it down by eleven. Their loud conversations and barking laughs had echoed into the hotel lobby. They were sloppy. Small bits of intel had slipped, and she'd picked them up as she'd passed by on the way to her room. More than one man had mentioned "last year" or "three years ago." The gunrunning was systematic and long running. A guy jeered another about not having the right clothes for his shitty detail in a cold freight car. Another man alluded to trouble he'd avoided at a truck weigh station, "Just sitting and eating my apple, looking pretty and innocent." Their voices lowered when they spoke of collecting and transporting money, but they were still reckless enough to let anyone within fifty feet hear. So they rode shotgun with the guns, collected the money at the final destination and carried it back to the base of operations: Morris Flats.

She'd communicated everything she'd gathered to Automatik and Ben while resting in her room in preparation for the night's action. He'd been in the bar, surrounded by the security men, for about a half hour, pretending to drink a beer and watch a basketball game. From their reckless conversations, he'd been able to identify most of them as former Marines, even down to two units out of Florida. The connections to Kit Daily were strong. Ben had understood when he'd worn out his welcome at the bar and had retreated to his own room as well. Both of them had communicated via their app when they'd heard the drunk men stumbling and laughing and insulting each other along the hallways.

The security men weren't on alert yet. They felt safe in Morris Flats. First mistake. She knew to feel safe was a sure way of getting blindsided. But what did it mean that she felt safe with Ben?

Separated by the floor and only in electronic contact, Ben's presence had surrounded her. He was an operator who could be relied on. His awareness extended to minute details about the men and the environment. It wasn't just his training or time in the wars. Ben had an innate ability to zero in on just the necessary details. It was how he'd found her.

Out in the night, she dissolved into the shadows of the street and followed the deepest corners like an inky river. No one could see her. Except Ben. If she was brave enough. If she could trust him to be caring and gentle with the delicate, newfound hope she carried.

Two blocks away from the hotel, her senses prickled. She wasn't alone. Her hand hovered over the pistol on her chest. A figure separated from the angular silhouettes of the building before her. Ben. He stood in his black tactical gear among the gas pumps of the derelict service station they'd chosen as rendezvous. She approached, and the features of his face emerged in the dim streetlights. His face was still all business, but his eyes were keen. He gave her a nod and extended a fist. She bumped it, and the two of them moved away from the gas station and to a weedy ditch behind it.

Train tracks striped the other side of the ditch. Without speaking, the two of them slipped into the shadowed side of the ditch and trekked forward toward the train yard. Their steps were quieted by soft dirt. Ben led and avoided any extra noise by looping around collected trash and fallen branches from nearby trees. He'd point all these obstacles out for her, always moving, always scanning forward and to the sides. She maintained her own watch of their perimeter and rear, keeping a hand on Ben's upper shoulder for silent communication.

His strong body balanced perfectly as he navigated. She'd known those muscles, not just in combat. Holding her. Giving her his power to crash against. Matching her and challenging her to find more pleasure. And now he was out on a secret detail with her. The memories of their sex made her breath run hotter in her chest, but they didn't cloud her judgment. She and Ben had fit together in the backseat of that SUV, and they fit together during a silent insertion into hostile territory.

She only needed to tighten her fingers for Ben to halt his progress. He looked at her. She tipped her head behind them, in the direction of a solitary civilian car two blocks away. The two of them remained completely still until the car continued away and disappeared into the north side of town.

When the sound of the engine faded, replaced by the brittle weeds shivering in a biting breeze, she and Ben resumed their progress. The smell of engine oil and axle grease announced the approach of the rail yard.

Ben suddenly stopped and crouched low. He motioned with his hand toward their eleven o'clock position. A police car patrolled up and down the streets in a serpentine pattern that covered all the corners. It wasn't a normal scan of a quiet town, keeping the citizens safe.

She brought her ear close to Ben's mouth. He whispered, "Perimeter sweep."

For the rail yard. They both waited until the police car finished the sector and cleared to another area. Silence descended again. Ben climbed up the opposite side of the ditch while she followed. A ten-foot cinderblock wall now separated them from the train tracks they'd been following. He made quick hand gestures to indicate that he'd help her up first, then he put his back to the wall. She readied herself and approached him quickly. His cradled hands supported her first step. Her other foot pressed off his shoulder, then she was easily on top of the wall.

The tracks glowed like a spiderweb covered in dew on the other side of the wall. Lights shined farther north in the heart of the train yard, and exhaust billowed from idling engines. The warehouses were black rectangles, voids in the landscape. She spotted no movement in the immediate area and waved Ben forward.

He ran up the wall toward her. She leaned down with her hand outstretched. His momentum and her strength carried him to the edge of the wall with her. They both swung over and jumped down to the other side.

They clung to the thick shadow at the base of the wall and remained motionless. The border had been crossed. Hostile territory stretched out in front of them. Once she was sure no one had detected them, she attached her night vision monocular to a telescopic sight and scanned the area around the warehouses four hundred yards away.

Ben crouched next to her. She knew he was

watching their immediate surroundings as her visual recon eliminated her peripheral vision. His hand rested on her back and would communicate any trouble.

She finished her assessment, brought her body closer to his and whispered in the smallest breaths, "Motion lights on the corners. Eighty percent coverage. We can shoot the gaps in the overlap."

He tapped his hand on her back to signal his readiness. She sprinted away from the wall and across four sets of tracks until she found the next pool of shadows in a hollow between two switching towers. Ben slid in right behind her.

No detection. She pointed in the direction of the next run, and Ben nodded. Now that she was on point, he covered their rear. The switch was seamless. He showed no ego about following her orders. She slipped out of the hollow and ran to the broader swath of shadows created by the warehouses.

Ben stayed on her hip and ran backward the last few yards until they settled into the new cover. They were still about three hundred yards from the warehouses, but there was little between them and the tall, wide buildings.

She and Ben crouched low and approached slowly. Their boots crunched on the gravel, but someone would have to be right on top of them to hear it. She recalled the position of the motion lights and angled their path so they'd be between the spread of the sensors. The two of them stopped every ten or so paces to assess their surroundings.

So far, no one had spotted them and there were no people working on this side of the warehouses.

But there was activity on the far end. A metal door screeched open and slammed shut. The sound cycled again. She pointed to her ear, and Ben nodded. He'd heard it, too. It could be one person coming and going, or two people entering the warehouse. At two hundred yards, she and Ben were still too far to hear any voices. Tension charged her limbs. She had to be ready. They had no cover if there was trouble coming.

She pressed forward with Ben in careful increments. The warehouse was silent after the two door slams. One hundred yards away, the voices emerged. Clipped, orderly sentences, but she couldn't make out the words.

The pressure of the stealthy insertion increased and her pace became even more deliberate. They were twenty yards from the side of the warehouse. The motion detectors would be able to see them from this point forward. A row of unlit windows, ten feet off the ground, lined the short side of the warehouse they approached. If a light turned on outside, the men inside would be able to see it. But whoever had hung the security sensors hadn't done as perfect a job as she would've. If she was correct, there should be a narrow gap in the spread she and Ben could ride to the wall of the warehouse.

She charted her path and still expected a light to turn on with each step forward. She had to be ready for anything. Quick gestures told Ben that if the floods hit them, she'd break to the right. The train yard continued in that direction but gave way to a scrubby swamp, which would be easy to hide in. Ben nodded, then held up three fingers and made the symbol of a person walking. At least three men in the warehouse. He'd picked out the voices. She gave him a thumbs-up and motioned for them to continue.

Ten yards. Now she heard the distinction between the talkers inside. It sounded like they were on the far side of the building, muffled by quite a few crates. No laughing or joking. The talk seemed to be all logistics. Whatever their business at the moment, they had yet to turn on any interior lights on this end of the warehouse.

She and Ben made it over the last few yards of open ground and pressed their backs to the warehouse wall. From here they'd have about six feet of leeway to work along the building's perimeter before the sensors caught them. She breathed to calm the tension and drew imaginary borders around the safe zones where they could operate.

Pointing at her eyes then the window above them, she told Ben she wanted to take a look inside. He again cradled his hands, and she stepped into them, then onto his shoulders. The man was like a steady mountain beneath her. She slowly peeked up into the window. Stacks and stacks of crates stood in stark, black contrast to a pool of light glowing on the far side of the warehouse. Three men gathered around a work table and stared down at a laptop computer. One of them periodically pointed to different areas of the warehouse. She couldn't identify the men, but they had the same bearing as the collected truckers and guards who she and Ben had spotted at the state park meeting. And they wore assault rifles slung over their shoulders.

She tapped Ben with her toe and conveyed what she saw via hand signals while still scanning the warehouse. He squeezed her ankle as he received the information. The men inside continued their business. She remained on watch. Ben didn't move or show any signs of fatigue.

The smell of military gun oil filled her nose. She ached to get inside the warehouse to see what was in the crates. She'd get her chance. One of the men closed the laptop, and the three of them filed out of the warehouse. The last man turned out the light, and welcome darkness blanketed the space.

A quick inspection of the window revealed foil tape around the glass and magnetic contacts poised at any opening point. The security system couldn't have been any newer than the 1990s and hadn't been well maintained. She unsheathed a slim knife from her boot and slid it between the corroded metal frame and window near a latch. The blade flaked rust away and tripped the latch. The hinges squeaked, and the window swung away. Quick panic flashed. She grabbed the window before it swung away from the magnetic switch.

Two centimeters. Any more, and the alarm would go off. She steadied herself, put the knife handle in her teeth and freed up a hand to dig into one of the pockets of her tactical vest. Delta operators were more than shooters. She'd been trained in safe cracking, security systems and lock picking, and equipped herself for most eventualities. Tonight's countermeasure was a simple magnet she attached to the tip of her knife and slipped through the window and onto the alarm sensor.

But there was always the chance the technique would fail. She tapped on Ben's shoulder, prepping him for the possibility to run. He squeezed a response, ready. She eased the window open, past the point where the alarm would trip. Silence. Tension released from her neck and jaw. She and Ben remained ghosts.

The window louvered to the point where it was wide enough for her to crawl through. She hauled herself up and lined her belly on the edge. As he'd done before, Ben took one step back, then ran at the wall. He clasped her hand and brought himself into the open window next to her. They swung to the interior of the warehouse and dropped down to the floor.

She hit the hard concrete and hurried to cover behind a tall stack of crates. Ben disappeared just a few feet away from her. Neither moved for a moment as they assessed the new environment. As soon as she was sure they were alone, she returned to the wall and pulled on a long chain attached to the window to close it.

Their tracks covered, the two of them pressed

farther into the warehouse. Yellow rail yard lights shined into the space from the opposite windows, giving just enough detail to navigate. The pallets and shipping boxes around them were coated in old dust and smelled of damp wood. These weren't the guns. But she and Ben couldn't just rush to the other side of the warehouse, as much as she wanted to. Their path curved, methodical, through the stacks of goods.

Ben poked his elbow into her arm, then pointed at a section of crates across the main aisle down the middle. She recognized the silhouettes. Wood, metal and hard plastic boxes. Military issue.

She and Ben skipped across the center aisle and crept behind the stacks of containers that reeked of gun oil. Some of the boxes still had their original shipping labels, along with their requisition numbers and destination base. Florida. Kit Daily's old unit.

Ben hissed, "These fuckers are barely trying to hide."

She carefully undid the latches on a long plastic container and opened the lid to reveal a long row of 9mm handguns wrapped in plastic and accompanied by two extra magazines each. "This is trouble when it hits the streets."

"Or if someone's trying to start a war." He tipped his head toward another crate. She knew the contents from its familiar shape. M249 SAWs. Someone would pay a lot for a fully automatic light machine gun like that. And they could do a lot of damage with it.

"Tracker." She unwrapped a pistol from the container before her and used a multi-tool to unscrew one of the grip plates. Ben placed a black tracker just a little larger than a grain of rice on the underside of the grip plate. It had a light coating of adhesive and stayed in place while she secured the plate back to the gun. They repeated the process for three more pistols, then closed the case. These were the same type of trackers he'd distributed in the bracelets, and as long as they were within range of a cell phone tower, they could be found.

Cracking open the wooden crates would've made too much noise. And it would've been nearly impossible to hide the signs of tampering with the tools she had at hand. She focused instead on an aluminum container that bore the dents of years of use. Inside were six U.S. military-issue M4 assault rifles, complete with optics on the top and flashlights and laser sights on the front rails. Ben lifted one out and slipped a tracker into the hollow grip. She had the next one out as he put it away, and they tagged all the weapons.

He closed the aluminum container and pointed at the crate of M249s. "I want those SAWs." Anger edged his whisper. "Tracking them isn't enough. I can foul the gas regulator. Two shots, and it'll blow."

"Do it," she agreed and helped him undo the metal latches on the plywood crate. They set the lid aside, and he pulled one of three machine guns out of their foam cocoons. It wasn't the quietest operation, even though he moved deliberately. Metal clanked against metal, and the sounds crept out into the warehouse.

He set the butt of the weapon on the ground and snapped open a blade from a multi-tool. The blade wedged into the gas regulator below the barrel and released it from its seat. He pulled a small tube of what looked like clay from one of his vest pockets, pinched off a small amount and kneaded it between his fingers.

She placed her mouth next to his ear. "I didn't know SEALs were that crafty."

He winked at her and continued to work the two-part epoxy for another few seconds. "Delta ain't the only tricky group out there."

"But we don't exist." She took hold of the SAW while Ben pressed a bit of the epoxy deep into the gas regulator with the tip of his knife. "If you look at my Army file, the only extracurricular you'll see is the women's golf team."

He chuckled and reached forward to replace the regulator on the weapon.

The far doors clanged open. The light turned on at the front and invaded their shadows. The lid of the crate was open. Ben held the regulator, and she had the SAW in her hands. She gripped it close to suppress its rattling parts and moved as far from the light as possible without echoing her footsteps into the warehouse. Ben disappeared next to her. He crouched low, poised. His body wasn't tense, but it was clear he was ready to leap into a fight if he had to.

The frustrated voice of Len the foreman barked out. "I thought we went over all this. Come on, Rob, it's not that fucking complicated." He walked down the center aisle, forty feet away from their position. Len spoke as if explaining to a child. "Green paint means it goes on a truck. Red goes on the choo choo train. So you don't mix and match them in the staging areas. If they're all the same color, then they're easier to load. Get it?"

Another man defended himself. "Yeah, I got it. It's just that your system doesn't account for final destinations. Look…" He strode farther up the warehouse. If he spotted the lid off the crate, the battle would begin.

Adrenaline readied her. She knew how not to lock up with panic, but all of her muscles were taut in preparation to move. Ben silently slid his pistol from the holster on his vest. She balanced the SAW in one arm and did the same. For the first time in Morris Flats, her finger was on the trigger.

The man continued, "Red, red, red. But if we put them all on the same train car and they're set for different destinations, we're fucked."

Len sighed out loudly. "That's why they're all grouped in the staging area. Batch by batch. But if you throw truck shit on a train, it messes the whole thing up."

"So you're saying that from here…" The man kept walking up the aisle. She watched Ben aim his

pistol in the direction of the voices. The man had
no idea of the danger and was nearly yelling. "All
the way to here is one load for a train."

"That's right." Len patronized him. "Nice and
organized until you guys find odd cargo to throw
in here and fuck it up." The two of them were ten
feet from the open crate. She scanned for multiple
escape routes. If she fired a shot, she would have to
run. "All I need from you is to ask before you start
slinging that shit around and screwing the whole
system."

Silence. How far would they go? If the argu-
ment continued, it could carry them right next to
Ben and Mary.

"Fine," the man spat. "But that means you can't
bitch at me or the guys when we're coming and asking where things go."

Ben maintained his steady aim.

Len grumbled, "Then it's a fucking deal." His
brisk footsteps receded up the aisle.

The other man remained motionless. Had he
spotted the crate?

"Get some coffee." Len shouted from the other
side of the warehouse and swung the door open.

"Yeah." The man called back, then muttered,
"Fucking asshole." He finally shuffled away from
Mary and Ben's position. After a few moments,
the light in the warehouse turned out and the door
slammed.

Ben let out a long breath. She released the tension that had strung between her shoulders. But nei-

ther of them completely relaxed. She waited until all the currents of air the men had stirred settled, then holstered her pistol. Ben did the same, and the two of them quickly reassembled the machine gun.

She carried it back to the crate and replaced the weapon. Ben pulled the next one, and they sabotaged the gas regulator on it and placed a tracker in the hollow grip. They took care of the last machine gun in the crate then replaced the lid and latched it. No signs of tampering. Whoever bought the weapons wouldn't have any idea something was wrong until the barrel exploded and the bolt deformed.

The two of them ventured into another section of the warehouse, scanning over the boxes and cases in order to catalogue the illegal guns. Mixed in with the military weapons were other foreign-made models. AKs, pistols, submachine guns, as well as thousands of rounds of ammunition of all calibers.

"Oh, no." She stopped at one long, hard plastic case, designed to carry only one weapon.

"Damn..." Ben patted her shoulder with sympathy. "They got your family."

She opened the case and revealed a Barrett .50 sniper rifle, disassembled for transport. It was complete with two magazines, three boxes of match grade ammunition and a telescopic sight. She'd used this weapon to save a lot of lives, as recently as the Automatik operation against the Russian mob in the Mexican desert. "Tag it."

Ben pulled out one of his trackers. "Best spot?"

"Underside of the upper receiver." She lifted the

part so he could get at a hidden area within. Thankfully, he was quick. She replaced the upper receiver in its spot and closed the case so she didn't have to look at such a trusted tool bastardized for profit.

"Let's bounce." Ben pointed his thumb toward the window where they'd entered. "We got what we needed tonight."

He was right. They'd identified the guns, tied them directly to Kit Daily and tagged them for tracking. Every second in the warehouse and near the rail yard increased their chances of being discovered. And without the rest of their strike team, it would be a nightmare for the two of them to go against the massing security forces.

They backtracked through the warehouse, away from the guns and back to the older pallets that weren't going anywhere soon. Ben set up under the window. She pulled the chain to release the latch, and it swung wide with a creak. Once the sound died, she climbed Ben's body and reached the open window. He ran up the wall to her hand, and the two of them balanced on the edge. She pulled the window down until there was just a small gap. Ben jumped to the ground while she used her knife to retrieve her magnet from the alarm switch. All traces of their ingress were removed. She closed the window, sheathed her knife and joined Ben at the base of the warehouse wall.

She put together her night vision rig and scanned the area ahead, including their path back to the cinderblock wall at the far edge of the yard. Everything was clear. She led them through the gap in the motion sensors and farther among the train tracks.

They continued their methodical process during egress. The activity in the yard continued, but the warehouse remained dark. She and Ben reached the wall and moved in perfect sync. She climbed his body then helped him over. Once back on the ground, they slithered into the shadows of the ditch and followed it back toward the hotel.

The immediate danger was over. The bigger war was coming.

THIRTEEN

OFTEN, AFTER A successful mission, Ben and his team would celebrate with beers and cigars. But there was no victory now, even though he and Mary had made it back to his hotel room without being detected. She sat on the small couch, and he took the floor, leaning against the wall next to the window. Long, slow breaths helped release the buzzing tension. The operation, though, continued. The rest of the strike team needed to assemble in town, the plan needed to be set, then the gunrunners needed to be neutralized before they moved their goods. That was the thorn. Could Automatik show up in time?

"Wish I could crack open a beer with you." He unlaced his boots but left them on for now.

She stretched her legs out onto the coffee table. "At Art and Hayley's place. With those dumplings."

"And those bomb-ass nachos." And a quiet table, just him and her. Safe, with all the time in the world. He allowed himself to revel in the plan. Nothing big. A dinner. Something to hope for on the other side of the operation.

He kicked off his boots and hauled himself to standing at the edge of the window. The curtains were closed, but he could see through the edge that Morris Flats slept below them. Only the highway through the middle of town had any cars and trucks moving on it. The roads were clear. His vantage didn't see far enough to the east to cover the rail yard.

"Fuck this town." He hated seeing all those guns piled up, waiting for eager hands. And he hated the constant danger he and Mary were in. All they needed was a little protected moment. A couple of beers, and they might be able to figure out what they'd be after all this. His neck cracked as he tipped his head back and forth to stretch out the tightness from tonight's mission. "That could've gone to hell in a second."

She stood and walked to the opposite side of the window and peered down. "We both know hell."

Streetlights below carved her features in gold. A weary warrior who'd seen and done all the things he carried with him as well.

"Maybe that's why we were able to lift each other out of it." He moved away from the window.

She followed him into the middle of the room, her face still, eyes revealing depth. Finally, she spoke. "You're too good at this."

"You didn't say that when we were infiltrating the yard." He knew what she meant but couldn't meet her head-on.

"I trust you as an operator." She didn't look at him. "As a teammate."

"But not as a…" He waited for her to finish the sentence. She didn't, so he added, "Friend?"

"I have friends, but we don't spend time in the backseats of cars." She crossed her arms over her chest.

"Not my friends, either." The distance between them seemed harder to cross than miles of razor wire and claymore mines. "But we might be that. Might be more."

"Don't give me that 'friends with benefits' bullshit." Her hands dropped to her sides, like she was ready to fight. "That's just a convenient way of leaving an escape route."

"I don't need an escape route because I don't feel trapped." He stepped toward her. She stood her ground. He approached cautiously. He didn't know how to get around her defenses and frustration edged into him. "We can be friends, and we can be whatever else feels right."

"Like I said, you're too good at this." Her voice was flat.

He absorbed the jab and continued. "Because it feels right, doesn't it?" Any second, one of those mines could go off, but he couldn't stop now that he'd ventured so far.

She ventured into the danger with him. "It does."

His heart beat faster in a tight chest. "I can't be good at this," he told her, "because I've never done it before."

"I can't be temporary." She was still poised, ready for a fight.

"How could I get enough of you?" He wasn't interested in a fight. No games. No hustle. He told the truth, and from there, couldn't change the trajectory.

"But you are good." She slid forward noiselessly. "Too damn slick, Ben Jackson."

"For you." He met her in the middle of the room. "Only you."

Her warm hand slid over his chest and curled into a fist, gripping his shirt. His frustration and trepidation burned away. He held her waist, pulled her closer. She smelled of the cool night and hot skin. He leaned down and kissed her. They met like a sigh, a release. Relief in the midst of the conflict.

She breathed deep and rested her head on his shoulder. "Why don't you brief the team? I'm going to get ready for bed."

The memory of the cold sheets edged into his calm. "You spending the night?"

"Can't stay away anymore." She smiled, and a broad heat opened up inside him.

With her fist still balled in his shirt, she shook him, then released him and walked to the bathroom. He sat on the couch and updated Automatik on everything they'd found during the night's recon. Mary reemerged after a few minutes and helped recount details like the requisition numbers on the crates and the final base destinations. The timeline for the strike team's assembly was sped up, but there was only so much they could do. A quick influx of strangers would take a simmering situation to a boil.

Mary perched on the arm of the couch and rested her forearm on his back so she could read over his shoulder as he typed on the phone. It was as easy as when she'd climbed him to get to the warehouse window. They didn't need words all the time.

They finished the debrief, and he placed his phone on the coffee table. Going over the list of weapons found had wound the muscles of his neck tight. It was difficult to speak through his clenched jaw. "Those guns can't hit the street."

She rested her palm between his shoulder blades, reminding him to breathe. "We're going to stop them."

"The SAWs, the Barrett…" He turned to her. "Those are for psychos with big agendas."

Her eyes were grave. "No one's going to get their hands on them."

He had to share her conviction. Doubt wouldn't accomplish their mission. "Kit Daily's going to fight."

"He's a dinosaur." Her lip curled. "And his security is lazy and confident."

"And we're neither." Weariness ringed his joints and tugged them down. He stood and ambled toward the bathroom. "We're ghosts."

Her words floated like smoke behind him. "The bullet they'll never see."

The day officially ended with the brushing of his teeth. He completed his other nighttime needs and returned to the room to find Mary standing next to the bed with her tactical vest in her hand.

Her shape was barely visible, but her husky voice shot a flash of heat through him. "I'm slipping into something more comfortable." She released her pistol from its holster and placed it on the nightstand, then laid her vest out on the floor within reach.

The mission didn't let up. Even with the two of them alone in his room and the bed welcoming them. He arranged his own gun on his night table and knew the backup was close in his luggage. A folding knife and a flashlight joined his sidearm, all within reach.

Clothing rustled on the other side of the bed. Mary unbuckled her belt and slid out of her pants. Her lithe shape crawled over the white sheets, then disappeared into them. He took off his fatigues and pursued her. The bed was cold and crisp until he met the intensity of her skin. The lean strength of her muscles. The smell of her hair and the silhouette of her mouth.

He leaned up over her and dipped down for a kiss. She rose to meet him. Their limbs wound together. He ran his fingers through her hair. She stroked across his shoulders and back. His erection grew. She pressed her belly against it, but their bodies knew it wasn't the time. Not without complete safety. Their rhythm remained calm like a quiet sea.

All the cold was chased from the bed. The kiss ended, and they held each other. He listened to her heartbeat with his head on her chest and found peace in her steady thrum. She scratched lightly over his hair and rubbed his earlobe between her fingers.

They slowly untangled until they lay shoulder to shoulder. She draped her leg over his. He traced the bottom edge of her panties and stroked up and down her thigh.

It only took a whisper to reach her. "I don't know where you live. You got an abandoned warehouse loft where you oil your weapons and lift cinderblocks for exercise?"

"And you're in a glass brick condo with neon wall art and a circular bed covered in black satin sheets."

"You've been spying on me." It was hard to blame her for conjuring that, based on his reputation.

"I've got a place in San Francisco," she said. "In a tall building on a hill."

"Of course." He imagined her watching the city, the whole west coast, from her window. "High vantage."

Her voice darkened a bit. "And multiple escape routes."

"I get you." He rested his hand on her thigh. Even home didn't always feel safe.

"You do." She wedged her hand under his ass.

"Automatik has some financial perks, but do they cover San Francisco rent?" He tried to see her in a city without her tactical gear on. "I pick up outside work consulting, and my apartment's not that prime."

"I'm mostly covered." She paused, and he wondered if that was all she'd disclose. "But I still get out in the daylight. I teach self-defense for women at a few gyms around town."

"Sweet. That's the good work." He could see how her calm and attention to detail would make her a great instructor. "I wish they didn't need it."

"Me, too." Her voice heated for a moment. "But until then…"

He leaned toward her. "If you ever want a demonstration dummy, call me."

She chuckled and pinched his butt. "I don't think my students would want to see what I do with you once I get you on the ground."

"Yeah, that's like tenth-degree black belt level, top secret, no-holds-barred hand to hand."

She grew more pensive. "But really, it might be good for them to have you there for some of the training. As the bad guy and the good guy."

"San Francisco to San Diego, is that long distance enough for you, sniper?" Risky, making plans and commitments like that. Even the suggestion sent a tremor of possibility up his back.

She turned and looked at him, light gathering in her eyes. "I can make that shot."

No promises. It was how they operated. If she said it, she meant it. And he'd do anything to find a way.

They drifted into comfortable silence. Her breathing slowed next to him. A dream took her skimming along sleep, her arm twitching. He re-

mained awake and allowed his body to sink into
the mattress. Aches and tension in his joints and
muscles dissolved. She woke with a sigh and sat
up slightly on her pillows. With Mary on watch,
he allowed himself to drift away. Tonight's mission
was over. The operation would resume tomorrow,
after they'd taken their shifts resting. For now, he
was safe with the most dangerous woman he knew.

SUNRISE SLICED THROUGH the gaps in the curtains.
Ben was already awake. Mary had been breathing
steady next to him, but he knew she wasn't sleeping. They'd traded off sleeping and watching most
of the early morning. About a half hour before day-
break, he'd made eye contact with her, confirming
they were both awake. But they remained motionless, resting before the next stage of the mission.
An uneasy twist churned in his gut. The next stage
was undefined.

He sat up and stretched his arms, neck and back.
"Do we wait? Collect more intel?"

She eased out of the bed, then disappeared behind it for a second. With a quick breath, she popped
back up again. Then down. After ten burpees, she
performed a brief yoga routine that revealed the
long strength of her arms and legs.

He was watching the swivel of her waist above
her panties when she answered, "I've been thinking about that, too." The shake of her head revealed
she struggled with the uncertainty as much as he
did. "Security forces are in town. Cops are block-

ing roads. If we keep probing, they'll know something's up. Or they'll at least work really hard at getting us out of town."

"Ben Louis and Mary Long would probably just lie low. She still has work to do here, right?"

She calculated in her head. "Probably a little more scouting on the west side."

He stood and charged his blood by shadowboxing for a moment. "Ben Louis did everything he could here, but he'd stay because Mary Long's sticking around."

"Ben Louis is a dog." She smirked and took a little extra time pulling her pants on while he watched.

"Ben Louis is sprung." Something he'd never been. Maybe in high school, before he'd figured out the easier ways to fit together with a woman and not have either of them tangled up. But that wasn't going to work with Mary. They were knotted. And he wanted it that way.

It was her turn to watch as he dressed. Desire heated her eyes. "Mary's got it bad, too."

Seeing her like that and hearing her admit it made him burn, too. "I'm going to need more time with you." He crossed in front of the bed to her. "Slow time."

Sadness crossed her face. He knew why. Planning ahead could be dangerous. Determination was necessary for the mission, but he'd been trained not to expect too much from the future.

She fought through the doubt and gazed at him with open need and resolve. "We'll find that time."

He believed her. He'd battle to the end to make that happen.

The clock spun on their mission, but he stole a moment and held his hand out to her, palm up. She placed hers on it, and he lifted it to his lips and kissed her knuckles. "Guaranteed," he said and let her hand go.

She didn't say anything, but he watched her parted lips, the rise and fall of her chest with a long breath. Then the steel returned to her eyes, the hard mask of the warrior. But not cold with him. The woman was ready for today's mission. "So what would Mary Long and Ben Louis do this morning, after their night together?"

He considered. "They've been hanging out for, what, three days?"

"You do have more experience with this kind of thing than I do." She grinned, wry.

But it stabbed a little too deep. "We've all got history."

Her face grew serious. "I'm sorry. I won't make that a thing again."

He reached out and gave her hand a squeeze. "Thanks." Then he continued mulling her question. "They're both on the road for work… They're both climbing the ladder…" He looked at Mary and just wanted to wrap himself around her, take her to the bed and make love until sunset, eat a hot dinner, then keep going. "This place doesn't have room service, so they're not shacking up."

She ventured, "Breakfast in the lobby?"

"Not after their first night in bed." A pang of unease hit his gut. "I think they'd split up to have their mornings. Shower, brush their teeth, all that ordinary stuff you don't want to see after getting busy with a new hookup." The idea of parting ways chilled him. Not just because he wanted days and days to discover her body. The whole town was heating up around them.

"We should be operating together." She obviously understood the dilemma and chewed her bottom lip. "But I think you're right on all points. She just wants to take a pee with the door open and catch up on social media."

A laugh bubbled up through him. "Now I got that picture in my head. Thank you."

"Any time, sailor." She winked, picked up her bundled coat and tactical vest and walked to the door. He didn't want her to go, but he opened it for her. They kissed one last time with her partly in the hallway. For show. And for them. Their connection. Their promise.

She sauntered down the hall. He watched her all the way to the elevator.

Bad things were happening in town. Things were going to get worse.

THE MAN MOVED like shrapnel, closer to her heart with each rush of her blood. And the way her pulse raced with him, it would be all over for her soon. But was it dangerous? Was it death? It didn't feel like it. Not the way she wanted more of him. More time to savor his skin and energy. His quick wit. The way he understood her and listened to learn more.

Mary sat alone in her room, in the way her alter ego would have, in accordance to Ben's plan. But she wasn't Mary Long. Instead of pretending to work on her laptop while surfing social media and checking prices on vacation airfare, she oiled her guns. The .38 and the 10mm were laid out on a microfiber cloth across the bed. She checked and rechecked the actions. The clicking metal was as comfortable as if she was cracking her own knuckles. The sights were still aligned the way she liked them, though she did most of her shooting instinctually now and could place her bullet on a dime at twenty paces with her eyes closed. She loaded the pistols and put them away before taking out her big single-shot break barrel.

The Barrett they'd found in the warehouse could reach out to a mile. She could touch and not be touched. But with the pistol's short barrel, she'd be lucky to get half that distance. Though she wasn't lucky. She was good. A sniper with a pistol. Stuck in a town full of menace. With Ben. At least there was a bright spot.

He messaged her phone, and she put the gun down.

Do you really golf?

She responded, Like a sniper. Calm, cool and accurate.

I suck at it. Can you teach me?

Her first instinct was to shut down more plans for the future, but her experience with Ben was starting to convince her that she needed to live. I'll get you swinging

Some nice courses in SoCal. Can we get Harper in on it after my private lessons? He's worse than me.

She was challenged further out of her solitude. The idea of socializing with her teammates lost some of the trepidation it usually stirred up. Ben helped bridge her. She answered, First thing you guys need to do some yoga to loosen your hips.

Her phone buzzed with another message. Automatik had run the information she and Ben had supplied. According to friendly on-base sources, the military was already aware of the missing shipments. They were actively looking and starting to make noise. She acknowledged the report and sent a message back, reiterating their need for a full assault team soon.

The response didn't warm her heart: First insertion after midnight.

She marked the time on her mental clock and responded, Understood.

The communication ended.

Ben messaged, Gonna be a long day. I'll see you out there. Stay sharp.

Always, she replied. You, too.

She finished checking over her pistol before putting it away in its case and hiding it in the false compartment in her luggage, along with her tactical gear and 10mm. The metal wouldn't be cold long. If the military knew the weapons were missing, then the gunrunners would get word. That was why they were on high alert, and it could explain the amount of private security who'd arrived over the last couple of days.

Her and Ben's recon operation could turn quickly into a fight against the world. She'd been in those battles and had made it out. Any man who'd been a SEAL as long as he had must've, too. But it seemed so much more complicated because it was Ben. Not just a fellow soldier. A temptation. A hope for a future that contained pleasure and comfort and not just war.

She arranged herself in Mary Long's clothes and headed out of her room. Her thoughts stormed behind her as she walked down the empty hallway. Ben was her teammate; she'd do anything to protect him. That hadn't changed. But if any son of a bitch out there hurt him, she'd be particularly brutal with payback.

The idea of him being hurt drove heated anger high into her chest. She had to breathe it down before exiting the elevator in the lobby. Seeing Ben near the breakfast tables lit a different kind of fire in her. Down her belly and around her hips. Another breath barely calmed her. She didn't want to be calm. She wanted to be out of that damn town and alone with Ben in a place where the time was theirs.

When she saw he talked to another man, her frustration receded and she went on alert. Ben and the man knew each other, but she didn't recognize the Latino, who was a bit younger than Ben. Their casual postures didn't reveal conflict. Ben spotted her and quickly moved his eyes away. He brushed his hand subtly across his thigh, flicking his fingers toward the door.

She understood and kept moving through the lobby. Who was Ben talking to? If he signaled her away, it must be trouble. She passed three men she remembered as hired security, drinking coffee and lounging in low chairs. They weren't aware of the danger she felt. It was a poison cloud, sinking lower over the whole town. Only a matter of time until it took them all.

FOURTEEN

HE WAS GETTING really tired of cold breakfasts of yogurt and cereal. But if he could endure living for a week on two days' worth of MREs during a surveillance op on the Pakistan border, he could make it through this. Though a full spread of pancakes, bacon and eggs would've been much better if Mary was sitting across the table from him.

This morning's brief text conversation with Mary had almost made him feel like a regular man talking to his woman until the Automatik status report interrupted them. He'd watched Mary's responses pop up and knew she felt the clock ticking tight as well. Kit Daily and his crew would want to move the goods soon, so they weren't all stacked in one place. Which was exactly why Automatik had to strike here and now. Midnight might be too late.

The way a man made his way directly across the lobby toward Ben, it seemed like the big dance was about to start. The Latino guy in a heavy flannel shirt and jeans was vaguely familiar, but Ben couldn't place him. Definitely not from the teams, or Automatik. A genuine smile spread across the man's face. He wasn't there to fight.

"Whoa, I mean…" He seemed almost awestruck. "I didn't know we had a genuine SEAL with us."

Shit. He was a Navy man. Ben finally placed his face among the deck crew of the Shearwater, an aircraft carrier he and his team had used at times as a mobile base. Ben smiled back, despite the sense of dread that washed over him. "*Former* SEAL," he corrected.

"Once you get that trident, like, does it ever go away?" The man extended his hand. "Lucas. Lucas Lara."

"Yeah, from the Shearwater in the Mediterranean." Ben shook his hand. "Ben Louis."

"We never officially met, but I remember you and your Team." Lucas beamed as he looked at Ben.

Mary appeared in the lobby, looking as fresh as if she'd slept all night and woken on a bed of rose petals. He'd already been made by Lucas and had to keep her as far out of the spotlight for now. He broke eye contact from Mary and motioned a signal he hoped she'd understand. Of course she did. Purposeful, but not hurried, she navigated through the lobby and out the front doors.

Lucas was oblivious. "I tried for SEAL training but never got accepted."

Ben sat back down to his uninspiring breakfast. "If you still want the experience, douse yourself in cold water and eat a pound of sand."

Lucas laughed, but a sadness haunted the backs of his eyes. "But I'm surprised we'd get a guy from the Teams on Pulaski's run."

"Pulaski's what?" Things went from bad to worse. An irrational hope that Lucas had just happened to be passing through town slipped away, and Ben felt like he was starting to lose traction on the ground.

Lucas's eyes went wide. He glanced around sheepishly and sat opposite Ben. "You're not?" He winced and tried to explain. "It's just part-time work for a local honcho. I'm taking shifts for a trucker going across country."

"I've met Chief Pulaski." Best to stay as honest as possible. "I didn't know he was hiring for side jobs."

"He's retired Navy, like us." Lucas gestured at himself and Ben, then vaguely at the other guys sitting in the lobby. "He does this a few times a year and helped me and some other dudes from the ship pick up gigs."

Ben seethed inside. He needed to get this intel to Mary and Automatik. Pulaski was Navy. Daily the Marines. They pulled from their old contacts for the guns and the manpower to move and protect them. The fuckers abused their power and put citizens at risk. They put citizens in the ground.

The sadness in Lucas dragged his face down. "It's my first time on the run. Hard to find good gigs these days." He absently massaged a point in the front of his shoulder. An old injury? Probably the reason he wasn't in the Navy anymore.

"Tell me about it, bro." Ben maintained an outward cool while inside he was ready to tear down the whole town. "I'm out here hyping sports equipment for a company I didn't start, I don't own stock in…" He pulled one of the bracelets from his bag and gave it to Lucas. "Freebie, man. Maybe it'll help with that shoulder."

Lucas looked genuinely moved. "Thanks, Ben." He slipped the bracelet on. "Big ol' SEAL, I thought you'd be in the movies or something by now."

Ben laughed. "I'm too pretty for Hollywood."

"You're too real, man." Lucas fiddled with the bracelet and tested his shoulder. "Not like those plastic actors."

Ben's coffee was cool enough to taste how bad it was. "If I go to Hollywood, you be my agent."

"Fuck yeah." Lucas put out his fist, and Ben bumped it. "We're trucking soon. You got to meet the other Shearwater guys. Might've been after your time, though." He stepped away from the table and talked to a couple of the other men in the lobby, one white, the other looking Korean-American. They glanced Ben's way with more curious caution than Lucas had shown.

Lucas returned to the table with the two men and made the introductions. "Ben, this is Frank and Chul."

Handshakes all around.

Ben saw they weren't as excited to meet him as Lucas was. "How's it going, guys?"

They all went through the usual bullshit of talking about making a day wage and getting by and hardly being able to wait until bikini-wearing barmaids start throwing the icy beers their way in any beach town down the road.

Before the conversation strung too thin, Chul gave Lucas a pat on the back. "We should head out and report in."

Chul and Frank receded, and Lucas lingered for a moment. "Good luck with the sales thing. I'll see you in Hollywood, man."

"Hell yeah, Lucas." Ben shook his hand. "Ride safe."

They parted ways, and Lucas bounded to his friends as they exited the hotel. Ben casually returned to his food. Nothing out of the ordinary. After a minute, he took out his phone and updated Automatik with what he'd learned. He informed them and Mary that he'd been recognized by a former Navy sailor. The news would flow quickly through town. The clock accelerated. It might become impossible to lie low and wait for the rest of the team. He needed to be operating with Mary. They needed to be ready on the trigger.

MORRIS FLATS WAS a ghost town. Mary encountered no other cars as she drove what open streets she could. The police had blocked more intersections with cones and sawhorses, creating straight shots for the trucks into the train station where they could load up, then get directly on the highways that would take the guns to every corner of the country.

Ben's latest message echoed like a rifle shot. He'd been identified. Now she understood why he'd waved her off at the hotel. He might've been compromised, but had kept her out of suspicion. For now. As soon as the information about his past made the rounds, everyone would look at her differently as well because they'd been seen spending so much time together. And with the town on lockdown the way it was, there was no telling what the gunrunners would do with unwanted variables.

She understood the connection between Pulaski and Daily as top dogs. They leveraged their military backgrounds for power. Anyone who didn't follow their way was easily intimidated. Fitting then that a group of former military operators like Automatik would be the ones to drive a stake through the heart of their gunrunning operation.

But it was seeming less and less likely the strike team would show up in time. A full assault starting at the borders of Morris Flats would take too long and would alert Pulaski and Daily in advance. They'd be able to get guns out of town before the team hit the rail yard. That was where the fighting needed to start. And end.

Without Ben, she felt like she was orbiting off balance. They should be together now, covering each other's backs. Now that he wasn't trusted by the powers in control, nowhere would be safe for him.

She drove for another half kilometer and spotted the mayor and her husband parked near a blocked intersection. Their SUV doors were open and they stood in the street, the mayor on her phone. When Mary parked behind them, the mayor wrapped up her call and hung up but still clutched her phone. Her gaze bounced up the street and warily back to Mary.

Mary got out of her car, and Eddie approached with a smile and outstretched hand. "Well, this is no fun for you. You'll have to come back in the summer when we're all in our backyards grilling."

She shook his hand, and then Donna Limert's, before giving a nearby traffic cone a light kick. "Seems like this is more than just road work."

The mayor waved off her concerns. "That's just the easiest explanation. Chief Pulaski runs his men through these drills, and they all get very excited. Cars and trucks make a little bit of noise through town, and then it's all over." She smiled without conviction. "Really, no big deal at all."

Mary ventured, "If any prospective buyers see it, we can just upsell it as an active and attentive police force."

"I like that, Mary." Donna still glanced up and down the street. "I'll bet you could sell me a snow cone in February."

Eddie chuckled, but his neck remained tense.

Radio voices blurted from inside the open SUV. Police chatter. "Squared away north of Maple."

"Outstanding." It was Chief Pulaski. It should've been a dispatcher.

Mary split her attention between the radio and the mayor. "Catch me on a day when I've had a couple of cups of coffee. I'll sell you your own house and take Eddie's commission."

The Limerts looked like smiling mannequins. Beneath the plastic grins, they rotted just like Kit Daily and Pulaski, making the acid churn in Mary's gut.

The police chief continued on the radio. "Car 77, break off. We're taking on water and need to right the ship."

He sounded more like a Navy man than a cop, and his vague metaphor couldn't be good news. He was ordering his men on some sort of damage control mission.

A man's voice responded, "Copy. Rolling in one minute."

Worry started to crack through Donna's usual polish, though she tried to remain bright. "See, those guys really know what they're doing. If you do a zip code search for this area, you'll see there are very few crimes."

Eddie added, "And a great ratio of officers to citizens. A lot of protection."

Protection for the gunrunning. "That's a huge concern for potential buyers." What assignment had Pulaski given car 77? And where was Ben?

The officer from car 77 announced, "We're going out on a 10-29."

Mary tightened when she heard the police code for a check for warrants. It gave them rein to stop whoever they wanted and question them. They were hunting. And there'd been a target on Ben's back since he'd confronted those cops on his first night in.

Pulaski answered, "Keep sharp. Unknown variables, right?"

"Roger that."

The radio quieted, but the voice inside Mary's head screamed for her to get out of there and help Ben. She maintained a smooth exterior. "I guess today's not the day to find a coffee shop to read in."

The mayor seemed relieved to be rid of Mary. "Probably just want to hang out at the hotel until all the excitement dies down."

Eddie nodded in agreement, maintaining his artificial grin.

Mary acquiesced with a wave and headed to her car. It was a struggle not to run, slam her door and screech away into the town. But she walked at a normal pace and pulled out her phone. Once in the car she messaged Ben, warning him of trouble coming.

No answer.

Driving through town looking for him would be a bad idea. The police were searching and could wrap up her and Ben in one maneuver if they wanted. She needed to operate on her terms.

She hung a U-turn and cruised back to the hotel. Not to sit and read, but to gear up and get to the high ground where she could find Ben and protect him.

Her heart pounded. The trigger had been pulled, and the hammer was falling.

BEN HAD FELT backed into a corner at the hotel. Word would be out about him, and he didn't want to sit and wait for the fallout in a building with too many blind spots and less-than-ideal egress. But driving on the Morris Flats streets wasn't much safer. Blocked intersections locked the town down into a maze with no escape. The ramifications of him being identified as a former SEAL hadn't caught up to him. But they would, and he had to be ready.

His phone buzzed in his jacket pocket with a message from Mary. Before he had a chance to park and check it, a police car swung around a group of traffic cones on a side street and lined up directly behind him. Their lights weren't rolling, and there were no sirens. If he pulled over now, he'd look guilty.

Maintaining the speed limit, he cruised through town, hoping to find a bar or restaurant where he could park and go in as justification for being out. But everything was shuttered. The citizens knew who the streets belonged to.

After two blocks of driving extra cautiously, but finding no exits from the road or places to park, he saw the police lights turn on behind him. The siren chirped once. He was already pulling to the curb when a voice commanded, "To the right and stop the engine."

He complied and kept both hands in plain view on the steering wheel while watching the angry cop and another he recognized from the rec center step out of the car behind him. The partner took up a defensive position at the sidewalk to cover the scene.

Angry cop strode toward Ben's car with his hand

ready over his service pistol. He reached Ben's open window but didn't venture too close. "License, registration and proof of insurance."

It was a bullshit stop. Ben hadn't done anything wrong. But he knew better than to argue just then. "License and insurance are in my wallet." He slowly pulled it from his back pocket and removed the cards for the cop.

The more ghostly members of Automatik had supplied him with a New Jersey driver's license and other relevant IDs for this op. But how far did the fake identity go? Or were the local police even interested in running his info at all? Most likely they were just looking for a reason to make things deadly.

"I'm sorry, I wasn't aware of breaking a law." Ben kept his voice even.

Angry cop just stared at his ID, then back at Ben's face. "Registration."

"It's a rental." Ben shrugged.

A vein showed on the officer's forehead. His nametag read Green. He spoke through bared teeth, impatient. "Then you should have paperwork."

"In the glove compartment." Ben pointed at it, then reached slowly for the handle.

Green slid back and gripped the handle of his pistol. "Step out of the car."

Ben froze. Fury raged through him. He'd done nothing to escalate the situation. It was all a fabrication, an excuse for Green to draw his weapon.

The officer reiterated louder, "Step out of the car. Now!"

If Green pulled his gun, Ben would have to reach for the compact automatic strapped to his ankle. No negotiations. This was clearly a setup, and Ben would have to fight his way out. For now he kept his hands up except to open the door.

The backup officer was also ready with his hand on his gun, but it remained in his holster. He looked more worried than angry and wouldn't be the first to shoot. Green had a hard-on to let the bullets fly. Then plant a gun in Ben's cold hand to justify the shooting.

"It would help if I understood why you pulled me over." Ben remained even and rational.

"You shut up right now. Shut up, and I'll ask the questions." Green worked himself up further. He was smart enough to keep a good distance between them. Ben couldn't charge him and would have to duck and move fast as he pulled his hidden piece if he wanted to survive what Green was planning.

Because there was no other way out. Words weren't working. The deadly outcome of this traffic stop had been decided before Green and the other cop had even turned their lights on.

Tension rose in Green. He'd snap any second. Ben found his battlefield calm. Amping himself up to meet the cop's aggression would just tighten his joints and get him killed. One flinch from Green, and Ben was ready.

The right rear tire of the police car exploded.

Green drew his pistol but aimed it up the street, in the direction of the rifle shot that cracked after the bullet had impacted. Ben moved before the crooked officer could pull the trigger. He dove forward and rolled and came up within striking distance of Green.

The other officer also had his gun out but made himself as small as possible in a building doorway, eyes wide and scanning the street. He was in no position to help Green.

Ben engaged quickly with a punch to the side of Green's neck. The officer swung his gun around. Ben grabbed his wrist and kicked him in the side of the knee. Green buckled to one side but was strong and pushed back against Ben. The cop's sidearm fired, and the bullet struck a brick building across the street.

Glass shrieked and shattered from the back window of the police car. Another rifle shot. Mary had Ben's back. Where the fuck was she?

He chopped an elbow into the side of Green's head, then locked up and twisted his arm. The cop grimaced and shoved hard into Ben, pushing them both back a step. Ben regained his balance and torqued Green's arm until his hand jerked open and the gun fell out.

They both looked at the pistol on the ground. Green surged for it. Ben drove a knee into his chest and splayed him out backward. Grabbing the pistol, Ben ran toward a gap in the buildings on the far side of the street, sure to keep the parked cars between him and the other cop who still took cover.

Another distant shot dug a chunk of the street out next to Green. Ben glanced back to see him scurry to safety in front of his police car instead of giving chase. But he did bark at the other officer, "Davis, don't let him—"

A bullet tore through the left front tire of the police car.

Ben made it between the buildings and kept running. Behind him, the two cops shouted at each other, and the rifle shots continued. But Mary wouldn't keep firing for long. Not in daylight, in an urban setting. She'd have to move soon to keep them from identifying her position. These last few rounds were just to keep the cops pinned down long enough for Ben to escape.

She'd cleared his path, and he snaked through the alleys and sides streets. Police sirens started blaring through town. He was able to keep hidden as the sounds gave away where the cars were and which direction they traveled. The rifle shots were silent. He had to find Mary. It was them against the world now.

The war had started.

_____

FIFTEEN

SHE COULD'VE KILLED THEM. Both of the cops who'd stopped Ben were crooked. They worked for the gunrunners, not the citizens. The traffic stop had been a setup from the start, with the primary officer primed to start shooting as soon as he'd gotten out of his patrol car.

But leaving two bodies on the street, both in uniforms, would've made things a million times worse for Ben and Mary. As it was, police sirens swirled through Morris Flats below her. She lay prone on the roof of a one-story building, two blocks from where she'd put down covering fire for Ben. A false edge to the roof blocked her from the street view and unless the local PD had air support, she had the run of the tops of the buildings.

After hearing the start of Ben's setup from the police radio in the Limert's SUV, Mary had hurried back to the hotel and collected her gear. Daylight prevented her from fully equipping herself, but she'd gotten her boots on with her jeans and had stuffed her tactical kit in a duffel bag. From the high vantage of her room, she'd seen Ben's car and the police car paralleling him one block over. The hotel roof was too far and too high for the single-shot pistol. She'd rushed out and tried to look as casual as possible as she'd walked out of the hotel and into town, where she'd stuck to the alleys until she'd found a ladder to the roof of a building.

Neither officer from the traffic stop had expected Ben to have backup. They'd strutted like they were invincible until her first bullet had hit. When she'd started shooting, Ben had taken over. He could've used the officer's gun against him but knew what she did about the escalation. His fight had been efficient, and then he'd run.

But to where?

The police cars continued to zip over the streets. If they'd found him, or even a trace, they'd concentrate in that area. He remained undetected. A siren blasted past her position and stirred the cold air. The fall sun tried to push through a white hazy sky. A clearer day would've provided better shadows to hide in, but everything in the town blended in the flat light.

She pulled her purse close and found a set of earbuds with an attached microphone. The rest of her kit, along with the break-barrel pistol, was in the small duffel bag. Easy to ditch and hide if she had to pretend innocence. So far, Ben was the only one they were looking for. But they didn't want him as badly as she did. She plugged the buds into her phone and fired up the secure communication app.

"Are you online, Jackson?" One ear listened to the radio silence while the other was open to the world in case someone tried to climb up the service ladder one building away. "Jackson, I'm one floor up, north of the hotel and south of Edison Street." No answer. "Copy and respond." Her voice was even, but her throat tightened with concern.

She had eight more rounds for the long-range pistol. Would that be enough to hold off the entire police force from finding Ben?

A click, and an electronic connection hummed in her earpiece. Ben whispered, "You were my angel, shooting bullets from the heavens."

Her chest opened up with relief. "What's your position?"

"On the other side of the highway, in the lettuce. I had to go low."

"How far north?" The map of the town spread out in her mind.

"Past the feed supply place."

The highway was raised above the town level in that area, with greenbelts on each side. It was just south of where they'd ditched the car after the state park op. "I don't have an angle on you from here."

"I have to move soon. The cruisers stopped buzzing and are crawling now, picking through town."

Her sector was quiet. She peeked her head just over the false wall to survey. "You have two rollers in your area, both on the other side of the highway." The cars crept over the streets like poisonous insects. And from the south, more trouble. "Security forces moving out on foot. Two per street, heading north. Submachine guns and sidearms."

"Fuckers," he muttered. "They wearing walkies? Linked to the police?"

She pulled out her long-range pistol and peered at the men through the scope. "Doesn't look like it. They're communicating by cell phone. One shooter, one talker." Any other details were unnecessary. She ducked back below the wall before the sun caught in her optics and flashed her perch to the enemy.

Ben's voice hushed further. "I'm getting bottled up. You up for a distraction?"

The pistol was still in her hands. "What do you need?"

"How about hitting that cell phone tower next to the highway?" It sounded like he rustled through foliage. "It's a little south of me, but it would draw them off."

The shot was within her range. "We'll take them back to the early '90s."

"Can you stick and move?" Concern spiked his voice. "Don't take the shot if it'll compromise your nest."

She glanced over the wall again, spotted at the cell tower in the distance, then located the closest security men to her. Three blocks. She could be two buildings over and down on ground level before they reached her spot. "I'm good."

"Hell, I know that."

"Get ready to fly." Two long breaths steadied her. She checked the pistol. Loaded. Safety off. Hammer cocked. She'd have to pull off the four-hundred-meter shot and get back under cover before she was seen.

One last breath. She held it halfway through the exhale and swung the pistol to the top of the false wall. The crosshairs in her scope lined up with the meatiest part of the cell tower. Heat shimmered from nearby chimneys, telling her that a light breeze moved from left to right. She compensated her aiming point, fired the shot and ducked back beneath the wall.

She gathered her gear and vaulted over the false wall on the north end of the building then jumped the three feet to the next roof over. The pitched angle didn't have much cover besides an HVAC stack. She glanced to the street below and didn't see any pursuers yet.

Cold air burned her lungs as she sprinted toward the next building north. She surged and leaped over the gap, landing with her chest against the low lip of the roof and her arms over it. The wind was forced from her lungs and she coughed to regain herself. The hard edge of brick dug pain into her arms. She pulled herself up and secured her duffel behind a large vent. Clipped voices echoed back where she'd fired the shot. She scurried across the roof toward a service ladder on the alley side.

By the time she hit the street, the two security men who'd been closest to her were both behind a parked car, aiming submachine guns up at her former nest. One of the men kept checking his phone with growing exasperation. Their eyes went wide when they saw her and they waved furiously for her to retreat.

"What the fuck are you doing out here, lady?" The first security guy wore a soft-shell jacket and a fleece cap pulled low over his eyes.

"Didn't you hear the guns?" The other man had dark sunglasses and a light beard.

"Are you with the police?" Her purse bounced against her hip as she strode across the street, the .38 within reach.

Ben's voice came through her earpiece. "Are you engaging? I'm in the clear and hustling to get to you."

Both security men hesitated. Then the man in the soft-shell answered, "We're assisting them."

She looked over their weapons and fabricated a false realization of danger. "Because the mayor said the police were running some drills, and I thought they were just shooting blanks."

Sunglasses Man motioned her toward him with one hand, the other still holding his 9mm submachine gun, set to burst fire. "Come on over behind the car." He softened his tone like speaking to a child. "Sometimes these drills can get a little dangerous."

"Is anyone hurt?" She pitched her voice for concern.

"No," Sunglasses Man continued, "but it really isn't a safe place for you."

She stepped behind the car and stood within two feet of Sunglasses Man. "Not yet," she spoke firmly.

"What?" He tipped his head at her, confused.

"The correct answer to 'Is anyone hurt?' is 'Not yet.'" She stared into their blank faces.

Ben whispered, "Oh my God, girl, you are *the* badass."

Sunglasses Man hissed frustration. "Listen, lady—"

She jabbed him in the throat, grabbed his submachine gun and knocked him backward with an elbow to the chest. He stumbled into the other man, who still hadn't processed what was going on. Soft-shell Guy half held his own weapon and half supported his sputtering security teammate. She kicked Soft-shell Guy just below the kneecap and felt the tendon pop. He screamed out and twisted against the car.

The submachine gun locked into her hands. She slid backward and trained the barrel on the men. "Flinch, and you get a bullet, understand?"

Soft-shell Guy only grunted and clutched his knee. The submachine gun hung limply over his shoulder. But Sunglasses Man had regained his balance and his hand hovered close to the pistol in a drop holster on his thigh.

She told him, firmly, "You're not a hero."

His eyes were invisible, but she read his body. Uncertain, afraid and angry. Shoulders climbing toward his ears. Feet constantly shifting. The idiot reached for his weapon.

She pulled her trigger. Burst mode on the submachine gun spit three bullets at a time. She placed one in the man's biceps, the other in his shoulder and let the third punch into the side of the car.

Pain tightened the man's face. A groan choked in his throat, and he pulled his arm close to his body and clutched at the wounds.

Ben came through her earpiece, urgent. "That you shooting?"

No time to answer yet. She kicked the wounded man in the front of the hip. He spun to the ground, facedown.

"I work with heroes." She leaned over him. "You're not a hero." She took the man's pistol and pointed the submachine gun at Soft-shell Guy. "On the ground, on your face."

The man's mouth twisted with hate and he complied. She stripped him of his weapons and a satchel of extra magazines, slung the second submachine gun over her shoulder and filled her purse with both men's sidearms. They didn't need any more attention. She sprinted away from the car, back toward the building where she'd stashed her gear.

She muttered for Ben, "On the move again."

"Copy." His breath rushed as if he was running. "Approximately five blocks from where I think you are."

"Two security down. I have their weapons." She reached the alley and sped up the ladder on the side of the building. "Back in the clouds." The architecture hid her from the view of the two compromised security men. If they'd watched her run, they'd only seen her swing around the back of the building.

"Hustling," Ben responded.

She hurried to her stashed gear, grabbed the duffel and took off again. "North." But there were only three more buildings on this block, then an empty lot. She jumped the gaps between the roofs and stopped at the last one. A sign protruded eight feet up the front, giving her cover from the street. But for how long? Police sirens started to pierce into her sector.

Ben announced, "Four blocks."

Security men would come, too. Without clear egress, any run she tried would be a fight.

"Three blocks." His hurried footsteps came through his mic.

She whispered, "Pinned behind a bakery sign."

"I'm—" He cut off, then grumbled, "I've got to clean up some trash."

A police car pulled onto the street just below her hiding place. She couldn't see it, but heard the tires rolling slowly. Hunting.

SIXTEEN

THERE WERE TWO men between Ben and Mary. Their backs were to him as they stalked fifteen yards up the street, submachine guns at the ready. He might be able to sprint across an intersection without detection and swing around their field of view. But a police car crawled one block parallel, blocking that path. And it was closing in on Mary.

He warned her through the mic, "Patrol car northbound toward you."

"Copy," she replied, terse. "Another one already here."

Ben had to take the street. "I'm incoming."

He leaned from the cover at the corner of a building and aimed Officer Green's pistol at one of the security men's legs. The man wore camo fatigues tucked into combat boots. The way he and the other man, who had a backpack heavy with gear, talked to each other, Ben could see they weren't longtime partners. A good operator wouldn't have to use words at all.

Ben fired a single bullet into the thigh of the man in camo fatigues. He spun to the ground and immediately started firing his submachine gun in Ben's direction. Bullets sprayed in an uncontrolled panic.

The man with the backpack joined in, not bothering to find out what they were shooting at.

Chips of brick and concrete danced around Ben, and he ducked back behind cover. The firing stopped. The wounded man groaned, and Ben heard his foot dragging as he stumbled across the sidewalk. Metal weapons clanged together. Ben knew if the other man was that close, he was helping his wounded partner and wouldn't be quick on the trigger.

Ben couldn't let them get to cover and pin him down. He peeked out, pistol first, and spotted them nearing the gap between buildings on his side of the block. Their weapons were in disarray, and fear crept into their eyes. He snapped off two quick shots, then sprinted across the street. The first bullet hit the wounded man in the other leg, taking him to the ground. The second bullet grazed the shoulder of the man with the backpack. He flinched and fired where Ben had been.

Still at a dead run, Ben shot wildly at the men to keep their heads down and their aim off. They flattened themselves on the sidewalk, and the backpack man dragged the wounded man into the gap between the buildings. Ben found his own gap on the opposite side of the street and had more room to move.

Eight rounds remained in Officer Green's pistol. Ben's ankle piece held eight more.

Mary spoke into his ear. "You're drawing one of the police cars."

Across the street, the wounded man sat on the ground and propped himself against a wall, his weapon in shaking, bloody hands. Backpack man stood at the corner of a building, scanning up and down the block with his finger on the trigger.

Ben was invisible for a moment. He glanced down the gap where he hid. A wood-and-metal fence spanned the buildings, too high to climb his way to the street behind. He saw the moving police car through the gaps in the boards. It would be on him after two right turns.

"I see him," he told Mary. "You know, today started out real nice." Feeling her next to him in bed had been a delicious slice of the impossible.

"Yeah," she whispered. Like a dream.

The man with the backpack was sloppy and left his lower leg exposed as he peered from his corner to cover the street.

Ben lined his sights up with the man's shin. "Then a motherfucker tried to kill me." He fired a single shot, hit his target and knocked the man to the ground. The scream echoed over the street. Ben didn't wait for a response and charged up the sidewalk farther away.

But as he ran, the police car turned onto the street. The two wounded security men shouted the cops in his direction and didn't stop yelling as the car peeled away. Ben reached an intersection before they could catch up and made a hard right. To the left and half a block away, the bakery sign stood faded in the flat sunlight.

He rushed closer to Mary's location and immediately bounded for safety next to a long, low appliance showroom. Another cop car parked at an angle twenty yards up the street, doors open and the officers out. One of them spotted him and immediately drew his pistol. The other followed suit, and they both fired without thinking.

Ben's cover held. To his right, the other cop car screeched to a stop, and the officers jumped out and took cover behind their vehicle to pin him down from another angle.

Mary snapped, "What the fuck is going on down there? Are you hit?"

He answered, "It's my gift to you."

"You should've brought flowers."

The second set of cops also fired blindly, wasting bullets on the brick wall.

The rounds were coming in head height, so he ducked low and fired twice at the cops on his right. One bullet tore through a tire, and the other struck an officer in the foot. "A firefight seemed more appropriate for a woman like you."

Intense fire came from the first cops while the second set dealt with the wounded man.

Mary's voice was dead calm. "It feels good to be appreciated, Ben."

Bursts of automatic gunfire snapped out from high. Metal, glass and plastic shattered in the street. The shooting from the cops stopped, and Ben poked out of cover to see them cowering from a barrage coming from the rooftop. His heart jumped when he saw Mary standing partially concealed next to the tall sign with a barking submachine gun in her hand.

The first police car buckled from the onslaught. Tires burst, and the machine shed pieces of itself over the cowering officers. One of the cops scurried to safety on the other side of the car. Ben went cold with rage when he saw the cop aim up at Mary.

Ben shot him through the forearm, and the gun flew out of his hand. The uninjured cop from the second car turned his pistol toward Ben and drove him back to cover. More blasts crackled from Mary and rained down on the second car.

Four bullets remained in Officer Green's pistol. Ben pulled the compact 9mm from his ankle holster and held a gun in each hand. Sirens approached, winding his clock for escape tight. He and Mary had to be gone before backup arrived.

"You've got the eagle eye up there, what's the best way out?"

She responded, cool, "North. Let them see us turn west and draw them into the heart of town where they'll tie themselves up. We double back east and hit that green ditch near the tracks."

"I like it." He crouched, ready.

"I'm going to need suppressing fire while I get down to street level."

"Say when."

"Stand by." Clothing and gear rustled through her mic. "Bring hell."

He broke cover, fired twice at the car on his

right to keep those men pinned and sprinted to the left. The cops at the first car remained low. The wounded one crouched by the rear wheel and gripped his forearm. But the other man was a threat. He popped up and aimed his pistol at Ben.

Two bullets remained. Ben sent them at the man, hitting him in the elbow and the side of the ribs. The officer buckled to one side and fired. The shot punched into the giant window of the store behind Ben. Glass rang like a deep bell.

Ben cleared past the police car, and Mary sped around the side of the building to meet him in the street. She unslung a submachine gun and tossed it to him. It was a welcome weight. He tucked the empty pistol behind his belt but kept the backup in his other hand.

Relief washed over him as he ran next to her. "I think I love you."

She glanced at him, face hard, but emotion in her eyes. "You're just saying that because I gave you a bigger gun."

They swung to their left through the next intersection. The cops on the street behind them shouted into their radios. Sirens stabbed out through town and drew closer to their area, pressurizing it. Following Mary's plan, the two of them altered their course in a jagged line. First north for a block, then back east toward the train tracks.

The ruse worked, and their path was free from patrol cars. They found the green ditch along the tracks and slid to the bottom then climbed into the thicker foliage on the opposite side. The different sirens of paramedics and ambulances wailed in the hazy air. The wounded were being tended to.

Ben and Mary remained still, both covering different approaches to their hiding spot. She smelled of gunpowder, which was just as good as roses.

He pulled out his earpiece and kept his words a secret between them. "I'm kissing you right now."

She also removed her com rig and whispered with a smile in her voice. "I'm kissing you back." He warmed as if she really was.

"Now I'm stroking your hair." The paramedic sirens stopped. They must've arrived at the wounded men. "And running my fingers down the small of your back."

"You like danger?" Her body remained at the ready next to his.

"Of course." He peered through thick reeds and didn't see any movement on the street next to their ditch. "Why else would I kiss you?"

"I'll give you danger." She glanced behind them, where the cinderblock wall bordered the train yard.

"Bring it." He pulled out his phone and tried to update Automatik with the latest developments. "Fuck."

"What?" She tensed.

"We cut ourselves off when we took out the cell tower." He punched through apps on the phone. "I can't accelerate the timeline for the strike team insertion. They should start moving in now that we've gone silent, but it won't be until after nightfall."

"Sunset in…" She watched the sky. "Over an hour."

"Last social media I'm seeing before the feed went dead mentions gunfire in town, but there's a total news blackout otherwise." He put his phone away. She shifted to address her duffel. While Ben covered the street, she snapped her tactical vest into place. The large break-barrel pistol hung in a soft case on her back.

"You got range with that thing." He patted it. "Thanks."

"Anytime." She rummaged in her purse and handed him a 10mm automatic. "Pillaged from the security assholes."

"I was getting hungry." He stripped the slide off Green's empty pistol, removed the barrel and recoil spring and scattered them in the dirt among the weeds. The new weapon went behind his belt where the old one had been.

"We can hit the buffet." She made a meaningful look to the cinderblock wall.

"The warehouse?" It had been a tight enough operation in the dead of night.

"All you can eat." Her grin was predatory.

"And what we don't take, we burn." Enough running and hiding.

They scanned the street, saw nothing and broke cover for the wall. She went up, then helped him over. Shadows had already collected on the other side, and they remained hidden to assess the terrain. Tracks crossed in front of them. Two hundred yards to the left were the warehouses and beyond them the loading operation. Some men worked, others stood guard with assault rifles.

She nodded to Ben. He returned it, gave her a wink and sprinted for the warehouse.

THE GUARDS IN the distance had superior range with their assault rifles. Mary would have to spray and pray with her short-barreled submachine gun if she and Ben were spotted. But years of doing business without resistance had dulled the guards, and they weren't covering all their sectors properly. She and Ben had a clean run to the first ditch between tracks, where they gathered themselves again and sprinted to the warehouse. Because of the flat daylight, they didn't have to worry about cutting a path between the motion detectors on the lights.

The two of them reached the wall and waited. Sirens continued to swirl in town, but that sense of emergency hadn't assaulted the train yard. She indicated the window to Ben, and he helped her to its edge. The broad doors on the other side of the warehouse were closed. All the loading was going on at the other warehouse, leaving them free to operate. She didn't know the status of the security system during business hours. To be safe, she used her knife to attach the magnet again and swung the window open.

She helped Ben up from the sill, and they both jumped down into the warehouse. Ben hurried to a crate and yanked the lid off. He pulled out two M4 carbines and tossed her one. There were enough magazines for both of them, but no bullets. They slung the carbines, and he stuffed the empty mags in his coat pockets while she put them in the pouches of her tactical vest. Ben took another two carbines from the crate to a set of thick metal shelves that supported older cargo. He jammed the barrels through a notch in the steelwork and bent them, rendering the weapons useless.

"We don't have to be subtle anymore." He left the rifles hanging on the shelving.

"You know what I want." She was already walking. He trailed just behind, watching their perimeter. The Barrett was still in its case where they'd left it. She opened the lid and assembled the massive rifle. "Bullets."

"Roger that." Ben took the point on the way toward the front of the warehouse. "Didn't see a lot our first time in. Maybe by the door."

His hunch proved correct. The first six pallets in the warehouse were filled with ammunition boxes in all calibers. While the sounds of trucks backing up and forklifts clanging against the sides of train freight cars swirled outside, she and Ben loaded their magazines and primed their weapons for combat. She was tempted to grab more and more of the guns around them, but they needed to remain light enough to move. The Barrett was already enough of a beast to carry.

With the mags for the Barrett full, she took out

more of the .50 ammunition and held it up for Ben. "Let's do some damage."

His eyes lit up and he bared his teeth. "Let's."

She used her multi-tool to pry the bullets out of several shells, leaving raw gunpowder to spread around the bases of the ammunition pallets. The wood was dry enough to catch, then send the flames higher to the boxes of bullets. For detonators, they left the shell casings on the ground with a little powder inside.

Two sets of footsteps sped up the concrete loading ramp at the front of the warehouse. The metal of an assault rifle ticked against its sling. Security guards. She and Ben immediately started up the aisle toward the back window.

The door flew open, one of the men speaking, "I don't fucking know. Cell phones went dead, and there was a shootout with that Navy SEAL who'd been prying in—" He fell silent when he spotted her and Ben and lifted his weapon.

Ben fired a quick burst as they retreated. The man fell dead, and his companion dove to cover behind a stack of crates opposite the one they'd sabotaged.

He shouted out the front door, "In here! They're in here!"

The man wasn't going to try and stop them himself, giving more time for retreat. She paused and aimed her assault rifle down the aisle and let a single bullet loose. It struck one of the empty shell casings on the ground and created a spark that ignited the gunpowder around the pallet.

White flames burst and hissed in thick lines. The wood pallet immediately caught fire. Smoke poured up and the boxes of ammunition started singeing. The other security guards who arrived at the door staggered back when they saw the burning mass.

The delay covered more of her and Ben's escape. Moving with the Barrett slowed her down, but she still managed to climb Ben to get up the wall to the window. She helped haul him up, then they both hit the ground on the other side.

Explosive pops shot through the inside of the warehouse. The fire had grown hot enough to set off the ammunition. Metallic bangs ricocheted in the large space, followed by frantic yelling from the security men. A fire alarm went off.

With their back to the exterior wall, they had a decision. To their right was the town. Left, across more sprawling train tracks, a wide swamp stretched into obscurity beneath thick trees.

Ben tipped his head that way. "Let's get wet."

It was the only choice. "Town's too dangerous."

They started running. Ben's powerful body handled all the weight of his weapons. "I'd rather take my chances with the cottonmouths than those fucking mercs."

Several security men from the loading area came around the side of the warehouse. Rifle shots crackled, and bullets whizzed past them. Adrenaline flashed in her legs as she charged toward safety.

She and Ben ran in jagged lines, never presenting a steady target. The train tracks were set on high mounds of gravel, and the ditches provided good cover. When they reached the bottom of one, she grabbed Ben's sleeve and pointed him down the ditch, where they'd be able to move undetected. He hurried with her, then they both turned up the far side, exposing themselves for a split second before they slid down a mossy embankment toward the swamp.

Errant rifle fire chased them and punched through high leaves. The spongy ground stank of rotted foliage with each step. She and Ben stayed to the edge of the green water and found a relatively firm trail that pierced farther into the swamp. Trees gathered around them and the air grew colder with the damp. The flat light transformed, as if they were viewing the world from inside a green glass bottle.

The gunshots halted behind them, replaced by running footsteps. At least eight men pursued them into the swamp. Her and Ben's feet started to splash in shallow water. Their high path had disappeared into a broad plateau. They veered right into thicker foliage. Ben motioned them behind a dense thicket, where they halted and prepared for an ambush.

They were too close for the Barrett. She leaned it against the tangle of branches and readied her assault rifle. Silent hand gestures between them indicated which sectors they'd cover, who'd shoot first, then which way they were going to retreat after firing.

The swamp fell quiet. Bubbles gurgled in the shallows, and leaves conspired with brittle voices in a light breeze. She heard her breath, and Ben's. The rough of his thumb made a faint rasp against the grip of his assault rifle.

Clumsy splashing announced the coming security men. They slowed as they got into denser foliage. Flashes of tan canvas and denim coats appeared through the leaves. Two men led in a crouch, their weapons ready. But unaware they were being watched. The man in Mary's sector scanned ahead, and the barrel of his weapon swept toward her.

She fired a single shot that sent the man backward into the shallow water. Ben's round streaked just after hers, finding the other security man and knocking him to the ground next to a jagged tree stump.

The other security guards couldn't be seen, but their guns opened up in a frantic answer to her and Ben's deadly precision. Foliage chopped apart around them. They ran to the arranged exit route, where the trees absorbed the bullets.

Soft dirt and shallow water made it feel like she was running in slow motion. Not to mention the weapons that weighed her down. But she'd trained for years under all kinds of conditions and had fought real wars through sand and mud and snow. Ben didn't show any signs of giving up, either. He glanced behind them as they escaped and held up five fingers, then one more. The security men weren't quitting.

Her and Ben's progress through the swamp made
too much noise for her to pick out the sound of
their pursuers. If the men were smart, they'd spread
out in a line that could march forward to contain,
then kill. But they weren't smart. Real intelligence
would've had them running as far out of range from
her as possible.

Water splashed shin deep, then to Mary's knees.
They wove through the straight trees spiking up
from the swamp. About twenty yards ahead, a clus-
ter of shattered stumps would make perfect cover.
She pointed Ben toward it.

Gunfire cracked. A bullet pierced the moss ten
feet at her right. Rib-high water churned as she
powered forward to the cover. More bullets skipped
past or sent bark flying from nearby trees.

Ben turned and sent suppressing fire back at
their pursuers while she continued to charge for the
stumps. She made it to a thick trunk and set up with
her assault rifle braced against the soft wood. The
security guards showed themselves in a haphazard
group, eighty yards away. They shot and ran, giving
the rounds little chance of hitting targets. But Ben
was still exposed. She had to tip luck to their side.

She fired a burst at the men. One of them spun
to the side, hit in the hip. The others dove for cover.
Ben half ran, half swam to the stumps with Mary
and set up his own rifle.

The low winter sun sank to the west and dimmed
the swamp around them. Shadows stretched long
and slithered on inky water. A fat spider crawled

along a crack in the trunk next to her. In a few minutes, there would be no light to see the spider.

Ben whispered, "Think they're patient?"

"They're not paid to wait," she answered.

"Fuck." Ben cocked his head, listening. "Clock's ticking for all of us."

Semi trucks rumbled in the distance to the west. A lot of them. The ones that had been staged at the state park were streaming into the rail yard. Even with the improvised sabotage she and Ben had left behind, there would still be enough cargo to move. They were doing it now, before the Automatik strike team could show up. And while she and Ben were pinned down in the swamp.

SEVENTEEN

THEY COULDN'T AFFORD a long standoff in the swamp while the guns bled out into the country on trucks and trains. Ben's mind spun through tactical scenarios that might end this encounter so they could get back into town where the real problem was. The sun was setting, but he didn't want to wait until nightfall to try a flanking maneuver on the security men. The swamp slowed movement down too much. He needed something fast.

"Can you spare a round from the Barrett?" He kept his voice down, knowing sound traveled better over water.

Mary kept her eyes on the stand of trees where the men had taken cover. "You got it. What's the plan?"

"You see that skinny tree leaning to the left?" The late light turned the wood ghostly pale.

"Yeah."

"The tree it's touching, I want you to put a hot one through its trunk, two feet from the water line." He stared down the sights of his assault rifle. "I'll sweep."

"One buzz saw coming up." Water rippled around her as she switched from her rifle to the Barrett. "Ready?"

"On you." His finger rested on the trigger.

The sniper rifle boomed, and the empty shell casing ejected and sizzled in the water near Ben. Birds scattered in thick clouds. The tree trunk shattered exactly where he'd wanted. It was completely severed and tipped to one side. The other tree leaning on it also fell.

The security men fled from cover. Ben released quick bursts, and men fell. Mary's rifle cracked again, and the bullet streaked through two security men at once. They flew back into the water and their weapons spun in the air.

Mary's shot echoed through the swamp like an angry god. The psychological impact was as great as the bullet's. The remaining three men turned and ran, helping the man who'd been hit in the hip on the way. They all splashed clumsily, leaving a clear path and obviously not caring about stealth.

Ben and Mary let them go. Pursuit would just prolong their time in the swamp and wouldn't get them closer to stopping the gunrunners. After testing the silence in the swamp, he pointed a suggested route to the southwest.

She nodded and added, "I need a high vantage to stop those trucks."

The tallest building in town. "The hotel."

They made slow progress through the swamp to the south. The water reached higher and higher on them. Mary held her sniper rifle over her head to keep the parts clean. He knew his assault rifle and submachine gun would be fouled by the sludge and moss, but should still fire well enough to get

him through the night. The stolen guns would be
destroyed after they took care of Daily and Pulaski
and their operation.

The ground grew more solid under their feet as
they headed west toward the edge of the swamp. But
they maintained a careful pace, pausing every few
yards to assess their surroundings. The sun sank in
the distance. Gloomy foliage massed around them.

His jeans were soaked and frigid, shoes flooded
and heavy. Cold night came on strong. In the dim
light, Mary's face revealed no weakness, only focus.
The physical discomfort and the reeking swamp
were easily ignored when he took in how badass
she was. They paused at a stand of trees, ten yards
from dry ground.

He kept his voice no louder than the high leaves
rustling in the cutting breeze. "You make this look
good."

A small smile cracked through. "I'll bet you say
that to all the operators you go into battle with."

"Just the beautiful ones with .50 rifles and tita-
nium nerves." He bumped his shoulder against hers,
and she pressed against him a moment.

They broke their cover and progressed to the
edge of the swamp. Firm dirt and the night's cover
made for faster travel. Streetlights glowed in town,
and the sound of trucks continued in the distance.
The two of them crossed several sets of train tracks.

He asked, "You have any C4 in your purse?"

"I wish." She kicked one of the steel rails.

Sabotaging the tracks would've given him huge

peace of mind. But if they wanted to stop the flow of loaded trains from the yard, they'd have to do it manually.

They reached the first road at the edge of town. Several low buildings housed auto mechanics, tire shops and other light industrial works. They were all quiet and closed, even though normal business hours would've had them open.

Ben muttered, "Morris Flats belongs to Kit Daily."

Mary added, "Not for long." She hefted her Barrett and hustled across the street to the corner of a building. He joined her there, and they scanned ahead. The hotel was approximately one kilometer away. The roaming police cars were smart enough now to keep their sirens and lights off. Private security men could still be out on foot.

The immediate path forward was clear, and they moved to the front edge of the building. One block away, a police car crept through an intersection. As soon as it cleared, Ben and Mary sped over the street and took cover behind a cyclone fence laced with wooden slats. The police car continued to move away, clearing space for them to proceed toward the hotel.

On the next block, Ben spotted two armed security men patrolling on foot. Their weapons were held against their chests, barrels down. Not ready at all. Mary saw them as well and shook her head. They both knew engaging them would only draw attention, even if they were able to end the fight quickly.

Instead, they widened their route but stopped and

retreated to a safe spot behind a Dumpster when a police car entered the area. It traveled up the block, using its searchlight to illuminate alleys and doorways, but didn't reach far enough to see them. The security guys waved to the car, which turned its headlights off then on in response. The sound of the car's engine masked the sound of Ben and Mary skirting behind the guards and the police.

The car pressed farther to the side of town and shined its light into the swamp. Ten minutes too late. Let them think Ben and Mary were still up to their chests in mossy water. Every extra second to operate freely brought them closer to shutting the town down.

Ben and Mary approached the facilities side of the hotel. The loading dock and garbage area were quiet. They used their old route up the metal ladder to the barren patio. Ben was without his gear, so Mary made quick work of the service stairs lock and then they were inside the building.

"Roof." She pointed up and started to ascend the stairs.

He tapped her shoulder to get her attention. "I need to kit up."

She looked over his soaked jeans and heavy, sopping jacket. "Yeah, you're a mess."

They charged with as much stealth as possible up to the third floor. He cracked the door open and peered into the hallway. Empty. He pulled out his damp room key and slipped out, Mary close behind him.

With a quick swipe of the key, they were into his room and locking the door behind them. Mary carefully laid her sniper rifle on the ground and pulled out her phone. "I'll try to update the team."

He pulled off his jacket and polo and replaced them with a long-sleeved shirt and his tactical vest. No time to change his shoes and pants. The found weapons were incorporated into his load out, and he was ready to go. "They coming to the party?"

She stowed her phone, lifted her Barrett and looked him up and down. "Sexy," she growled.

The chill of the damp clothes burned away as his pulse kicked. "You and me, Mary. We're going to make some noise."

One moment before they were back in the battle. He walked to her and kissed her. She returned it. He was rocked by how fearless she was. They parted and walked to the door, fully armed.

She whispered, "With the cell repeater out, we can only rely on proximity, and no one's close enough to our position for contact."

The complication twisted in his gut. Communication was key during an assault like this. "We'll do what we can to keep our eyes on them from above." He opened the door and checked the hallway.

The hotel security guard stalked between Ben's door and the entrance to the service stairs. Ben used hand signals to indicate how many men and the position to Mary. As far as he could see, the man was unarmed.

Mary mouthed, *H2H.*

Ben slung his rifle and drew his knife. Mary squeezed his shoulder, letting him know she was ready, and he burst into the hallway. The guard shuddered with shock when he saw Ben coming. His fists came up in a fighting stance, but he back-pedaled from Ben's continuing pursuit.

Mary trailed at Ben's hip, her big gun on her back and her assault rifle aimed at the guard. She whispered a clipped, "On the ground, on the ground."

The guard seemed conflicted between fear and duty. His fists remained, but his legs wobbled. Ben came on strong and jabbed to the man's face with his empty hand. The guard flinched and raised his hands to protect his jaw. Ben followed up with a solid punch to the man's solar plexus. His sputtering breath smelled like coffee and stale cigarettes. A pained grimace spread across his face. The guard collected his arms to his chest. Ben brought the butt of his knife down on the man's head, just strong enough to knock him cold.

Mary covered the hallway while Ben dragged the unconscious guard by his collar into the service stairs. Then they switched positions, with him holding his assault rifle at the ready while she pulled the boots and socks off the guard and removed the laces. She tied the guard's wrists and ankles to the metal stair railing with the laces, then stuffed one of the socks in his mouth. He snored.

"Brutal." Ben took the pepper spray from the man's belt and the phone from his pocket.

Mary didn't bother looking at the guard again. "He picked the wrong side." She took the stairs two at a time toward the top of the hotel.

The door to the roof was locked, and this time Ben had his tools. After a few seconds of scraping, the door opened and a cold wind gusted down.

Mary faced it, calculating. "I'll have to compensate for that drift."

They walked out onto the roof and closed the door behind them. Large HVAC vents and fan units stood on the asphalt surface. He and Mary stepped over the wide pipes and ducts that snaked over the roof on their way to the front corner of the building. A four-foot wall rimmed the perimeter of the roof. Mary immediately deployed the bipod on her sniper rifle and set it at the top of the wall to sight through the scope.

She smiled. "We have the high ground."

Ben took out his phone and attached the earbud. "Still no contact with the strike team." If they were even in the theater of operations.

From the corner of the building they had a view of the swamp to the far right, the rail yard next to it in the distance, then the town spreading out beneath them.

Mary scanned over the territory with her scope. "They're too good. I won't be able to see them."

He used a monocular from his vest to scout below. "But we have targets."

Two trucks hauled their cargo away from the rail yard. More were being loaded from the warehouses. The sabotage had done damage, but men worked around the smoldering corner of the building to move crates and pallets. Diesel exhaust puffed from several train engines. It wouldn't be long before they spread the guns across the country.

The trucks had straight shots through town because of the roadblocks. Not that there was anyone out except the police. Patrol cars continued their sweeps, shining searchlights into every corner. The two cars he and Mary had disabled had been towed up onto the sidewalks to clear the way.

Mary kept her eye to her scope, cheek to her rifle, and tracked movement down below. "How about a roadblock right by the highway? That'll bottle things up."

He swung his monocular view over to one of the trucks. It was a block away from an on-ramp. "Second truck is heading for a different highway. Can you get them both?"

"With you as my spotter."

He shifted his perspective to take in the heat exhausting from a roof vent on a building below. "Crosswind, left to right."

She made an adjustment to her scope. "Speed?"

"No more than ten knots." The tractor trailer started to climb onto the curving on-ramp.

Mary's voice remained calm. "I want that truck."

"Send it."

The rifle boomed. Ben kept his eye on the monocular and saw the truck lurch a moment later. Fluids hissed from below the cab. A man jumped out and ran as flames spread over the street and up the truck. There was no way for another vehicle to get up that ramp.

"Good kill," Ben informed her.

Mary was already on to the second truck. It skirted lower through town and closer to the hotel. One police car escorted in front of it and another behind.

He panned his view along the truck's path and told Mary, "If you tag it after this intersection, with the cab in the middle of the block, the trailer will block the cross street."

"I like your mind, Beans," she growled. "Same wind?"

He checked the heat streams. "Unchanged."

"Traffic's a bitch." She fired another bullet.

The fuel tank on the cab exploded in a ball of flame, and the truck screamed to a stop. The driver leaped out the passenger door. Fire raged higher and consumed the cab. The cop car behind the truck nearly slammed into the trailer. It backed up and tried to get around but couldn't and had to make an awkward U-turn in the street to make its way to a clear path.

The front patrol car sped up for a moment, then screeched to a halt. Smoke jetted from its engine block. White fire flashed from the shadows of an alley and the car sagged as its tires exploded.

Ben breathed new life. "There's our team."

The relief in Mary's voice reflected his own. "Fuck yeah."

Below, the two officers stepped out of their car with their hands raised. They walked carefully into the path of the headlights and got to their knees. Two figures detached from the shadows, dressed in tactical gear, faces covered. They removed the cops' weapons and handcuffed them before dragging them to the sidewalk and leaning them against a building.

"Sant and Raker?" she asked.

He watched the two men dissolve back into the murky night. "Looks like Raker's cowboy bowlegs."

She exhaled a quick laugh. "Harper and Art are out there somewhere."

"Hopefully everyone's at the party." But there were no other signs of the Automatik strike team in town. "Tak and Marks are just Green Berets, but they can shoot straight."

"Support vehicles are moving to the first truck." She aimed her rifle back in that direction. A police car rocketed through the streets, knocking traffic cones out of its path toward the burning truck.

Ben watched through the monocular. The fast car made a difficult target to predict for a bullet that had to travel over half a mile.

Mary murmured, "Here comes a surprise." Her rifle barked, and the round streaked down. Ben saw its concussion wave distort the heat streams from the buildings. The hood of the police car blew off, and steaming fluids jetted into the air. Flames ripped high, and the car fishtailed to a violent stop.

The officers scrambled out and were almost immediately met by two of the armed security men. The group of four hurried into an alley, guns drawn and ready.

"That wasn't Chief Pulaski in the car." Ben refocused away from the monocular to his phone and brought up the tracking app. "I'll bet he's farther north, sticking close to the train yard." Without the cell repeater, there was no content on the map. "Tracking is a no-go. I can only use proximity, like the coms."

"Our team needs to know the battle plan." Frustration tightened her voice. "They're running blind down there."

He knew what that meant and put in his earpiece. "You secure up here?"

"I've got your back." Her eye remained at her scope, but a smile curled her lip.

"That's just an excuse to look at my butt." His gear hung secure to his rig, ready to move.

"You know it." She glanced away from her rifle for a second to wink at him. He absorbed as much of her heat as he could hold, clutched it close in the core of his chest. She put her earbud in and turned back to her rifle. "Talk when you can, we'll see what we can pick up."

He kissed her on the top of her head and whispered, "We're going to end this and then we're taking our time."

"Promise me." She didn't look at him. Her words shook him.

They both knew operators didn't make promises.

"I promise." He left, wishing he could just rain fire on the whole town and wipe it off the map, then be alone with Mary. But there were good people in Morris Flats. He and Automatik needed to be surgical about removing the cancer of Kit Daily, Pulaski and the Limerts.

His eyes took a second to adjust to the fluorescent lights in the service stairs. He crept down, past the hotel security guard, who'd regained consciousness but knew better than to try struggling or yelling.

"Patio door," he informed Mary before stepping back into the night.

They were still close enough for the communicator to work. "Roger that. Path ahead looks clear."

"Thanks, angel." He moved out onto the patio and down the metal ladder into the loading area.

"Emergency services are rolling out to the truck fire at the on-ramp." She spoke even and clear, eyes above the world. "They're leaving the other one to burn. Loading continues at the rail yard."

"Copy that." Thick smoke rose into the black sky a few blocks to his left. Sirens howled, and lights flashed against the nearby walls. He proceeded to the right, toward the shadows surrounding the low industrial buildings.

The connection with Mary thinned. "No visual… armed security…sector…" Then silence. It tore him apart to continue forward, farther from her and toward the danger. He'd lost her voice, but knew she was up there, watching over him. And he knew he'd do everything he could to complete this operation and get back to her.

EIGHTEEN

SHE WATCHED BEN slip across a street, then disappear. The shadows swallowed him. She knew how he expertly navigated the night. But she couldn't hear his voice, couldn't tell him what she saw or get the reports of his actions. A cold ache gripped her chest.

No one below had spotted her after the three shots. Emergency services scrambled, and the police cars sped through the streets haphazardly. Yet she felt exposed. Did it make her vulnerable, feeling what she did for Ben? Did it make her a bad operator? Reckless with emotion?

Mary put her crosshair on the hood of a police car that approached Ben's territory. Then she moved the aiming point, compensating for the speed of the car and the travel time of the bullet. She squeezed the trigger and sent the round splitting the night air. A second later, the car sprayed engine fluids and swerved to a sideways stop. Flames licked out under the hood, and the two officers bailed out.

Ben remained hidden.

Another truck motored toward the highway, one on-ramp north of the one she'd shut down. The distance would stretch the effective range of the .50, but if she could block that escape route, too, the extra time it took the trucks to get out would allow Automatik to operate below.

The truck cab was red and white, the cargo container worn yellow. On the other truck she'd aimed for the vital organ of the fuel tank. But at this range, she could only narrow the bullet down to the engine area. She scanned ahead of the truck's path. The on-ramp curled into the highway. If she was late with the shot, it would miss any substantial mechanics and allow it to escape. She sighted on the curve of the on-ramp that would place the cab's profile flat to her shot. And waited. And kept her nerves from winding too tight. The truck still didn't appear in her scope. Her heartbeat threatened to throw the shot off. She took a breath in, let it out halfway, then held it. It was the last bullet in this magazine. Reloading would take too much time. There was no second shot.

The truck broke into her field of view. She aimed high to account for bullet drop and fired before the truck reached her crosshairs. The path of the round cut through the sky and arced down. The truck drove directly into the kill zone and was hit in the engine block. Sparks and fire burst, followed by thick black smoke. The truck was dead, and the on-ramp was impassable.

She was a hell of a warfighter and that hadn't changed. But the tug she felt for Ben every time they were apart, and the flash of bright heat he brought when they were close, had raised the stakes.

Nothing could happen to him. She'd fight every last man in this town to keep him from being hurt.

TWO SHOTS HAD streaked down from above. Mary brought lighting down on the town. Ben had seen the aftermath of the police car. It still burned, abandoned, by the time he'd lurked a block away. There'd been no sign of the police officers. The result of the other bullet was unknown, though he was sure it had hit its target with maximum impact. He wished she could report her action. Even just to hear her voice.

The town was a mix of chaos and complete silence. Like every other war zone.

Ben moved when the path was clear and hid when activity sped past him. Another police car patrolled three blocks away. It swept with its searchlight but didn't stop and stayed clear of the burning wreck of the other car in the area. The armed security details had become more cautious. They crept slowly at the edges of buildings, weapons ready. Ben had seen two of them at an intersection parallel to his and swung farther to the east toward the train tracks.

He hid himself in a stack of car body parts and brought up the tracking app on his phone. Finally he was close enough to have a view on movement. Pulaski was north, near the train yard. His officers were spread throughout town. The civilians Ben had given the bracelets to were all home. Good. He hoped they had the lights out and stayed away from the doors and windows. Lucas Lara, the retired Navy aircraft carrier man who'd made Ben at the hotel, roamed the streets. There had to be at least one other security man with him. Even these small details gave him an advantage.

"Jackson on the ground," he whispered into the mic of his earbud for anyone close enough to hear.

"Man," his SEAL teammate Harper answered, "I didn't know there were any friendlies down here."

Ben breathed easier with more of his team in the hellish town. "'Bolt Action' Mary's on the roof keeping an eye on us."

Art Diaz broke in. "We saw her damage."

"What's your twenty?" Ben gathered himself to head back into the firing lanes.

Harper maintained a low voice. "Feels like the middle of town. Hardware store and a bank."

"Six blocks from me." Ben moved out.

Sant's distinctive British accent added to the conversation. "Raker and I are further west of center. Mercs drove us north of the truck Mary took out."

Ben calculated the area. "Stay on your line. We should all be sweeping east toward the rail yard. That's where the real business is."

"Roger that," Sant confirmed.

Ben came to the end of an alley and scanned the street. Nothing visible. Every corner could hide gunmen or crooked cops. He burst across the street. Gunfire crackled. Bullets whizzed past him, off target. He made it into a gap between a restaurant and a yarn shop and kept running. The gunfire broke off and footsteps chased him.

A man yelled out in pain, and Ben heard him crash to the ground behind him. A moment later, the distant .50 rifle shot reverberated like thunder. Mary had tagged one of his pursuers, and he made it to the next street without incident.

Harper snapped onto the airwaves. "Was that Mary?"

Ben sidestepped up the next street and bolted for another alley. "We snaked a fifty from the warehouse. I've never seen such beauty as her raining lead."

"Sounds serious." Harper chuckled.

Ben didn't know how to articulate to his friend and teammate all that had happened between him and Mary in the seriously short time frame. "Dead serious."

He approached the center of town, where the grid of streets provided long sightlines and poor cover. Ducking into a secure doorway, he checked his phone. Lucas was south of him, near where Mary had stopped the truck so it blocked the intersection. No other blips indicated hostiles near him. He looked up and saw the sign for the hardware store one street to his west.

"Nearing you, Harp," Ben announced.

"We're at the edge of the bank parking lot, in the weeds."

"See it." He sped in that direction, knowing that while he was exposed over the street, Mary covered him. For now, the area was quiet. A stand of trees and bushes bordered one side of the parking lot. The slightest human movement within the camouflage drew him.

Harper and Art stood against a broad tree, both covering different areas. They wore their tactical rigs covered with gear and magazines and carried assault rifles. Art's knit cap was pulled low over his brow. Harper wore a bandana and no helmet and smiled broadly when he saw Ben.

"There's my Jackson." Harper extended a fist. Ben bumped the side of his against it. "You in one piece?"

"All squared away." He readjusted his gear after the sprints along the streets.

Art just stared at him, a little smile in his eyes but mouth grim as usual.

Ben challenged, "You got something to say, marine?"

Art turned to Harper. "I told you it was trouble to send him and the sniper on assignment together." Ben puffed up to counter Art, but the man was dead right.

Harper kept his eyes on his sector but squinted, incredulous. "You never said that. You never say anything."

Art muttered, "You just weren't listening."

The two men gave space for Ben to take a position by the tree. Nothing could approach without them knowing.

Harper ventured, "Anything we need to know?"

"It's all good," Ben answered, and he meant every word.

Harper responded, "That's all we need to know."

And the conversation was over.

Art shifted his feet. "So what are we shooting at and when are we shooting at it?"

"Major trucking's bottled up through town, so we need to press into the rail yard." Ben laid out the plan as far as they could take it. "Suppress security forces and stop the trains. Two warehouses, one damaged, both full of weapons still as yet to move out."

Art growled, "Point the way."

Tak's voice crackled on the comm, "We copy that. North of your position. Converge?"

"Negative," Ben replied. "You're the north flank. Sant and Raker are south. We'll take the middle. Converge on the rail yard."

"Roger," Tak answered. He grew more urgent. "Shit, you have heavy hitters heading to your neighborhood. Too fast for us."

Marks, his teammate, added, "Loaded tractor trailer and an oversized tow truck, big enough to clear one of the wrecks clogging the on-ramps."

Ben, Art and Harper all stood ready, looking for movement. The approaching trucks rumbled. Ben amped himself up for the next action.

"Police escort?" Ben asked.

"None." Tak whispered; he must've gone into deeper cover. "Only see one patrol car, and he's prowling our sector."

The trucks grew louder.

Harper moved from the cover of the tree. "It's our party."

Ben readied his weapon and spoke into his mic, "North and south teams, we'll see you at the rail yard."

"Copy that," Tak answered.

Sant replied, "Affirmative."

Ben wanted to hear Mary's response. She was isolated on her perch, the way she normally operated, but it seemed too detached from the flow of information. He needed any indication that she was still safe up there.

Diesel engines gnashed and howled, pushing their vehicles too fast on the city streets. Ben and the others broke their cover and sped toward the intersection where they were headed. A tractor trailer blew into view a block away. Right behind it was a huge tow truck. When they hit the intersection, the semi continued forward, and the tow truck made a hard right to turn north.

Ben made his decision quickly and barked it out. "Truck first. We'll catch up to the tow as he's trying for the on-ramp."

Art and Harper were with him, scrambling over the bank parking lot, through the bushes at the back edge and to the next street. Ben and Harper both aimed at the streaking truck while Art covered their flank.

Ben claimed, "Airbrakes," and sent a burst of

bullets into the base of the cab, where the hoses led to the trailer.

"Tires." Harper fired in a tight pattern, shredding the rubber around the wheels.

The air hoses popped and screamed, and the tires on the trailer locked up and screeched along the road. The cab listed, bent over where Harper had destroyed the front tire. The truck wasn't going anywhere. But the driver remained in the cab. Too scared to fight? Or…

Art announced, "Trojan horse," confirming the trouble Ben felt in his gut.

Three security men appeared on the top edge of the cargo container and opened fire. Ben, Art and Harper scattered. Ben found cover behind a low wall while the other two made it to a stand of trees lining the street.

The opposing force kept them pinned down with a steady barrage. Ben poked his weapon over the wall and fired blind, just to open a little space. The security men paused, and he rose above the wall to fire at their receding shapes. Art and Harper also shot at the men, chipping pieces of the trailer away but not hitting anyone.

An urgent clock burned into Ben. "They're wasting our time."

Harper responded on the com. "Diversion away from the tow."

"You guys bring grenades?" Ben was only equipped for recon.

Harper's answer arced through the air and landed

on the roof of the truck. One of the security men scrambled toward the grenade and swung his rifle at it. Ben fired at the man and clipped him in the arm. But the man still managed to knock the grenade down. It burst into the side of the cargo container and tore a hole in the metal. The other two security men came to the edge again and fired down, continuing the stalemate.

One of the guns fell silent. Then the other. Ben heard Mary's voice in the lingering echo of her distant rifle. She was safe and she was telling him to knock out the fucking tow truck. Ben broke cover and ran up the street in the direction of the blocked on-ramp. Harper and Art joined up with him.

Harper marveled as he sprinted, "She's good."

"The best." Ben didn't know enough words to describe her.

The three of them ran up a block, turned east for two, then north again. They paralleled the highway. A hulking truck burned across the on-ramp ahead. The massive tow truck had backed up to it and hooked to the long trailer. Ben calculated the distance from the wreck to the hotel. A hell of a shot, at the functional limit of Mary's rifle. Out here, he couldn't expect the same precision she'd shown on the security guards at the last engagement.

But her bullets did streak through the air and punch into the side of the tow truck. It kept grinding, though, and started to pull the trailer and truck down the on-ramp. Ben and the others were only about a hundred yards away.

Art set up behind a tree and fired into the tires of the tow truck. The thick rubber was picked apart but stayed mostly intact, and the tow kept motoring. Harper and Ben dove behind a short cinderblock wall surrounding the yard of a nearby house and set up their weapons to fire on the truck.

Bullets raked at them from the right. Three more security guards shot from behind the cover of a row of concrete street barricades. The longer they kept Ben and his team pinned, the more space the tow truck cleared.

Ben tapped Harper and indicated he was going to swing farther to the right for a different firing position on the security. Harper nodded and handed him a grenade and held up two fingers to show how many he had remaining.

Staying low against the wall, Ben crept as far toward the shooters as possible. Their position gave them a perfect vantage over the area, even keeping Art suppressed behind his tree. When he'd gone as far as he could, Ben peeked up to get the enemy's position, pulled the pin on the grenade and threw it.

One of the security men shouted, "Grenade!" and they stopped firing to scramble.

Ben rose above the wall in time to see the explosion and flying chunks of concrete. But the men remained below the barriers. Only a glimpse of one of them flashed in a gap. He shot at the shape but wasn't sure if he'd hit him. Harper and Art opened fire as well and kept the men pinned.

Another goddamn delay. Frustration clenched

Ben's jaw. The tow truck would clear the on-ramp in a minute. And God knew how many train cars were loaded and on the move by now. Ben vaulted the wall and moved in a wide arc to flank the men while they were still occupied by Harper and Art's barrage.

He couldn't see enough of them to target but could tell the men were working on something rather than just huddling away from the raining bullets. He hustled to cover at the corner of a house and warned the others over the com, "Bad news coming."

"Shit." Art spoke between bursts from his weapon. "I see it. They're manning a SAW."

Harper blew out a frustrated breath. "We're not that heavy."

Ben stole a glance from his cover. One of the men braced the light machine gun on the barrier and another held its belt of ammo. "Be ready to take them out."

Harper called back, "With what artillery?"

The security man behind the SAW pulled the trigger and sprayed lead toward Harper's hiding place.

Ben readied himself. "Here it comes."

The SAW choked, interrupting the flow of bullets. The front of the barrel exploded and the bolt torqued, twisting the weapon out of the man's hand. He fell backward, and the other men stood, shocked. Harper and Art didn't miss a beat. They snapped off precise rounds that took out the two standing men. Ben rushed the position and fired at the remaining security man as he was trying to recover a rifle on the ground.

The immediate threat was neutralized, but the tow truck continued less than a block away. Harper and Ben approached it, and Art hung back to maintain cover for them. The driver had a spiteful look on his face as he went through his gears to drag the screeching truck.

Harper kept his weapon down but took a grenade from his vest and held it up for the driver to see. The man's eyes widened. Harper made a big show of pulling the pin, then underhanded the grenade so it skipped along the pavement and rolled beneath the tow truck. The driver leaped out and ran, dropping the large revolver he'd had hidden.

A second later, the explosive went off with a loud pop. The tow truck barely moved, but the underside was gutted and immediately started leaking fluids. Several parts of the drive train hung down, shattered and immobile. The on-ramp remained blocked.

Behind Ben, somewhere in town, a high-powered rifle fired a single shot. It wasn't Mary.

He nearly shouted into his mic. "Report. Anyone have eyes on that shooter?"

"Negative," Tak answered.

Sant came back, "No visual, but he's on a rooftop somewhere to the south."

"What was his target?" Ben assumed the worst.

Raker drawled, "Looks like it might've been the hotel."

Ben could barely breathe. "That's Mary." Cold fear rushed along his arms. He checked the tracker on his phone. The blip indicating Lucas moved steadily toward the hotel. Did that kid have a sniper rifle? Ben's chill disappeared into hot anger. He ran and barked orders to the others, "Get to the train yard. We'll be there."

The communicator was no good at this range. He had to eliminate any threat coming her way. He had to get to her.

NINETEEN

A SON OF a bitch was shooting at her with a hunting rifle. The bullet crashed into the face of the hotel, two meters low and to her left. She could tell from the sound of the shot that the weapon had a long barrel and a wood stock. The hired security goons would've brought something more tactical. Mary bet that one of the local crooked cops had gone home to pick up his personal piece. But it didn't matter if that rifle had only taken out deer up to this point; the gun had no ethic and didn't care who it was aimed at.

The muzzle flash had faded by the time the bullet had reached up to her. The limp streetlights only illuminated parts of the rooftops in town below her. Plenty of hiding places. And whoever was down there was savvy enough to wait and watch for her own telltale blast to target. But he wasn't good enough to get her on the first shot. And now that she knew he was down there, she wouldn't let him get away.

She'd watched Ben's action at the tow truck. Her bullets weren't enough to stop it from range, but he and Harper and Art had taken care of the problem nicely. A vengeful satisfaction had washed over her when she'd seen the SAW explode in the hands of the hired security.

But the battlefield pleasure had been short-lived. The counter-sniper had played his hand, and she'd had to shift her view from Ben's sector to the closer rooftops. After that, Ben was gone. She had no idea where he or his team had disappeared to. The action in town quieted. Only two police cars still patrolled.

The sniper below was impatient. He'd tried his shot before he had a positive target. He would leap at bait. One round remained in this magazine. She targeted the hood of one of the police cruisers and let the bullet fly.

Without waiting to see the damage she'd done, she picked up her Barrett and hurried to her left, near the center of the hotel face. Below, the yellow flash of the counter-sniper's rifle winked. He was on the roof of a building five blocks north of the hotel. A facade protected him, and the nearest streetlamp didn't reach far enough to reveal his shape. His bullet smacked the hotel where Mary had last fired from. Still low, but closer to her position.

Mary slapped a fresh magazine in her Barrett, threw the bolt forward and set up to fire. Her scope reached out to where the sniper was, but there was no definitive target in the darkness that would guarantee a hit. If she had com with the team below, she could ask for a flare to illuminate the area. But silence persisted in her earpiece. Ben and the others must've been making their way to the train yard by now.

If she couldn't send up a flare, she might be able to make one. Up the block from the man's rooftop was a transformer on a power pole. She'd have to be quick, and re-aiming for a follow-up shot after the heavy recoil of the .50 was always a challenge.

She practiced the move. Targeting the transformer, then swinging the crosshairs down to where she thought the counter-sniper was set up. The transition was too bumpy and she tried to keep the pressure from fueling her frustration. No margin for error. She ran through the motions again, smoothing them out a little. If she didn't get him with her first try, he'd know she was on the move and would disappear until she gave her position away again while trying to protect her team on the ground. The man below had time on his side. But she had a solid-gold trigger finger.

Deep breath. Exhale halfway and hold. She shot the transformer, and a bloom of yellow sparks erupted. Sliding her view to the target rooftop revealed the counter-sniper in the glittering light. He was swiveling his head from her area to the transformer and back to her. The man put his eye to his own scope, and she fired. Her bullet chipped through the top of the facade he hid behind and struck him in the chest. The rifle spun from his hands.

Threat dispatched.

But the battle was far from over. Four security men swarmed the police car she'd tagged and set up a perimeter for the officers who were out on the street with pistols drawn. The one remaining patrol car had picked up speed and was heading right toward the hotel.

Time to move out. But without clear communication from Ben and the team, she had no idea if they still needed her support from above. And she had no idea what kind of ground fighting she was jumping into.

BEN'S LUNGS BLAZED and his muscles ached. He had to run faster. He'd seen the exploding transformer and heard Mary's shots. There had been no final response from the enemy sniper, and he knew she'd eliminated that problem. But it wasn't Lucas with the high-powered rifle. His tracker was at the edge of the hotel and getting closer to her.

Ben's com was still too far away to reach her. To warn her.

A block parallel to him, a police car hurried south toward the hotel.

"Sant, Raker, can you intercept that roller?" He barely had the breath to speak.

"Affirmative," Sant answered.

Ben had to slow at an intersection, then sprinted through when he saw it was clear. "Leave it operational. I need the wheels."

"You got it," Raker twanged. "Engaging now."

Gunfire crackled two blocks away from Ben. Shouting. More shots. Silence.

Ben rounded a corner to see the car idling with its doors open and the back windows shot out. The two officers lay facedown on the sidewalk, hand-cuffed, faces red with anger. Their weapons had been stripped and were in the hands of Sant and Raker, who covered the men and the area from the safety of a half-walled patio.

"Thanks for the ride." Ben saluted his team-mates.

"Cheers." Sant nodded back.

Raker asked, "You want us?"

Ben slid into the passenger seat and across to the driver's, closing the doors as he went. "Stay on mission."

Tires screamed. He stood on the gas and sped to-ward the hotel, driving with one hand and checking his phone with the other. Lucas had made it inside.

"Mary. Mary." He still wasn't close enough but had to keep trying. "Hostiles in your area."

He plowed through a barricade of sawhorses. Three blocks from the hotel. Too damn far. His heart pounded faster than the engine roared.

"Mary!"

The car bounced over the sidewalk as he took a corner too tight.

A faint voice answered, "...don't have eyes on you."

He leaned forward, urging the car faster. "I'm in the patrol car. You have hostiles coming at you."

She came in clearer. "I read. I read. I see you."

"What's your twenty?" The hotel loomed a block away.

"Rooftop," she whispered. Was Lucas already up there with her?

Ben sped over the hotel parking lot. He swerved to avoid a row of cars and straightened out in time to bust over the curb and smash through the front windows of the hotel. The impact jarred him. The car slid sideways on the cubes of safety glass and sideswiped a huge planter. He threw the car into neutral and ran to the stairs.

Rushing could kill him. He'd already announced himself at the front of the hotel, so surprise was out of the question. He cracked the entrance to the stairs a sliver and peered into the bright white. With the first landing and set of steps clear, he swept inside.

Mary murmured into his ear, "I detected movement in the stairwell and backed out."

He remained silent, motionless, though his pulse pounded. Two flights up, maybe three, a boot shifted on metal stair. The butt of an assault rifle scraped against the painted concrete wall and the hair on the back of Ben's neck stood up. He eased forward and looked up the center of the rectangular spiral created by the railing.

His voice barely reached the mic. "Three men. Third floor."

"Copy," she whispered back. "I'm clear back if you want to engage."

He steadied himself, sighted along his assault rifle and fired up at the men. One was struck in the leg and yelled out. The other two immediately started pouring lead in Ben's direction. He sped up the stairs on inspired legs to the first landing and hugged the wall. Bullets popped through the metal railing and pinged off the steps where he'd been.

During a pause in the firing, he glanced up again. Lucas and Chul remained on their feet, weapons pointed down. Frank wrapped a field dressing around his shin. Ben fired up at them and sprinted to the second-floor landing. They fired down in an erratic spray. Above them, the tied-up security guard screamed through his gag.

Ben popped the empty mag from his rifle and knew they'd hear it. Another barrage rained down the center of the stairwell while he reloaded. He stomped on a step as if he was rushing them, and they leaned over to fire in that direction. Ben snapped off three quick rounds. Two hit Chul in the chest, and the third dug into the wall above him. The man slumped forward on the railing, dead.

Frank dragged himself forward and fired a handgun as fast as he could pull the trigger. Ben was forced back. A cold sweat along his arms told him how close he'd been to getting shot. He edged along the landing for a different view above. Lucas gripped a submachine gun across his chest and stared into the high distance, instead of where Ben was.

"Lucas!" Ben shouted up to the guy who looked like he wanted to be far away from the battle. "You know what's coming. You know you can't fight it."

Frank hissed, "Don't listen to him."

"Chul's dead," Ben barked. "Frank's next. You didn't sign up for this, Lucas."

"Fuck you!" Frank screeched.

"I already shot you, deckhand," Ben yelled back. "You don't get to say shit to me."

Frank's answer was another magazine full of bullets in Ben's direction. But the reload was slow, and Frank's injured leg limited his mobility. Ben countered quickly with a single shot into Frank's center mass.

The man grimaced and wheezed but still managed to finish loading his pistol and fall back away from Ben's field of view. His gurgling voice commanded Lucas, "Get that fucker. Kill that fucker."

"You're not going to do that, Lucas." Ben calmed his tone. "You're not going to come up against this Navy SEAL and win."

"Do it!" Frank spat, blood in his lungs. He exposed his arm and hand and pointed his pistol across the landing at Lucas.

Ben double-tapped his trigger. One bullet went through Frank's wrist, and the other tore the gun from his grip. His scream dwindled quickly. There wasn't much life in him. But Lucas remained armed and a possible threat.

"You don't want to take your chances with me, Lucas." This part of the firefight was over, but the tension still hummed in Ben. He reached out with all his senses for any additional threats. Lucas's ragged breathing was the only sound. Ben rose two steps closer to the third-floor landing. Lucas flinched when he saw him. The Navy man didn't aim his weapon at Ben, but gripped it in his fists.

Ben kept his barrel pointed at Lucas. "It's not a fight you can win."

Lucas slid out of view. "S-stop."

"You were supposed to be a truck driver. This is your first time doing it, right?" Ben crept closer. "Are you really ready to die for motherfucking gun-runners?"

Mary's voice graced Ben's ear, and her words floated down from above. "Don't fight."

Ben reached the last landing before Lucas and saw Mary one floor higher. She held a submachine gun down on Lucas. A profound pressure in Ben's chest unwound with the sight of Mary, uninjured, on her feet and still at war.

She continued to move toward Lucas. "Put down your gun. This isn't your fight."

Ben approached, and the two of them converged on the nervous man. "She knows, Lucas. It's the only way you get out alive. You're not a fucking merc. You don't want to be here. This isn't the truck driving job you signed up for."

The weapon shook in Lucas's hands. His watery eyes glanced from Ben to Mary and back. "I... can't. You...stop."

Mary was almost tranquil, despite her shining submachine gun. "Dying hurts, Lucas." She took a deliberate step to the side so he could see Frank and Chul's bodies. "It isn't quiet, and there's no reward."

His mouth quivered. His hands loosened on his gun.

"Drop it," Ben commanded. "On the ground."

Lucas took a shaky breath and released the weapon. The clatter bounced up and down the stairwell. While Ben covered him, Mary approached, stripped the pistol he wore on his hip and kicked the submachine gun into a corner. She searched over him briefly, found no other weapons and stepped back.

"You're alive," she announced.

Ben cocked his head toward the bottom of the stairwell. "Get gone. Get as far away from this town as you can."

Lucas bolted down the stairs without another word.

Ben stepped up to Mary, wanted to wrap his arms around her, wanted to carry them both far away from the chaos and death. But he stayed on alert, and she did as well. The heat in her eyes, though, reflected what he was feeling and he ached to kiss her.

"You good?" he asked through clenched teeth.

"You know it." The quirk in her smile made him burn even hotter.

"Fuck yeah, I do." He stepped closer and brushed his shoulder against hers. It was all they could do. She leaned into him for the touch. Then proceeded with him down the stairwell.

"The streets look like a mess." Her voice rasped. They'd been awake and in the field for quite a while.

"Thanks to you." He covered a landing. She proceeded down the stairs, waiting until he caught up. "Take care of the counter-sniper?"

"Done." She clipped a nod.

"Where's the fifty?" They reached the first-floor landing.

"On the roof." She tapped a pouch on the small of her back. "But I took the bolt."

He gripped the door handle and looked to her. She nodded. He creaked the door open. After scanning out for a moment, she tipped her head in the direction she wanted to go. He pushed the door farther. She exited, him trailing just behind her. They both aimed in different directions to cover their path.

The short hallway opened to the elevator bank, then the lobby. The police car still idled, glass like ice on its roof and hood. Cold wind howled in through the broken window. The night was black outside the hotel.

Mary pulled up, wary, and slid to cover behind a brick planter in the lobby. She must've sensed trouble. He trusted her instincts and set up behind a pillar next to the front desk, his weapon ready.

Two security men crept forward past the shattered window. They entered the lobby on opposite sides of the police car, assault rifles leading the way. Glass crunched under their boots. They were cautious but still hadn't spotted Ben and Mary.

She shot first, tagging one of the men in the shoulder. Ben followed with a round in the other man's leg. They both went to the ground, clutching their wounds and losing their guns. Ben and Mary rushed them before they could recover from the initial shock. He took the rifle from the man closest to him and tossed it, and the man's sidearm, into the police car. Mary stripped the weapons from the other man then jumped into the passenger seat.

Ben jumped behind the wheel, threw the car in reverse and floored it. Cubes of glass sprayed until the tires caught and sped the car backward. A metal frame on the hotel's front window caught the open driver's door and tore it off. The car bounced down the curb and lurched when Ben yanked the gearshift to drive.

Mary braced herself against the dash. "You want me to drive?"

"Really?" He floored it and peeled away toward town. "Would you rather shoot or drive?"

She huffed a breath and pulled her rifle across her lap. "I'd rather shoot."

"Then stop complaining about my driving and get your finger on the trigger, woman." Cars and trucks burned on the streets. "Because we're heading straight down the barrel."

TWENTY

"WOMAN?" SHE WAS gratified to see Ben suitably concerned with her tone of voice; he tore his eyes from the road to glance at her expression. She raised her eyebrows and repeated, "Woman?"

He had to return his gaze to the road in order to steer past a burning police car and abandoned tow truck. "You're not *my* woman," he explained. "I can't own you. But you are *the* woman." He pounded the side of his fist on the steering wheel and huffed with frustration. "How do I say it? You're all woman." The car bounced over a curb, and Ben muscled it back onto the street. "You're everything."

When he looked at her again, a truth resonated in him. A calm amid the chaos around them. It was gone in a blink. He refocused on the road and gunned the engine. But she still felt his depth and the answering resonance in her own chest.

Bullets flew across the street, and still she knew that all of life wasn't just a lonely war.

Ben jammed the car to one side, opening up a firing lane for her. She poked her assault rifle out the window and let loose a burst. Their attackers scattered.

"Is that the cavalry?" Raker asked urgently over the com.

"Incoming." Ben straightened out the car.

Sant broke in. "We're pinned by a plumbing supply store. Shooters are in a ditch below a high wall."

"I know it." Ben stomped more speed from the patrol car and explained to her, "Sant and Raker are south, Art and Harper middle and Tak and Marks are north into the train yard."

The push would back the gunrunners against the swamp and concentrate the fight. There was no more high ground for her to protect the team from afar. She tightened the straps on her vest. "It's going to get big."

"Fuck, yeah." Ben sat up straighter and scanned ahead. "Get ready to bail." He drove with one hand and pulled his rifle across his lap with the other.

She held her gear to her and gripped the door latch. Ben sped half a block up, screeched around a hard right then eased off the gas. The plumbing supply Sant mentioned was up on the right. Beyond it was a frontage road, then the long ditch she and Ben had used to move invisibly through town. All that good cover would make it difficult to uproot any shooters in there.

"Now!" Ben released the wheel and dove out the side of car.

She yanked the handle, threw the door open and leaped. Hard concrete slammed into her hip and shoulder. Pain shot across her upper back. The impact rolled her forward, and momentum tried to tear the rifle from her grip. She stopped her roll and got her bearings in time to see the car bounce over the curb on the far side of the frontage road and fly into the ditch.

Ben ran behind the destruction, rifle barking as the security men broke cover to avoid the impact. She scrambled to her feet and joined him. The car angled down sharply and crashed, bending metal and breaking glass. A man stumbled through the weeds and tried to turn his submachine gun on her. She snapped off two rounds and sent him into the bottom of the ditch.

Sant and Raker added to the fight. Bullets flew back and forth. She flattened to the ground and fired at the security men, who panicked and abandoned their calm and discipline. Ben maintained his cool. She didn't take her eyes from the conflict to look at him, but the curt, confident bursts from his weapon told her everything she needed to know.

And just like that, the battle was over. The last of the gunshots faded. The wrecked car idled. There was no more fight left in the one security man remaining. He walked out of the scrub with his hands high and a shaken look on his face. Sant stripped him of his remaining weapons and bound his wrists behind his back with a zip tie. Raker then secured the restraint to a stop sign pole.

"Who the fuck are you guys?" The security man was more defiant when it was clear they weren't going to kill him.

No one from her team answered. They moved

away from the man and collected back near the ditch. Mary informed Sant and Raker, "Over that wall you're on the tracks, and about four hundred yards north are the warehouses."

Sant and Raker nodded their understanding.

Ben looked over their gear. "Any more ordnance?"

Raker tapped a pouch on his chest. "Couple of grenades."

"If you can spare them, take out some train tracks so they can't move out." Ben bumped his knuckles on Raker's shoulder. "We'll see you in the badness."

Sant extended his fist to her, and she knocked hers into it before they moved into the ditch, above where the fight had just happened. Raker and Sant hurried up the other side and disappeared over the wall. She and Ben continued north through the weedy cover.

Behind them the tied-up security man shouted, "Who the fuck...?" but he ran out of breath. ATF, FBI, military police would all be sweeping up after Automatik did the heavy lifting and would collect this man and anyone else too wounded to run away from the fight.

She whispered to Ben, "Glad we're just making a mess and not cleaning it."

He suppressed a laugh. "Gonna take a lot of spin on this one."

Sant announced in her earpiece, "Three hundred yards from the warehouses. Security swarming the whole yard. No movement with the trucks, but the trains are still being loaded."

Ben asked into the mic, "Harp, what's your twenty?"

"One block from the entrance to the train yard," he answered. "Got hung up with a little resistance while you were crashing the car."

She and Ben were losing their cover. The ditch started a gradual rise toward the parking area in front of the rail yard. As the weeds thinned her tension rose. Ben motioned to his left, toward the town buildings, and Mary gave him the thumbs-up.

He told Harper, "We're coming to you."

"I'll put a kettle on." Harper kept talking as she and Ben climbed out of the ditch and sped across the street to the buildings. "And Jackson, you should know that your com is always live. It's dangerous, man. You had me getting all choked up during your dashboard confessional back there."

Ben paused at a corner, put his hand over the mic on his earbuds and whispered to her. "I meant every word."

She might've blushed, and also covered her mic. "You'd better." Eyes open, she kissed him. He returned it and breathed her in during the all-too-brief touch.

They parted, and Ben released his mic. "Don't be afraid of your emotions, Harp. They get toxic if you bottle them up."

"He's right," Art growled.

Mary checked over the street before breaking

from the shadows and hurrying toward the area where Harper and Art should've been. Ben ran sideways with her, covering their exit. Shots popped off toward them, and Ben returned fire until they were safe behind another brick building.

"Glad to see that Delta operator kept you in one piece." Harper gave them a wave from one building north. Art crouched next to him, rifle pointed up the street.

Ben feigned surprise at her and spoke broadly into the mic, "Delta? You told me you'd learned how to shoot in the Girl Scouts."

"No," she corrected him. "I told you I shoot like a girl. That's why I always hit my target."

"Damn straight." He winked at her and licked his lips.

And here, in the middle of a battle, she blushed. Heat across her chest, up her neck and into her face. All the places she wanted him to kiss her. She took a long, calming breath and tried not to think of the places she wanted to kiss him back.

Luckily Harper interrupted, "What's the action, Jackson?"

"We just took fire from someone on the south edge of the parking lot." Ben peeked around the edge of the building. "It's got to be crawling with security forces."

She plotted the approaches from their current placement and suggested, "We can press, two teams, top and bottom, pinch in toward the middle."

Harper came in first. "I like it."

"Agreed," Art announced.

"I'm in," Ben said. He reloaded and brought his rifle to his shoulder.

She gave him a spank on the ass and slapped a fresh magazine in her own weapon. Her watch showed it was ten minutes until midnight. "Move out."

Art and Harper stalked forward and swung north. Ben led the way. She trailed close, hugging the wall at their backs. Parked cars provided too much good cover for the security men on the other side of the street. Yellow lights on the buildings carved the area into bright arcs and opaque shadows. For now, she and Ben were hidden.

He stopped and leaned in to her. "They're itchy. I'm going to send one."

"Do it."

Ben fired a single bullet, and it was answered by a spray from three gunners. Their wild shots picked apart the bricks in front of her. She tracked the flashes for the man on the right and took him out. Ben did the same with the man on the left. They both concentrated on where the middle shooter had been, but he'd found cover by the time they shot and the rounds dug through the metal of a nearby car.

Harper and Art engaged their enemy with a flurry of shots. More men scrambled through the dark, their shapes too fleeting to make targets. The windows of the administration buildings were unlit, but she saw the metal blinds shifting as people inside watched and waited.

One quick silhouette was familiar across the front porch of the buildings. Len the foreman ran with a shotgun in his hands. She fired at him, but he was already gone. Her muzzle flash drew attention and bullets from more men behind the cars. She and Ben returned bullets while moving farther forward and to their right. As Harper and Art shifted higher, the four of them would be able to squeeze the security men in the parking lot.

Len's shotgun boomed toward Art and Harper's area. Other shots followed. She and Ben hurried their pace, carving a path with bullets that scattered the men to cover.

Harper spat through the com, "Ah fuck, I'm hit."

Cold urgency rushed through her. Ben fought harder forward, taking out two men and pinning a third behind a barrage.

Art's voice maintained the calm of a seasoned soldier. "Leg shot. He's good. Pulling him back."

Ben growled, "Pushing up." He pressed on, uprooting the hidden man and dropping him. She kept up, letting her training and experience take over. Action led to reaction, with no thought in between. Their sector was quickly cleared, but the men on the north end of the parking lot remained and fired toward Art and Harper.

If those men swarmed, then it could be the end for her friends and teammates.

"Len!" she shouted.

The foreman shifted from the formation and looked up, confused. She shot him through the hip and chest. His shotgun clattered against the concrete, and he fell into another shooter.

Ben followed up, firing at the other man and taking his attention from Art and Harper. Bullets streaked toward her and Ben, and they took cover behind the cars. A hand grenade went off near the security men, and one screamed. Art must've found a good hiding place and was able to finally counter the attack.

She and Ben took advantage of the distraction and rushed the flank. The security men had no plan for a two-pronged assault and were overwhelmed. Only one was smart enough to surrender. She zip-tied him to a steel fence post before retreating from the lot to find Art and Harper.

The two men were behind a low wall that surrounded a patio. Harper held compression on his thigh while Art kept watch, weapon ready.

Ben slid to his friend's side and removed a medic pouch from the man's vest. "Shit, Harp, this is just going to give you a sexy limp for a few weeks." He unpacked supplies and quickly dressed the wound. She set up next to Art and scanned for more enemies.

Harper smiled through the pain. "You know I got a thing for physical therapists."

Ben secured the bandage. "We'll make sure he's real good-looking. How about a surfer this time?"

"Done that." Harper winced and shifted so he could man his weapon. "Find me a guy working his way through med school. Maybe with glasses."

If Art was surprised by the talk, he didn't make a sound. It was more than she'd ever learned about Harper's private life. But she hadn't spent much heart-to-heart time with her Automatik team. Socializing over a few beers only got so far beneath the surface. Opening up with Ben had started to connect her more to all of them. She knew she didn't have to keep them at a distance anymore and craved the time to share more than just passing stories.

Ben gave his friend a pat on the shoulder. "I'll be on the lookout. You good?"

"Prime-time." Harper slapped a fresh mag in his weapon and threw the bolt.

Art shifted at the wall to give Harper space. "We'll cover your six from here." Their setup at the corner of the patio wall gave them a broad view of the entrance to the rail yard.

She was able to see past the admin buildings to the loading area. High work lights revealed forklifts shuttling pallets from the warehouses to the freight cars. Train engines idled, ready to drag their deadly cargo across the country. Kit Daily and Chief Pulaski stalked through the activity, shouting orders to the scrambling men. A security detail of at least fifteen shooters made a perimeter around the whole operation.

"Nearly midnight." She showed her watch to Ben. "They'll be gone by then."

"Let's rock." He patted her ass and vaulted over the wall.

They reached the parking lot and edged toward the gap in the buildings that marked the entrance to the yard. Far to her right, a hand grenade exploded with the sound of shattered metal, followed by bursts of automatic gunfire.

"Some tracks are jacked," Raker barked on the com, "but we're pinned."

Tak radioed, "Inbound from the north, but will hit resistance in a second."

Ben rolled his shoulders. She steadied her breath. They arrived at the end of the building and readied their weapons. Twenty yards out, heavy machinery made good cover. Twenty yards beyond that were the armed security men and the heart of the gun-running operation. The shooting and shouting continued to her right.

She looked at Ben for final confirmation.

He blinked slow, ready, and announced, "We're punching them in the gut."

They both fired at the security guards and sprinted into the rail yard.

TWENTY-ONE

THE INITIAL BURSTS took out one security man and scattered the rest for cover. Ben and Mary reached a thick, battered tractor. It absorbed the rounds sent back at them. His friend's blood smeared his hands. He couldn't allow another drop to be spilled. Not tonight. Not by any of the guns Kit Daily and Pulaski were trying to push.

The two honchos continued yelling at their men to keep loading the train cars. Smoke billowed from the corner of the sabotaged warehouse, but the work continued through the doors and over the ramp.

Ben glanced around the corner of the tractor. Pulaski strutted behind the line of security men, fury on his face. Officer Green lurked at his side, flexed tight as usual, cranked on the violence. He gripped an assault rifle tight enough to squeeze the sap out of it.

More shots came after Ben ducked back behind cover. Mary switched places with him and sighted down the barrel of her weapon, barely peeking out.

"I have a shot." Her ability to go from quick action to absolute stillness was amazing. "Let's chip at the right edge. Give Sant and Raker a break."

Sant chimed in, "Sounds brilliant to us."

Ben crouched above Mary and aimed out where she indicated. Just at the base of a loading crane, a fragment of a man's leg was visible. Mary fired and, with a nearly impossible shot, clipped the man. He stumbled forward, right into her second shot. Another shooter behind the crane popped out to retaliate, and Ben dropped him.

Some of the fire that had been directed toward Sant and Raker swung around to Ben and Mary. He sent a spray at these men, just to keep them honest, then returned to safety behind the tractor.

Clipped bursts chattered from Sant and Raker's position, silencing two of the security men's guns.

"Obliged," Raker huffed, on the run.

The right edge of the security perimeter collapsed. Mary tapped Ben, then darted from the tractor to a steel shack at the base of a switching tower. There was only room for one person there. He hated seeing her alone, farther into enemy territory, but it wasn't because he doubted her abilities. She motioned toward her next destination, an unloaded flatbed rail car. Ben indicated he'd cover her move and set up at the corner of the tractor.

She ran, and he swung around in time to see a security man aiming at her. Ben eliminated the man and sprinted out to join her at the wide steel wheels.

"No! No!" Kit Daily shouted like a twelve-year-old four-star general amid the crackling gunfire. "You're paid for a reason, and that's to load these trains." One of the massive diesel engines revved higher.

Activity popped at the north side of the yard, followed by the com announcement from Marks, "Tak and Marks are on the scene."

Sant sassed with his full British accent, "Green Berets put lead in your boots?"

Tak's comments were interrupted by sporadic gunfire. "We'll have you back to your bangers and mash in a minute, Sant."

"Fuck that," Sant scoffed. "Chicken tikka."

Ben interrupted, "I'm going to have whatever Hayley's cooking."

Art grunted approval. "You got that right."

"Shoot first, dinner later." Mary grounded them all. Then she put her hand over her mic and burned him with a look. "And I'm going to need you alone for a few hours."

Blood rushed to pound in his ears. The idea of that much time with her made him all kinds of hungry. He wrapped his hand around his mic. "I've got just the place."

"Not the backseat of a car." She shook her head.

"Luxury, woman." He drew out the words, knowing she watched his mouth.

Her lips curled in a smiling sneer, and she shook her head at him. She slayed him.

He released his mic and informed the team, "Stirring it up."

Mary pointed the way around the flatbed and ran to the next set of wheels. He glanced under the carriage as he followed and saw Pulaski and Green, the angry cop, were still rushing in the open, trying to rally the security. When Ben got to Mary's side, he motioned that he'd go around the back of the flatbed first because he had a target. She slid out of his way, and Ben crept around the corner.

"Drop it, Green!" His shout startled the officer, who fired a round into the dirt, then started to yank his rifle toward Ben.

Ben didn't give him the chance. Two rounds put the crooked son of a bitch onto the ground. Pulaski gaped in shock and staggered toward the cover of a forklift.

He reached for the pistol on his hip, but Mary commanded, "Don't! Don't!" She swung past Ben and pressed toward the police chief with her weapon ready. He shook with indecision. She tried to make up his mind for him. "You're done, Pulaski."

"What are you?" His hand hovered over his gun.

"I finished you." She moved a little closer. Ben watched for any other activity, but the fighting was only taking place to the north and south of them.

Pulaski decided. His face scowled with hate and rage. He reached for his sidearm, and Mary shot him through the shoulder. But the man didn't go down. Hissing through his teeth, he tried to use his other hand to grab the weapon. Mary fired again, piercing that arm. Pulaski spun into the forklift. His legs started to give out but he kept trying to force himself standing. Mary maintained her rifle on him, and Ben approached.

"You motherfucking—" Ben cut off Pulaski's curse with a fist in his face. The man finally fell.

Ben stripped his weapons, cuffed him with his own handcuffs and left him bleeding and mumbling in the greasy gravel.

Metal clashed in mechanical thunder. Train wheels turned. A set of three freight cars slid toward the south, pulled by a churning engine. The workers who'd been loading abandoned their equipment and fled back toward the empty black of the swamp.

"Shit." Raker was out of breath. "That train's heading for clean tracks."

Ben turned to give chase but stopped when he saw two men running on the ground next to the last freight car. One man was larger and slower. Bad knees. "Kit Daily," Ben called him out.

The train pulled away and revealed Kit Daily and a security guard standing among the tracks less than a hundred feet away. Mary fired before the guard could. Daily didn't even look at the man fall. He drew his .45 and sent sloppy bullets toward Ben and Mary. They dove for cover behind a mound of gravel and leaned their backs against it.

She tossed her rifle aside and drew her pistol. "Empty."

"I'm close." He didn't know how many rounds he had left in the mag, so he unslung his primary weapon and clicked the safety off on his submachine gun.

Mary dug her heels into the dirt and coiled. "He doesn't have range with that automatic in those old hands."

Ben felt her ready tension against his shoulder. "And his reload's going to be slow."

They rose together and turned to face Daily. He fired and fired, bullets tumbling high and wide or digging into the dirt far in front of Ben and Mary. The confidence he usually wore had been bleached away in the harsh work lights. His last round spun into the forklift back by Pulaski, then the slide locked open on an empty chamber. He reached for another magazine on his belt.

Ben and Mary both shot at once. She tagged him just above the knee, and Ben punched through his shooting shoulder. Daily howled louder than the train engine. The whole yard seemed to stop and listen to his pain and rage. His boots scraped and kicked over the gravel, but he couldn't find any footing. A long groan punctuated his fall. His wounded leg remained outstretched and he jerked to one side.

He wasn't done. Daily dragged himself backward and tried to reload his gun. Ben and Mary scrambled over the gravel mound and charged him. He managed to get a magazine into the pistol and snap the slide forward. Ben reached the downed man and kicked the gun from his hand.

Daily ground his teeth and winced. "Who…the fuck…are you?"

Mary searched him roughly for any more weapons and only came up with a pocketknife. She stood, foot on his shoulder to pin him. Anger rose in her eyes. She still pointed her pistol at Daily's head and could end his life in a blink. Her tight mouth barely moved when she told him, "Balboa13."

The stone face of a warrior returned, and she stepped away from Daily. All he could do was squirm. Ben understood her anger. But there'd be no satisfaction in killing the man. His disgrace would have to be loud, and take down his whole rotten network.

"Clear," Tak announced from the north.

Sant responded, "We're on the train and stopping it."

Art joined in. "Harper's holding up. Sirens approaching. We used the sat phone to call in the federal street sweepers."

Mary walked away from Daily, took a long breath in, held it, then exhaled. "Dust us off."

Ben moved to her side. She leaned on him and allowed him to lean on her. They stood that way while the rest of the team assembled in the center of the rail yard. Harper limped and used Art as a crutch. The lanky Marks looked like he'd just shown up after a round of golf, not a smudge on him. But his Japanese-American teammate, Tak, was covered in soot and had a long tear down one of his sleeves. Sant kept things cool and easy, as usual. Raker smiled genially, despite the series of bleeding scrapes on his jaw and neck.

The thumping of a helicopter soon drowned out the coming sirens. An unmarked Blackhawk landed toward the back of the rail yard, near the edge of the swamp. It stayed on the ground only long enough to collect all the Automatik operators. Ben strapped into the jump seat next to Mary. Their thighs pressed against each other. Their teammates tended to injuries or just allowed their bodies and minds to relax.

The helicopter rose, and he could see the flashing lights of the federal authorities whose job it was to bring the law and clean up the broken town. Mary also looked down. She traced the train tracks with her finger. He understood. The higher they went, the spread of the tracks went wider. They'd stopped it. A knot uncoiled in his stomach.

And a new excitement grew. He brought his lips close to her ear and spoke over the helicopter's motor. "Ben Louis and Mary Long are gone."

She looked at him with the realization. Was that apprehension on her face? He knew he felt it, but it wouldn't hold him back from chasing down what was next.

He asked, "Are you okay with that?"

Her answer was the question, "Are you?"

"I'm ready to be real."

TWENTY-TWO

COLD CHICAGO GLITTERED outside the tall hotel windows. But the bitter wind that had edged through the slightest gaps in Mary's clothes as they'd walked back from dinner couldn't invade the spacious suite. Most of the warmth came from Ben behind her. Closing and locking the door. Leaving the lights off so they could see the view with the curtains open.

His hands ran over her shoulders, firm enough to release some of the constant tension in her muscles. He helped her out of her coat and hung it next to his. She walked to the window and looked out at the city. Lit windows revealed strangers' lives. She was a stranger to them as well.

Ben stood behind her, voice as velvety as the wine they'd shared. "It was as far up as I could get you."

Twenty-five floors. "You know I like the high ground." Yes, he knew her. Small tugs, like hooks in her skin, remained as she tried to remove her armor.

He never rushed her. "There's no op on call tonight. No assignment. No target to take down." His hand rested on the small of her back, and a comfortable heat wrapped around her hips. "No bullets flying."

She leaned back into him. "I can't guarantee that."

He kissed her temple. "You already tagged me. One in the heart, one in the head."

She pressed into his kiss, letting the simple touch soak in. "You always know how to say the right thing to a girl."

"You packing?" He snuggled her closer into his chest.

"Always." The compact 9mm was constantly within reach in her purse.

"Me, too." Sadness threaded through his words.

She understood the constant caution. The distance from the everyday life those people on the other side of the window had.

Fresh energy rose in Ben and he wrapped his arm around her waist. His motor never let him get too down for too long. He took her up with him. "Nothing's touching us tonight."

She glanced back into the spacious suite. "Should've gotten separate beds."

"Oh, *I'm* touching you," he corrected and leaned his mouth close to her face. "If you'll have me."

"For a night?" Removing her armor was difficult.

He kissed her cheek. "I didn't plan an escape route."

She turned to look at him. His honest eyes helped the heavy steel fall away from her chest. And the need on his face, the real hunger, made her pulse race. The skin on her throat and the tops of her breasts heated. "We can escape together."

"Hell yeah, we operate well." He patted her ass and walked back into the suite. "I'm going to fill a bath."

She sat on the bed and unzipped the sides of her boots. "I have showered since we were crawling around in that ditch in Morris Flats."

Water rushed in the bathroom. Ben reemerged. "I know." He came to her and helped pull her boots off. "You smell like roses again."

The simple perfume was reserved for non-operational days and nights. Any distinctive odor during a battle could give away her position.

He ran his hands under her jeans and up her calves. She wouldn't have suspected it would be erotic until his confident move made her the nerves of her legs tingle. She leaned back on the bed to revel in the sensation. He removed her socks and tossed them aside.

"But you got to know something about me." His hands paused on her thighs. She leaned up with concern but saw the glint in his eye. "I don't do bubble baths."

"Do you soap?" She sat up completely and unbuttoned the top two buttons on his dress shirt, exposing smooth skin over defined muscles. She licked at him with her eyes and licked her lips.

"Occasionally." He snarled under her gaze and stood, removed his shirt and let it drop to the floor. City light carved his torso. Her breasts felt heavy and heat bloomed low in her belly. He waved her forward. "Let's get you naked."

She placed her hands in his and rose from the bed on slightly shaky legs. The pleasure and anticipation mixed with apprehension. She still wasn't used to being this open with someone. He unwrapped her scarf and helped her out of her sweater. Steam billowed from the bathroom door behind him, making Ben look mythical. She tried to let the fear fall away with her clothes, and removed her T-shirt and bra and brought her bare chest against his.

He growled. That need shook her, too. She kissed his collarbone. He stroked his hands through her hair. Her nipples grew more sensitive against him, and she was torn with wanting every sensation at once and drawing things out, one by one.

His fingers slid around the waistband of her jeans until they met at the button and the fly. Of course he was as adept at getting her out of her pants as he was field stripping a light machine gun. She kept her panties on and brushed past him, picking up her purse on the way to the bath. He kicked out of his shoes, socks and jeans and followed.

A wet, hot atmosphere surrounded her in the bathroom. The wide tub sat on a small platform in a corner, near another tall window with the curtains open. She placed her purse in arm's reach at the edge of the platform and tested the water.

"How is it?" Ben leaned in the doorway, wearing only his boxer briefs but holding his holstered backup pistol.

"Too hot." She turned the water off.

"Perfect." He dropped his underwear and strode

toward the bath. His arousal was already very evident. Her need flared, seeing him like that. Ready, inspired by her. He put his pistol down on the opposite side of the tub from her purse. First his toes tentatively dipped into the water, then his feet. He shuddered as he lowered himself into the bath. "Lord." He motioned for her to join him.

He hummed a little song of approval while she slipped out of her panties. She braced herself on his shoulder to climb into the tub. Her skin tingled, tight, as the hot water rose up her legs.

Ben dipped his hands in the water and brought the heat higher up to her hips and waist. She sat into the tub and let out a groan.

He nodded with sympathy. "It wakes up all those scrapes and bruises, right?"

Only four days had passed since their action in Morris Flats. After the helicopter ride, they'd scattered to different airports through the Midwest in order to fly back to San Diego for a debrief with the Automatik logistics team. Harper got the hospital attention he needed, and Art was reunited with Hayley.

She'd been left with too many questions after the operation had been marked complete. What now? What had been with Ben, and what was next? Part of the answer came with a text from Ben, suggesting separate flights to a rendezvous in Chicago. He'd picked her up at the airport and taken her directly to dinner. And now she was naked in a bath with him.

"But the bruises are worth it." She sank lower and leaned back onto Ben. He ran his palms down her arms. "Feds got what they needed. The mayor and her husband were rounded up trying to sneak out of town."

"Daily's active-duty Marines cronies were in irons as of two days ago." He stretched his legs out next to hers. "And the only news people see is that it was an internal, bloody conflict between factions within the gunrunning operation. But the high school got a big anonymous donation for its gym."

"You want a medal?" Her hands slipped under the water and over his thighs.

"I might have one or two of those somewhere." His palms slid over her shoulders and collarbones and down to rest at the top of her breasts. She squirmed, trying to get his touch lower. "Are you wearing yours?"

"How can a soldier who doesn't exist get a medal?" She took his hands and moved them over her breasts. Slick, hot skin rubbed against her nipples, and she arched her back.

He whispered, "You exist," and kissed the side of her neck and her ear and her temple.

These were more answers. Slow and savoring. Ben's attention to her, his understanding of her, hadn't wavered. He'd been bold and open all along. She was learning to believe him. She turned her head and kissed him. And with her lips on his, she tried to tell him how their connection woke up so much within her, the way his touch woke up the pleasure in her body. He communicated himself as well with his firm mouth devouring hers and never seeming to get enough.

One hand remained on her breast and the other skimmed down her belly. His erection grew stronger on her back, and her blood pumped with the possibilities. She spread her legs for him. Hot water swirled along her pussy, then his fingers lay firm over her. But he didn't move. She did. Swiveling her hips so he slid up and down her folds. She grew wet, but the bathwater diffused the slickness, giving a raw edge to the pressure of his fingers. Her blood kicked faster when he rubbed over her clit. The concentrated pleasure was too much, and she shifted so he moved lower along her pussy again.

His teeth bit gently into her shoulder. She gasped, filling herself with steam. Sensations bounced up and down her. His bite, his palm over her nipple, his fingers through her folds. She gripped his thighs and writhed to draw more from all these points. Water rippled and splashed against the inside of the tub.

But she couldn't get the pace lined up. Everything felt good, but it tumbled awkwardly through her without order. She stopped moving and sighed with frustration.

Ben released his bite from her skin and stroked his hand over the spot. "We've got time." He told her, "This is ours."

"I'm…" She turned and faced him. "I'm trying to understand that."

The lights outside glinted off his eyes and the water on his body. He reassured her, "You're doing it. You're already living."

She took a moment to hear him. To feel the heat of the bath winding into her muscles. To let the time spin out in front of her without it turning into a countdown. "Dry me off." She stood and stepped out to the soft bathmat. Ben followed and wrapped a large towel around her, more luxurious than she'd ever felt. The water soaked into the material, but the heat remained. She told him, "Get me wet."

He smiled, carnal, and looped an arm behind her shoulders. "Come with me."

Her training had taught her how to counter a move like this, and it was a pleasure to ignore her instinct for combat. He leaned low, scooped up her legs with his other arm and lifted her to his chest. She draped her hands around his neck and drew him into a kiss. There was enough trust for them both to reveal how much they wanted each other. The kiss progressed quickly as she opened her mouth, drawing his tongue in. Her breasts still tingled from the heat of the bath and his touch. Her pussy throbbed, wanting to find the pleasure again. He squeezed her tight to him, then took a moment to collect her purse and his pistol.

The air cooled as he carried her into the bedroom. She flew, free. Not weak. Or injured. But together with someone else who knew her. He set her down next to the bed. The towel slipped from around her chest and gathered at her feet. He placed her purse and his gun close and dragged the blanket to the foot of the bed, exposing the crisp sheets.

Nude and alone with Ben in the dark. Time and space all around them. Her head felt light and she enjoyed the rush. Her pulse hurried; her fingers throbbed. And her more sensitive areas felt like they could sense the smallest movement of Ben before he touched her.

He placed his hands on her waist and encouraged her to sit, then lie back. The sheets whispered, and the mattress conformed perfectly to her body. He leaned next to her, the smile in his eyes.

"Let's see if you're wet by the time I reach your pussy." His lips followed his words on her ear. The way her breath rushed with just the suggestion, she could almost guarantee she would be. He kissed the front of her throat, then trailed his mouth down between her breasts. His tongue flicked across her nipple, and she moaned. It tightened, and he toyed with it between his teeth. She lost her voice. His hands smoothed down her ribs and slid under her ass. Then his mouth kissed over her heart and down her belly. She pressed her heels into the mattress and lifted her hips for him. Warm breath spread over her mons. He used his shoulder to gently part her legs. "Can you feel it?" he asked.

"Yes." Her pussy pulsed, hot. Wet. "Find me."

He moved one of his hands and stroked down the front of her cleft. Her moisture gathered on his finger, and he slipped up and back over her lips. She rocked with him and moaned with him. She bucked when the flat of his thumb rasped on her clit. All the moving pieces that had seemed a jumble within her were falling into place. Ben's mouth on her pussy wound her into a single blazing sensation.

She arched higher and higher with each stroke of his tongue. The first hum of a climax centered through her. It grew, and she raked her nails over Ben's shoulders. He quickened his pace and took her breath away. Then he slowed and slid his tongue into her. The orgasm spiraled closer. He licked out of her opening and back to her clit. The release snapped through her, and she came.

Hard waves rocked her. Ben held her hips and kept his mouth against her sex. She ground out more of the pleasure until her muscles gave out. He lowered her to the mattress and kissed the front of her thigh before crawling up next to her. They wound their bodies together, and the last of the climax thumped between her chest and his.

As soon as her voice returned, she urged, "Stand up."

He raised his eyebrows at the gentle command but still complied. She brought herself to sitting on the edge of the bed and faced him. His body was poised, his cock rigid. She wanted to crash against him but let the moment draw out. This was the pleasure of time.

She rose. "Why don't you sit in that chair?"

"This one here?" He pointed to a little reading setup in the corner. "Or this one?" A larger arm-chair loomed on the far side of the bed.

"By the window." She walked behind him as he sauntered to the larger chair. "I want you to see this."

Ben eased himself onto the chair. "This is better than the back of a car, right?"

"Much." She kneeled in front of him. "But we're resourceful operators. We can adapt to any environment."

The muscles of his thighs firmed under her hands. She ventured higher, feeling the thick cords that moved him. His eyes blazed, locked on to her. She learned to savor the seconds as they stretched out. Stroking over his stomach. Smoothing her palm across his chest. She relished his quick intake of breath when she wrapped her fingers around the base of his cock. Solid and satin. He froze when she kissed the side of his shaft and flicked her tongue over his head.

She drew him into her mouth, and he sighed through clenched teeth. She tasted his musk and his spicy salt. Opening wider, she took him deeper. He pressed up, and she accommodated as much of him as she could. With her mouth and hand, she stroked his length. His body moved with her pace, under her control. His pleasure drove her desire higher. She rubbed the heel of her free hand across one of her nipples, and the bright sensation spread across her skin.

Their pace sped. He thrust farther into her mouth. She could lead him over the edge, but her own needs still raged. She moved her lips from him and looked into his focused face. "I have a condom in my purse."

"Just one?" he rasped.

"A box," she admitted.

He smiled like he was ready to devour her. "I have a box in my coat."

Any trepidation was forgotten in the tingling rush that swept up her legs, across her back and over her chest. She was ready to be devoured. "Get one."

He sprang from the chair and returned while rolling the condom on. She stood and placed her hands on his shoulders to urge him sitting again. He held her waist and moved her closer. She straddled him with her knees on the seat of the chair. The head of his cock slid along her pussy. She was still wet. More wet. Their eyes locked. They breathed together. She lowered herself onto him.

She sighed, and he growled. Swiveling her hips sank him in. He filled her and their connection spread sweet fire throughout her body. She gripped his shoulders. One of his hands curled around her waist, the other slid up to palm her breast. She ground together with Ben, absorbing the intoxicating sensations. She raised and lowered on his shaft and watched his face grow more intense.

Their speed increased. She leaned into his chest. He enfolded her with his arms. This was what she needed. Complete. Enveloping. Ben surged forward. She thought he might be coming, but instead he stood and carried her with him. He was still inside her as he walked them to the bed. Feeling him move her like that, balanced on his strength, almost had her coming again. She lay back on the mattress and hooked her heels behind his legs.

His thrusts moved her. She burned so bright with pleasure she had to close her eyes. Another climax edged closer. He gripped her thigh to his waist. His other hand spread over her belly and his thumb stroked down over her clit.

"Ah, yes," she told him. But she knew he already understood. "Yes." She punctuated the movement of his cock into her. "Yes. Yes. Yes." Faster. A rush of blood and barely enough breath. Harder. She drew him as far in as she could with her legs and let the orgasm take her.

"Yes, Mary." He didn't stop and pushed her to white hot. His urgency grew. Muscles tightened. He leaned down and pressed close, coiled his arms around her. The two of them welded together in their heat. A final thrust plunged him inside, and he came.

His body shuddered. The sparks of her own climax still bounced within her. Time slowed again. She basked in each moment. She slicked her hands over the sweat on his back and tasted the salt on his shoulder. Their breath rushed. Her heart pounded, then eased to a normal pace.

Ben rolled them to the sides and separated enough to look into her face. "Such a beautiful woman." He stroked down her cheek.

Emotion welled in her. She believed him. "Woman?"

He nodded. "Anything you want to be."

"I want…" She searched. She pushed away the fear of the unknown and ventured past the solitary and distant life she'd been living for too long. "To be here…with you."

"You are now." He kissed her. "And I'm going to hold on to you until you tell me to stop."

They both half leaned on the bed, and she shifted to get more fully on the mattress. Ben helped her onto the bed, then disappeared into the bathroom for a second. He returned without the condom on and slid up next to her. She reached down and dragged the cool sheets up over them.

"I haven't slept naked in a long time." Her purse and pistol were on her side of the bed.

His automatic was on the floor at the foot of the bed. He laughed small and thoughtful. "I can't remember the last time." He pulled her close.

She rested her head on his shoulder and spread her hand over his chest so she could feel his steady heartbeat. They'd fought wars together. They'd survived and would be called on to do so again. But that clock wasn't ticking just now.

"Tomorrow?" she asked.

Ben whispered a promise, "Tomorrow it's us."

* * * * *

ABOUT THE AUTHOR

NICO ROSSO DISCOVERED the romance genre through his wife, romance author Zoe Archer (aka Eva Leigh). He's published a wide range of romance stories including some with demon rock stars, a sci-fi space opera, steampunk Westerns and now romantic suspense with the series Black Ops: Automatik. When he isn't at his desk, he can be found in the workshop, building furniture and other projects for his new home with Zoe in Central California. Check out his website at Facebook.com/NicoRossoAuthor.

REQUEST YOUR FREE BOOKS!
2 FREE NOVELS PLUS 2 FREE GIFTS!

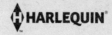

ROMANTIC suspense

Sparked by danger, fueled by passion

YES! Please send me 2 FREE Harlequin® Romantic Suspense novels and my 2 FREE gifts (gifts are worth about $10). After receiving them, if I don't wish to receive any more books, I can return the shipping statement marked "cancel." If I don't cancel, I will receive 4 brand-new novels every month and be billed just $4.74 per book in the U.S. or $5.49 per book in Canada. That's a savings of at least 12% off the cover price! It's quite a bargain! Shipping and handling is just 50¢ per book in the U.S. and 75¢ per book in Canada.* I understand that accepting the 2 free books and gifts places me under no obligation to buy anything. I can always return a shipment and cancel at any time. Even if I never buy another book, the two free books and gifts are mine to keep forever.

240/340 HDN GH3P

Name _____ (PLEASE PRINT) _____

Address _____ Apt. # _____

City _____ State/Prov. _____ Zip/Postal Code _____

Signature (if under 18, a parent or guardian must sign)

Mail to the **Reader Service:**

IN U.S.A.: P.O. Box 1867, Buffalo, NY 14240-1867
IN CANADA: P.O. Box 609, Fort Erie, Ontario L2A 5X3

**Want to try two free books from another line?
Call 1-800-873-8635 or visit www.ReaderService.com.**

* Terms and prices subject to change without notice. Prices do not include applicable taxes. Sales tax applicable in N.Y. Canadian residents will be charged applicable taxes. Offer not valid in Quebec. This offer is limited to one order per household. Not valid for current subscribers to Harlequin Romantic Suspense books. All orders subject to credit approval. Credit or debit balances in a customer's account(s) may be offset by any other outstanding balance owed by or to the customer. Please allow 4 to 6 weeks for delivery. Offer available while quantities last.

Your Privacy—The Reader Service is committed to protecting your privacy. Our Privacy Policy is available online at www.ReaderService.com or upon request from the Reader Service.

We make a portion of our mailing list available to reputable third parties that offer products we believe may interest you. If you prefer that we not exchange your name with third parties, or if you wish to clarify or modify your communication preferences, please visit us at www.ReaderService.com/consumerschoice or write to us at Reader Service Preference Service, P.O. Box 9062, Buffalo, NY 14240-9062. Include your complete name and address.

HRS15

REQUEST YOUR FREE BOOKS!
2 FREE NOVELS PLUS 2 FREE GIFTS!

HARLEQUIN®

I N T R i G U E

BREATHTAKING ROMANTIC SUSPENSE

REQUEST YOUR FREE BOOKS!

2 FREE NOVELS
FROM THE SUSPENSE COLLECTION,
PLUS 2 FREE GIFTS!

YES! Please send me 2 FREE novels from the Suspense Collection and my 2 FREE gifts (gifts are worth about $10). After receiving them, if I don't wish to receive any more books, I can return the shipping statement marked "cancel." If I don't cancel, I will receive 4 brand-new novels every month and be billed just $6.49 per book in the U.S. or $6.99 per book in Canada. That's a savings of at least 18% off the cover price. It's quite a bargain! Shipping and handling is just 50¢ per book in the U.S. and 75¢ per book in Canada.* I understand that accepting the 2 free books and gifts places me under no obligation to buy anything. I can always return a shipment and cancel at any time. Even if I never buy another book, the two free books and gifts are mine to keep forever.

191/391 MDN GH4Z

Name	(PLEASE PRINT)	
Address		Apt. #
City	State/Prov.	Zip/Postal Code

Signature (if under 18, a parent or guardian must sign)

Mail to the **Reader Service:**
IN U.S.A.: P.O. Box 1867, Buffalo, NY 14240-1867
IN CANADA: P.O. Box 609, Fort Erie, Ontario L2A 5X3

Want to try 2 free books from another line?
Call 1-800-873-8635 or visit www.ReaderService.com.

* Terms and prices subject to change without notice. Prices do not include applicable taxes. Sales tax applicable in NY. Canadian residents will be charged applicable taxes. Offer not valid in Quebec. This offer is limited to one order per household. Not valid for current subscribers to the Suspense Collection or the Romance/Suspense Collection. All orders subject to credit approval. Credit or debit balances in a customer's account(s) may be offset by any other outstanding balance owed by or to the customer. Please allow 4 to 6 weeks for delivery. Offer available while quantities last.

Your Privacy—The Reader Service is committed to protecting your privacy. Our Privacy Policy is available online at www.ReaderService.com or upon request from the Reader Service.

We make a portion of our mailing list available to reputable third parties that offer products we believe may interest you. If you prefer that we not exchange your name with third parties, or if you wish to clarify or modify your communication preferences, please visit us at www.ReaderService.com/consumerschoice or write to us at Reader Service Preference Service, P.O. Box 9062, Buffalo, NY 14240-9062. Include your complete name and address.

REQUEST YOUR FREE BOOKS!
2 FREE RIVETING INSPIRATIONAL NOVELS
PLUS 2 FREE MYSTERY GIFTS

Love Inspired® SUSPENSE
RIVETING INSPIRATIONAL ROMANCE

YES! Please send me 2 FREE Love Inspired® Suspense novels and my 2 FREE mystery gifts (gifts are worth about $10). After receiving them, if I don't wish to receive any more books, I can return the shipping statement marked "cancel." If I don't cancel, I will receive 4 brand-new novels every month and be billed just $4.99 per book in the U.S. or $5.49 per book in Canada. That's a savings of at least 17% off the cover price. It's quite a bargain! Shipping and handling is just 50¢ per book in the U.S. and 75¢ per book in Canada.* I understand that accepting the 2 free books and gifts places me under no obligation to buy anything. I can always return a shipment and cancel at any time. Even if I never buy another book, the two free books and gifts are mine to keep forever.

123/323 IDN GH5Z

Name	(PLEASE PRINT)

Address		Apt. #

City	State/Prov.	Zip/Postal Code

Signature (if under 18, a parent or guardian must sign)

Mail to the **Reader Service:**
IN U.S.A.: P.O. Box 1867, Buffalo, NY 14240-1867
IN CANADA: P.O. Box 609, Fort Erie, Ontario L2A 5X3

**Are you a current subscriber to Love Inspired® Suspense books
and want to receive the larger-print edition?
Call 1-800-873-8635 or visit www.ReaderService.com.**

* Terms and prices subject to change without notice. Prices do not include applicable taxes. Sales tax applicable in N.Y. Canadian residents will be charged applicable taxes. Offer not valid in Quebec. This offer is limited to one order per household. Not valid for current subscribers to Love Inspired Suspense books. All orders subject to credit approval. Credit or debit balances in a customer's account(s) may be offset by any other outstanding balance owed by or to the customer. Please allow 4 to 6 weeks for delivery. Offer available while quantities last.

Your Privacy—The Reader Service is committed to protecting your privacy. Our Privacy Policy is available online at www.ReaderService.com or upon request from the Reader Service.
We make a portion of our mailing list available to reputable third parties that offer products we believe may interest you. If you prefer that we not exchange your name with third parties, or if you wish to clarify or modify your communication preferences, please visit us at www.ReaderService.com/consumerschoice or write to us at Reader Service Preference Service, P.O. Box 9062, Buffalo, NY 14240-9062. Include your complete name and address.

LIS15

REQUEST YOUR FREE BOOKS!

2 FREE NOVELS FROM THE PARANORMAL ROMANCE COLLECTION, PLUS 2 FREE GIFTS!

YES! Please send me 2 FREE novels from the Paranormal Romance Collection and my 2 FREE gifts (gifts are worth about $10). After receiving them, if I don't wish to receive any more books, I can return the shipping statement marked "cancel." If I don't cancel, I will receive 4 brand-new novels every month and be billed just $24.76 in the U.S. or $27.96 in Canada. That's a savings of at least 29% off the cover price of all 4 books. It's quite a bargain! Shipping and handling is just 50¢ per book in the U.S. and 75¢ per book in Canada.* I understand that accepting the 2 free books and gifts places me under no obligation to buy anything. I can always return a shipment and cancel at any time. Even if I never buy another book, the two free books and gifts are mine to keep forever.

237/337 HDN GLDY

Name _____ (PLEASE PRINT)

Address _____ Apt. #

City _____ State/Prov. _____ Zip/Postal Code

Signature (if under 18, a parent or guardian must sign)

Mail to the **Reader Service:**
IN U.S.A.: P.O. Box 1867, Buffalo, NY 14240-1867
IN CANADA: P.O. Box 609, Fort Erie, Ontario L2A 5X3

Want to try 2 free books from another line?
Call 1-800-873-8635 or visit www.ReaderService.com.